"A powerful entry in a fine romantic fantasy series."

—The Best Reviews

"An excellent addition to her entertaining Highlander series."

—*Booklist*

THE DANGEROUS PROTECTOR

"One thing that Chapman does so deftly is meld great characterization, sparkling humor, and spicy adventure into a perfect blend."

—*Romantic Times*

THE SEDUCTIVE IMPOSTOR

"Chapman's skills as a storyteller just keep getting better. Utilizing warmth and humor, she makes this thrilling romantic tale both funny and scary. Great reading."

—*Romantic Times*

"One of the best books I've read in a long time. . . . A fun, sexy read!"

—*Old Book Barn Gazette*

"Engaging romantic suspense . . . surprising twists . . . Janet Chapman seduces her audience."

—The Best Reviews

TEMPTING THE HIGHLANDER

"Chapman breathes such life and warmth into her characters, each story is impossible to put down."

—*Romantic Times*

"A wonderful addition to Chapman's Highlander [series]."

—*Booklist*

JANET CHAPMAN

Secrets Of The Highlander

Pocket STAR Books

New York   London   Toronto   Sydney

Pocket Star Books
A Division of Simon & Schuster, Inc.
1230 Avenue of the Americas
New York, NY 10020

This book is a work of fiction. Names, characters, places, and incidents either are products of the author's imagination or are used fictitiously. Any resemblance to actual events or locales or persons, living or dead, is entirely coincidental.

First Pocket Star Books paperback edition February 2008

POCKET STAR BOOKS and colophon are registered trademarks of Simon & Schuster, Inc.

For information about special discounts for bulk purchases, please contact Simon & Schuster Special Sales at 1-800-456-6798 or business@simonandschuster.com

Cover design by Min Choi
Cover art by Alan Ayers

Manufactured in the United States of America

10 9 8 7 6 5 4 3 2 1

ISBN-13: 978-1-4165-0529-7
ISBN-10:   1-4165-0529-6

To Alex,
Hold on tight, Mr. Man,
as we explore the world together!

For those of you just joining us . . .

Thirty-eight years ago, an aging Scottish drùidh named Pendaär cast a spell to bring Laird Greylen MacKeage eight hundred years forward through time. Pendaär's plan was for Greylen to meet and marry Grace Sutter so they could have seven daughters—the seventh girl destined to be Pendaär's heir.

Except the magic got a bit out of control that fateful day, and not only did Greylen make the fantastical journey from twelfth-century Scotland, but so did three of his men and the six MacBain warriors they were battling at the time. Even their warhorses got sucked into the time-bending storm.

The ten men, finding themselves in a strange new land, did what any God-fearing warriors would do and sought refuge in the nearest church. There they met the old priest, Daar, who taught them the ways of modern society and eventually persuaded them that their destiny lay here, across the Atlantic.

The MacKeages and Daar moved to Pine Creek, Maine, where they bought several thousand acres of timberland, built a modern castle they named Gù Brath, and opened the TarStone Mountain Ski Resort. The six MacBain warriors, true to their hardheaded nature, decided to settle in Cape Breton, Nova Scotia. Five of them died within the next two years, chasing electrical storms in hopes they would be transported back to their natural time. Finding himself alone, Michael MacBain finally moved to Pine Creek, where he purchased a Christmas tree farm abutting the MacKeage land.

In *Charming the Highlander,* Greylen MacKeage, fully adapted to modern life, meets and marries rocket scientist Grace Sutter. And just as Pendaär had been promised by the powers that be, they had seven daughters—all born on the winter solstice: Heather, twins Sarah and Camry, twins Chelsea and Megan, Elizabeth, and finally Pendaär's heir, Winter.

As for the other warriors, in *Loving the Highlander,* Morgan MacKeage meets Sadie Quill and they marry and have several children. It's also in that book that Callum MacKeage marries Charlotte. As for Ian . . . well, you'll have to read *Tempting the Highlander* to discover what happens to him!

Michael MacBain falls in love with Mary Sutter, Grace's sister, within months of moving to Maine. But Mary dies just after giving birth to their son, Robbie. In *Wedding the Highlander,* when Robbie is just nine years old, Libby Hart arrives in Pine Creek and sends Michael's heart into a tailspin all over again.

Moving into the next generation, Robbie MacBain's story is told in *Tempting the Highlander*. Three years later, twenty-five-years-old Winter MacKeage comes face-to-face with her unasked-for destiny in *Only With a Highlander*. In this book you also get to know Greylen's and Grace's jilted (and very pregnant) daughter Megan MacKeage.

This is her story, in which Megan discovers a whole new kind of magic.

Chapter One

Megan MacKeage slipped out the front door of her home and strode across the footbridge guarding the entryway. Discovering she no longer was able to button her coat, she pulled it against her rounded belly and headed to the stable. It had been almost two weeks since anyone had last seen Gesader, and Megan didn't buy her sister Winter's explanation that the semiwild panther was merely hiding from the throng of people that had descended on Gù Brath eight days ago.

The social chaos had started with her and her sisters' birthday party four days before Christmas and wouldn't wind down until after the new year. The annual two-week-long celebration had become a tradition since Heather's birth thirty-three years ago—which had been followed by six more babies over the next ten years, all girls, all born on the winter solstice. As Grace and Greylen MacKeage's seven daughters had grown up and started traveling their own paths, the once-intimate gathering had expanded when the girls returned every December to Pine Creek, several towing husbands and an ever-increasing number of children in their wake.

Two weeks was too long for Gesader to stay away, Megan fretted as she pushed open the huge stable door, and walked to Goose Down's stall. "Hey, big boy," she crooned, giving the huge draft horse's nose an affectionate pat. "How would you like to help me search for Gesader?"

She lifted Goose's bridle off the peg under his nameplate and opened the stall door. "The snow is only up to your knees and there's no icy crust, so the trek should be easy." She slipped the bit in his mouth and tucked the bridle straps over his ears. "I haven't seen that black devil since before the solstice and I'm worried about him, even if no one else is." She led Goose into the aisle, hooked him in the cross ties, then leaned her forehead against his large, warm cheek. "What if he's hurt?" she whispered. "What if he got tangled up in a coyote trap or gored by a buck he was trying to bring down?"

Goose's only answer was a long-winded sigh. Megan headed to the tack room and wrestled the heavy saddle from its stand. "You have to help me sneak off without being seen, Goose, because I don't need any more lectures from anyone, telling me what I should and shouldn't be doing." She grunted, pulling the saddle free. "I'm pregnant, not incapacitated."

"They only lecture because they love ye," a rich-timbered voice said behind her.

Megan spun around with a gasp, dropping the saddle. "Kenzie," she sputtered.

She'd met the imposing highland warrior six days ago at Winter and Matt Gregor's wedding. Kenzie was Matt's long-lost brother, Matt had explained when he'd proudly introduced Kenzie to everyone who had gathered in the high meadow on Bear Mountain for the wedding. Or to be more precise, his *thousand-year-old* brother. For Matt was also known as Cùram de Gairn, a powerful drùidh who had traveled a thousand years forward in time to seduce an equally powerful wizard—who just happened to be Megan's baby sister, Winter—into helping him right a terrible wrong.

No one had been surprised by Kenzie's mysterious appearance, considering that Megan's father, Laird Greylen MacKeage, as well as her uncles Morgan and Callum MacKeage and Michael MacBain, were also time travelers.

Megan's mind reeled at the realization that the magic she had known since birth appeared to be spiraling out of control lately. Or maybe her head was spinning because she'd stopped breathing again—which seemed to happen whenever she found herself around Kenzie Gregor.

"A lass in your condition shouldn't be lifting heavy saddles," he said, his golden eyes dark with reproach. He picked up the saddle, set it back on its stand, then turned and walked out of the tack room. "Nor should ye be riding."

Megan stared at the door he'd disappeared through, taking deep breaths as she counted to ten. But when she heard Goose plodding back to his stall, she lost what was left of her patience. She ran into the aisle, swiped the reins out of Kenzie's hand, and led her horse back to the cross ties.

"I am quite capable of deciding what I should and shouldn't be doing," she said, striding back to the tack room.

Kenzie's golden eyes lit with amusement as he arched a brow at her glare.

"I understand you've barely been in this century a week," she said. "But you'll soon discover that things have changed in a thousand years. Twenty-first-century women—pregnant or otherwise—don't want men lecturing them. We can take care of ourselves."

"Marriage still seems to be the norm, though," he countered. "Which implies it still takes two to raise a bairn." His gaze dropped to her belly, then moved around the barn before returning to her. "Yet I don't see a husband out here helping you."

Megan's cheeks flushed with heat. No matter how civilized Kenzie looked with his modern clothes, clean-shaven face, and short haircut, he still had the mind-set of an ancient. "I don't care if you're older than time itself; you have no right butting into my business."

She spun on her heel and led Goose outside to the mounting stairs. But before she could brush the snow off the steps, large hands suddenly lifted her onto Goose's saddleless back. And before she'd finished yelping in surprise, Kenzie had vaulted up behind her.

"Where are we off to, then?" he asked with a resigned sigh, taking the reins from her hands.

Megan went perfectly still. "*We're* not going anywhere. You're going back to the house, and I'm riding up Tar-Stone Mountain to look for my . . . my cat."

Ignoring her dismissal, her unasked-for escort reined Goose toward the slopes crowded with skiers enjoying their holiday vacation.

Having had plenty of experience dealing with ancient-thinking men, Megan realized he wouldn't be ditched easily. So she might as well take advantage of his will-ingness to help her—as well as of the heat that radiated from his overlarge body like a blast furnace. And who knew, maybe some of his brother's magic had rubbed off on him, and Kenzie might be able to conjure up Gesader.

"The other way," she said, reaching in front of his hand to pull on the reins, turning Goose toward the nar-row tote road that ran up the forested side of TarStone. "Gesader is likely hiding in the woods. He doesn't much care for crowds."

Kenzie urged the Percheron onto the unplowed log-ging road. "Most cats would be snuggled up in front of a fire this time of year, instead of tramping through snow deeper than they are tall."

"Not Gesader," Megan said, deciding that riding bare-back was much more practical than using a saddle. Be-tween Goose's warmth beneath her and Kenzie's heat enveloping her, Megan felt like *she* was snuggled in front of a fire. Or else her hormones were acting up again. "If you're from tenth-century Scotland, how do you speak English so well?"

Kenzie reached around her to her open coat collar. "I've been practicing for several years. Ye should button up," he said, trying to fasten the top button.

She pushed his hand away. "I can't. My belly's getting too big. So you knew for several years that you were coming to this century? Is that what Matt needed Win-ter's help for? The terrible upset he caused to the con-tinuum that nearly killed all the trees of life—that was just to bring you here?"

Kenzie pulled her back against him by wrapping one

arm around her expanded waist. "More or less. *Gesader* is an ancient Gaelic word. Why did ye name your cat Enchanter?"

Megan made a production of repositioning herself, and leaned forward to take hold of Goose's mane again. Kenzie Gregor was a virtual stranger, yet he was acting as though they'd been best buddies for years. "My sister named him, as he's really her pet. I've only been back in Pine Creek four months. But with Winter spending so much time with Matt this fall, Gesader seemed to prefer my company to hers. And he's not a house cat, he's a panther."

"Maine has panthers?" Kenzie asked curiously.

"No. We have lynx and bobcat, and there have been rare sightings of mountain lions, but no panthers." Megan smiled. "Our cousin Robbie MacBain brought Gesader forward in time three years ago as a tiny cub. Robbie's our resident guardian who's in charge of keeping Pendaär in line. Or he was, before Pendaär lost all his magical powers." She shrugged. "Now I suppose Robbie must guard us from Winter and your brother. He's the logger married to Catherine and is baby Angus's father."

"Aye, I remember. He carried ye upstairs to bed last night when ye fell asleep in your chair." Kenzie chuckled. "And Pendaär is the cranky old priest who's always the first to sit down at the table and the last one to leave, who keeps eyeing me as if he thinks I'm wanting to steal the whiskers right off his face."

Megan laughed. "That's Pendaär, though everyone calls him Father Daar around the moderns. He was a powerful wizard before he passed on the magic to Winter. He was the one who brought my father and uncles to this century nearly forty years ago. But Daar sort of . . .

he often bungled his spells, and he ended up bringing three other MacKeage men here, as well as six MacBain warriors and all their warhorses."

She turned to look at Kenzie. "The MacKeages and MacBains were at war at the time, but Michael and Papa declared peace years ago. The MacKeages settled here in Pine Creek when they purchased TarStone Mountain. They built Gù Brath, got the ski resort up and running, then decided to find wives to rebuild their clan."

Kenzie shook his head. "But your poor father sired seven daughters instead."

Megan shot him a scowl and faced forward again. "Another thing you'll discover about the twenty-first century, Mr. Gregor, is that having a bunch of sons is no longer important. Thanks to modern technology, being female is more often a strength than a weakness. Women can do anything men can do." She shot him a smirk over her shoulder. "And most times, we do it better."

He tossed his head back in laughter, his handsome face bathed in the afternoon sun. Megan immediately faced forward again and started calling Gesader's name.

"Ye mentioned you refer to the old priest as Father Daar around the moderns. What do you mean by *moderns*?" Kenzie asked when she paused.

"It's how my father and uncles have always referred to the people here. Those who traveled through time are the old ones, and anyone of this century is a modern. What was it like, to travel through time?"

"Violent. Terrifying. Nothing I care to repeat."

"Robbie's wife, Catherine, accidentally traveled back with him once, and she said she never wants to do it again, either. She also said that when she landed in twelfth-century Scotland, she was naked." Megan grinned.

"Is that why she and MacBain had to marry?"

"No. In fact, today men and women can even make love without having a wedding—not that it's any of your business."

"Are we still talking about Robbie and Catherine?" Kenzie asked softly. "Ye sure do get prickly at the mere mention of marriage, lass. Why is that? Did the father of your babe not ask ye to marry him?"

"That's none of your business!"

"We're related now, are we not? Does that not make you my business?"

"Your brother is married to my sister," she countered. "That doesn't exactly make us kissing cousins."

Megan immediately slapped her hand over her mouth. *Kissing cousins?* Where in hell had *that* come from?

Kenzie laughed so hard she would have fallen off Goose but for his strong arm wrapped around her. "No," he said through his laughter, "that doesn't make us kissing cousins." His arm around her tightened. "So where *is* the father of your babe?"

"Burning in hell, I hope," she snapped.

"Tell me where he is, and I'll to go fetch the bastard."

"What for?" she sputtered, looking over her shoulder.

"To marry ye!"

Megan took a deep breath and faced forward again, reminding herself what century he was from. "I would never consider marrying a man who doesn't love me."

"Love has nothing to do with it, lass. The two of ye are having a bairn together, whether ye wish it or not."

"I am quite capable of raising my child without him."

"I don't doubt ye are. But does your babe not deserve to know his father?"

"He or she will have dozens of uncles and male

cousins. I have a whole family to help me here in Pine Creek. If Wayne Ferris ever grows a conscience and decides he wants to meet his son or daughter, I will deal with him then. In the meantime, I want nothing to do with the jerk."

"Does he know about the babe?"

"Yes."

Kenzie fell silent for a time, then softly said, "Our sister was abandoned by the father of her babe. Her name was Fiona, and she had no family to help her. Matt and I were off fighting wars, and our mother had died the year before. Fiona only had our father, and it's my understanding he'd started to lose his mind by then."

"What happened to her?"

"She died giving birth, and her babe died soon after."

Megan hugged her rounded belly. "I'm so sorry. I guess that pretty much explains why you're so concerned for me." She gave him a reassuring smile. "But I really will be fine."

Goose plodded onto a windswept ridge and the forest opened to a spectacular view of Pine Lake nine hundred feet below. Kenzie reined to a stop and dismounted, then helped her down.

"Aye, you'll be fine. I will make sure of it," he said. "Now, about Gesader," he added, gently gripping her shoulders. "There . . . ah . . . there's something I'm needing to explain to ye, lass, about your missing pet."

Jack Stone rested his arms on the door of his cruiser to steady himself, and trained his binoculars on the north face of TarStone Mountain. He started his search at the narrow fingers of snow stretching from summit to base, ignoring the skiers as he looked for more substantial,

four-legged movement. Satisfied the horse wasn't traveling up the edge of the ski slopes or along the chairlift
paths, Jack panned west over the dense spruce and pine
trees, stopping at occasional openings in the forest long
enough to determine each one was empty.

"Come on, sweetheart. Where'd you disappear to?" he
said softly. "And who are you riding with?"

Jack continued working his way across the mountain,
though he knew spotting his target in the rugged terrain
was about as likely as finding a teenage runaway in New
York City. But having beaten those very odds more than
once, he continued his methodical search with the patience of a hunter unaccustomed to failure.

"Bingo," he said, when the horse carrying two riders
stepped onto a granite ridge halfway up the mountain
ten minutes later. Jack tossed the field glasses on the seat
of his cruiser, strode to the back of the blue and white
SUV, opened the rear hatch, and grabbed his rifle case.
He looked up and down the remote road, then lifted out
the high-powered rifle that had not been issued with the
handcuffs and badge when he had become head of Pine
Creek's new police force last week.

With a derisive snort, he slid open the bolt of the rifle.
Some force. He was chief of exactly one deputy officer
fresh out of the academy, and a grandmotherly clerk.

Pine Creek, along with the neighboring townships of
Lost Gore and Frog Cove, had been growing in leaps and
bounds, the town selectmen had explained to Jack during his interview. And though they had the county sheriff's department and state police to back them up, the
three small resort communities wanted their own arm
of the law to call whenever someone thought it would

be fun to swap personal possessions between citizens.

Honest to God, those were the very words the select-men had used. Nothing had actually been stolen; a few gas grills, toys, holiday decorations, and mailboxes had merely been redistributed between houses, seasonal camps, and businesses. Jack had nearly offered to take the job for free, if a bunch of bored teenagers constituted Pine Creek's hottest crime wave.

He walked to the front of his truck and leaned on the hood to look through the scope attached to the rifle barrel. He spotted the horse, riderless now, and then the two people standing beside it. Without taking his eye from the lens, he turned up the magnification until Megan MacKeage finally came into perfect focus.

Jack sucked in his breath at the sight of her. Her shoulder-length red hair kept blowing in her face despite her attempts to tuck it behind her ears, her lightly freckled cheeks were flushed from the cold, and her eyes—which Jack knew were startling green—were narrowed against the noon sun as she looked up at the man holding her shoulders.

Jack had made the TarStone Ski Resort part of his daily rounds, fairly confident that if he were to drive past Megan, she wouldn't recognize him. Seeing people out of context of their known environment, especially when their looks had changed as much as his had, always made hiding in plain sight easier.

While cruising through the resort's parking lot this morning, he'd spotted Megan leaving her home on horse-back, snuggled against the chest of a man he'd never seen in town. Jack was good with faces, postures, mannerisms, and genetic heritages. And though the man had been a couple of hundred yards away, Jack hadn't seen any resemblance to any of the MacKeage and MacBain men he'd met, other than the guy's size.

Jack trained the powerful rifle scope on him now. He surely was a big bastard, at least a foot taller than Megan's five foot three. His shoulders were broad and he had the build of someone Jack would want on his side in a fight.

A cousin? Or an uncle, maybe?

Or a boyfriend?

The sound of a vehicle approaching from the direction of town ended his surveillance, as well as his speculation. Jack strode to the rear of his truck and set the rifle back in its case, then dropped the hatch just as a blue and white pickup rounded the corner and came to a sliding halt.

Officer Simon Pratt emerged through the cloud of powdered snow he'd created. "Your radio's not working," he said, peering in the open front door of Jack's SUV. "Hey, it's not even turned on," he added, reaching inside to the console. He straightened and frowned at Jack. "Ethel and I have been calling your cell and radio all morning, and I've spent the last two hours hunting you down."

Jack pulled his cell phone out of his pocket to check for a signal, only to discover *it* wasn't turned on, either. "Sorry," he said, turning the phone on before tucking it back in his pocket. "So what's up?"

"The bakery was broken into last night. The place is a mess."

"They *broke* in? And trashed the place?" he asked in surprise. "But that's not their MO. They usually just take stuff sitting around outside."

Simon shrugged. "The bakery's not open on Monday, so the owner didn't arrive until eight this morning. She'd planned to catch up on some paperwork, and found the back door busted open and most of her supplies scattered everywhere. She called our office, and Ethel and I have been looking for you ever since. We were just about to call the sheriff."

"Why?"

His question seemed to startle Simon. "Because we couldn't find you."

Jack gave him a level look. "Did it ever occur to you to just go to the bakery without me and process the scene?"

"Ah, sure, I did that, I mean, I *secured* the scene. I strung tape around the place and had the owner put a Closed Until Further Notice sign in the front window."

Jack plucked his binoculars off the seat and slid into his cruiser. "Then let's go have a look at your crime scene. On the way, try to recall what the academy taught you about processing a break-in."

"*My* crime scene?" Simon looked startled again.

"You took the call, didn't you?"

"Well, yeah. But you're the chief."

"And I won't always be available, will I? So since you're my second in command, I expect you to deal with whatever comes up." He lifted a brow. "You graduated with honors, right?"

Simon squared his shoulders. "I could process that scene in my sleep."

"Then I'll follow your lead," Jack said, closing his door.

He watched Simon stride back to his truck, looking a good two inches taller. Jack turned the key in the ignition and put his truck in gear, gave one last frowning glance at TarStone, and stepped on the accelerator.

Oh, yeah. He would definitely follow Simon's lead— because despite what his résumé implied, Jack didn't know squat about processing a crime scene, since his talents ran in a completely different direction.

Chapter Two

*M*egan looked at Kenzie as if he'd just sprouted a second head. He forced himself to remain perfectly still, though he wanted to pull her against his chest and soothe her shock. He just as desperately wanted to run deep into the forest in shame. He realized his grip on her shoulders had grown fierce and stepped back, tucking his hands behind him. He could only imagine how she felt. Until he'd actually said the words out loud, even *he* had started to believe it had been nothing more than a two-hundred-year-long nightmare.

"Y-you can't be Gesader," she whispered, her face as pale as the snow. "I've known him since he was a cub."

"You've known *me,* lass. You only need look at me, Megan, to realize it's true. Are these not the eyes of your pet?" he asked, touching his face under one eye, then covering his heart with his hand. "*I'm* the panther cub MacBain brought forward from twelfth-century Scotland."

She backed up a step, as if trying to distance herself

from what he was saying. "But you can't be Gesader," she repeated in a barely audible whisper, taking another step back.

His urge to comfort her finally won out, and Kenzie moved with lightning speed to gather her in his arms. She immediately started to struggle, so he simply sat down in the snow with her on his lap. "I lay dying on the battlefield when Matt found me a thousand years ago," he explained. "And that was the day my brother made his deal with Providence."

She went still and stared straight ahead at Pine Lake, her curiosity apparently overriding her horror.

"Matt had no way of knowing what his demand would set into motion," he continued. "I was the only family Matt had left and I was mortally wounded. So my brother accepted his calling as a powerful drùidh, on the condition that my life be spared."

She remained silent and rigid in his embrace. He took a shuddering breath and continued. "Only I'd already started heading for this incredibly bright light, ye see, that offered me blessed relief." He leaned in close, his chin brushing her hair. "I so badly wanted to experience what that light promised, but apparently Matt needed me more. Only it was too late for me to continue living as Kenzie Gregor, and I hung in limbo for what seemed like forever before I suddenly became a young colt— born of a mare right there on the battlefield."

Megan gave a soft gasp.

"I spent the next two hundred years as various animals. I lived, died, and was reborn hundreds of times as both wild and domestic creatures."

"Then Matt gained nothing," she said with no emotion. "You weren't Kenzie, you were an animal."

"Aye, but we still recognized each other, lass. And four times a year, on the solstices and the equinoxes, I became a man again for twenty-four hours."

"So your becoming a . . . an animal upset the continuum?"

He brushed a strand of her hair from her face and tucked it behind her ear. "Matt's deal with Providence was in blatant disregard for my own free will, Megan. I was never given the chance to decide if I would prefer death or life as an animal."

She turned her head to look up to him. "What would you have chosen?"

"Death. Which I finally did after two centuries, when I asked Matt to please find a way to allow me to die one last time, preferably as a man. He realized he needed help to undo his wrong, and began devising a way to meet your sister. He lured Robbie MacBain back to twelfth-century Scotland to bring the taproot from his tree of life, and me, forward to this time."

"Why did he need Winter's help, if he's such a powerful drùidh?"

"Besides being a drùidh, Matt is also a guardian, and guardians can't actually interfere in our lives. They can only guard us from the magic."

"He interfered in yours!"

"Aye, he did. And he so upset the continuum, we all nearly paid the price for it." He squeezed her gently. "But thanks to your wise and very stubborn sister, everything has worked out. I am myself again, I shall die a natural death one final time, and together with Providence and a bit of help from Talking Tom, Matt and Winter now have an even more powerful tree of life."

Megan suddenly scrambled off his lap, her face flushed

as she turned on him. "Winter! She's known all along!" she cried. "I've been so worried about Gesader this week, and she couldn't even tell me you were him!"

Just as quickly as her anger had come, her face paled again. "I . . . I've been crying all over you for the last four months," she whispered. She pointed an accusing finger at him. "You've been sleeping in my bed!"

Kenzie stood up, worried she'd back off the edge of the rise. "As a panther, Megan," he said, moving toward her. "Not as a man."

"I told you my deepest, darkest secrets." She took another step back. "I—"

He lunged, reaching for her at the exact moment she realized her peril. But instead of grabbing him for support, Megan used his momentum to knock him off balance. She gave him a surprisingly forceful push in the chest and bolted away.

Kenzie fell over the rise instead, landing in a snow-drift as deep as he was tall. "Megan!" he shouted. "Don't run, lass!"

She peered over the edge, saw that he hadn't fallen far but was stuck, then disappeared.

"Megan!"

She didn't return.

"Goose!" Kenzie called out, throwing his body back and forth to free himself from the snowdrift.

The horse's head appeared over the edge of the rise, his hooves knocking more snow loose. "I'll make my own way back. Go catch up with your mistress and take her home."

The horse disappeared, and Kenzie gave a snort. So Matt had figured right: he really *could* talk to animals.

* * *

Jack surveyed the small kitchen of the Pine Lake Bakery & Bistro. "What's that smell?" he asked the two people staring at him, apparently waiting for him to say something police-chief-like.

"I noticed it, too, the moment I stepped inside this morning," Marge Wimple said. The petite, gray-haired bakery owner wrinkled her nose. "It smells sour."

"Like rotting vegetation or something, only laced with sugar," Simon Pratt added.

"You go arrest that brat Tommy Cleary this minute," Marge said. "Everyone knows he's their ringleader, and the Cleary place sits right next to a bog. *That's* where this smell comes from." She pointed to a brown spot on the floor. "Where else you gonna find mud in the middle of the winter?" She then pointed her finger at Jack. "You put the fear of God in Tommy, and make him tell you who his accomplices are. Just look at what they did to my shop!" Her tearful gaze moved over the mess. "It'll take me a week to clean this place, and another week to restock all my supplies. That's two weeks right out of the middle of my busiest season."

Jack bent down and touched one of the brown spots. "I need a bit more than the fact that Tommy Cleary lives next to a bog to bring him in for questioning." He sniffed the mud. "This is definitely out of a swamp, but that's not the smell lingering in the air." He spotted a slimy substance on the edge of the smashed doughnut display case and walked over to sniff it. "It's coming from here," he said, moving aside and motioning for Simon to take a whiff.

"Whew!" Simon said, jerking upright. "That's rank. What is it?"

"The lab will have to tell us that."

"What lab?" Simon asked.

Jack frowned at his deputy. "The state has a forensics lab we can use, doesn't it?"

"Oh, yeah. Sure." Simon rushed over to his evidence kit. "I'll have Ethel give them a call to find out how we send them stuff."

"It's that Cleary boy and his brothers, I tell you," Marge said. "Joan Cleary lets those boys run loose like a bunch of heathens. Everyone knows it was them who stole my sign last month, and took Rose Brewer's moose antlers off the front of her store. We didn't get our stuff back for a entire week. A fisherman found them hanging on his ice shanty two miles out on the lake."

Marge stalked up to Jack. "We hired you to stop this foolishness, but it's only getting worse." She raised her finger again, clearly intending to poke him in the chest, but when her eyes met his she changed her mind. "What are you going to do about this, Chief Stone?"

"Deputy Pratt and I are going to fully investigate your break-in, Mrs. Wimple. We'll gather fingerprints and evidence, take a look around outside, and talk to people in the hopes that somebody saw something. You can start cleaning up once we give you the okay, which should be sometime tomorrow morning." He gave her what he hoped was a police-chief-like smile. "We'll keep you apprised of what's happening. Thank you for being so cooperative, Mrs. Wimple," he finished, turning toward the back door of the bakery.

He stopped beside Simon, who was scraping some of the mud into a plastic bag. "Take some pictures with that fancy new digital camera." He nodded toward the large evidence kit that would make one heck of a fishing tackle box. "Get some shots in here, then take some pictures of the grounds outside and the front and back of the store."

"Sure thing, Chief."

"My name is Jack," he told Simon for the umpteenth time. "White men stopped calling us chief several decades age."

Simon's eyes widened. "Y-you're an Indian?" he sputtered, his face turning a dull red.

"Half Canadian Cree," Jack said. "So stop with the chief thing, will you?"

"Yes, sir."

Jack gave a snort and walked outside, ducking under the crime scene tape before putting on his sunglasses. He stopped in the middle of the lane that ran between the stores and Pine Lake, and scanned the downtown business district. A lot of money had gone into the storefronts on the street side, but the backs of the buildings were even more impressive. No alley full of dumpsters and recycling bins here. The stores came within fifty yards of the shoreline, and the town had capitalized on that, building a park with benches, landscape trees, and strategically placed logging artifacts. The Pine Lake Bakery & Bistro was sided by a craft supply store, an art gallery, then an outfitter store, and finally a restaurant with huge windows facing the lake.

"Find out if that railing was already busted or if that break is new," Jack told Simon when the deputy came outside with his camera. "Is the discoloring on the doorjamb more of that slime?"

Simon leaned in close to look, then immediately jerked back. "It's the same stuff, all right."

"Take a photo of it," Jack instructed, turning to scan the snow. "What do you make of this?"

Simon walked up beside him and squinted at where Jack was pointing. "Those are tracks."

"But what kind of tracks?" Jack asked, carefully stepping over the snowbank beside them, then following the tracks into the otherwise pristine layer of snow as he scanned the ground in a fifty-foot circle. "They simply begin here all of a sudden," he said, pointing. "They come out of nowhere, like something flew in, landed here, and then walked to the bakery. Get a shot of this, too," he said, hunching down over one of the holes. "I can't make out the shape because something was dragged over the print."

Simon snapped several pictures, then continued photographing the path the tracks made. "They're too large to be from a bird. One of those para-skiing kites maybe?" he asked as he worked. "Or an ultralight airplane? A bunch of home-built ultralights fly around the lake on the weekends."

"Any in the Cleary family?" Jack asked, walking toward the frozen shoreline.

"Nope. The Clearys can barely manage to buy food. A small plane would have made a noise. Maybe someone heard something."

Jack shook his head. "There's no tracks where it took off again. Whoever came in here walked away."

"Or used Main Street as a runway."

Jack thought about that. "A hang glider or large kite makes more sense than a plane, even a small one. And dragging a glider might have made those tracks." He shook his head again. "But that's a pretty unusual way to arrive to a burglary. Maybe the tracks don't have anything to do with our break-in."

"But they head directly to the bakery," Simon pointed out.

"None of the other stores were broken into?"

"Nope. I checked the shops on both sides of the street. Everything is just as the owners left it last night."

Jack looked out at the busy lake dotted with tiny islands, zooming snowmobiles, ice shanties, and even a few pickups with plows on them. Hell, it was busier than Main Street out there. He looked back at the bakery. So, what had caused a bunch of bored teenagers to go from pulling a few harmless pranks to breaking and entering?

And what in hell had made those tracks?

Chapter Three

"*I* thought I'd find you down here."

Megan looked up from the computer screen and scowled at her sister. "Go away," she said, returning to the Internet page.

Of course Camry ignored her. She sauntered into Gù Brath's science lab, pulled up a chair, and cradled her chin in her hands as she also studied the screen. "I wondered how long it would take you to get bored working at Winter's art gallery." She reached over to hit a keyboard button to scroll down the page. "I'm surprised you lasted three months. Not Easter Island," she muttered, hitting the button again. "Or Costa Rica, either. It's too hot. There!" she said, pointing at the new Internet page. "You can go count Steller's sea eagles off the coast of Siberia. That's definitely far enough away to teach all of us a lesson."

Megan reached up and shut off the monitor.

Camry immediately turned it back on. "No, I think

you're on to something here, Meg. You should run as far and as fast as you can, and to hell with everyone. You're a fully grown woman, so why hang around here getting fawned over by a family who loves you?"

Megan looked down at her lap. "It's killing me, Cam. Mom and Dad treat me like a fragile piece of glass, afraid if they so much as look at me wrong, I'll shatter." Tears welled in her eyes. "Dad actually got down on his knee and tied my shoes for me yesterday."

Camry covered Megan's hands. "He can't help himself, coming from a time when being pregnant and single was just about the worst position a woman could find herself in. None of us can help being worried about you, because we love you. Mom said you came home in tears from your fieldwork in Canada, and cried for nearly a month when Wayne Ferris broke your heart."

"But everyone's concern is only making it worse. I came home looking for support, not pity. I certainly expected better from you. We're more alike than our own twin sisters, and I was positive *you* would realize I haven't turned into a helpless idiot. So how come you didn't tell me about Kenzie?"

"Ahh," Camry said, leaning back in her chair. "That's why you're searching for a job. So you can run away again, only this time from . . . from what, Meg? Why should Kenzie being Gesader throw you into such a tail-spin? It can't be the magic, since we grew up with it. So what is it?"

"Why didn't you tell me?"

"And just how was I supposed to explain that the panther you'd been sleeping with for the last four months was really a man?" She leaned forward. "Everyone knew how embarrassed you'd be."

"And none of you thought I would eventually figure it out when Gesader never showed up again? Cam, I told that cat *everything*," she whispered. "All my deepest, darkest secrets." She covered her face with her hands. "My God, I even told him how I'd torn off Wayne's clothes and made love to him under the stars!"

"And Gesader saw you naked when you got ready for bed. That's really what has you so flustered, isn't it? That, and even though you're not quite over Wayne, you find Kenzie mysteriously attractive. So who finally told you, anyway?"

"He did. And I *don't* like Kenzie that way."

"Why not? He's handsome as all get out, and he's seen you at your worst and doesn't turn tail when you approach. So what's wrong with liking him 'that way'? I'm tempted to flirt with him myself."

"He's a *warrior*."

Camry arched her brows at Megan's tone. "And just what's wrong with warriors? They make up most of our family, including our own generation. Half our cousins have served in the military."

"Which is exactly why I fell so hard for Wayne. *His* first reaction to a problem isn't to bludgeon it into submission, but to solve it peaceably. He doesn't have one confrontational bone in his body. He's interested in stuff I'm interested in, he's shy and gentle and sensitive, and he's got this endearing little clumsiness thing going on."

"The men in our family can be sensitive and gentle."

"Wayne wouldn't even know which end of a sword to hold," Megan countered, "much less how to shoot a gun. You should have seen him with the students out on the tundra, Cam. No matter how heated their petty arguments got, Wayne disarmed the situation without even raising his voice."

"He sounds like a nerd."

"He is. A wonderful, beautiful, sensitive nerd. And for an added bonus, he's only five foot ten, so I don't get a crick in my neck talking to him. I love the men in our family, Cam, I just don't want to be married to one. I want Wayne."

"Then go get him!" Camry snapped. "Instead of looking for a new job halfway around the world, get your sorry butt back to Canada."

"And do what?" Megan snapped back. "*Beg* Wayne to marry me?"

"MacKeages do not beg." Camry narrowed her eyes. "The Megan I grew up with would have fought for the man she loved. She sure as hell wouldn't be hiding in the family fortress, having a four-month pity party."

Megan lifted her chin. "I am not hiding. In fact, I'm planning to confront Wayne."

"When?"

Megan started scrolling down the page again. "Just as soon as I get my ducks in a row," she muttered. "That's why I'm looking for a new job. I'm going to become gainfully employed again and move into my own home, and *then* I'm going to track down Wayne and show him exactly what he threw away."

"*That's* the sister I grew up with." Camry's face suddenly brightened even more. "You know what this means, Meg? If you give wimpy Wayne the boot, you've broken the curse of us girls getting pregnant the first time we make love to our future husbands!" She bobbed her eyebrows. "Which also means I'm free to start dating again. Maybe I *will* go after Kenzie."

Only Megan wasn't feeling her sister's enthusiasm. "Why didn't the curse work for me? And are you . . . still a virgin?"

"No," Camry said softly, her face pink. "Were you?"

Megan shook her head. "I've had other relationships."

"Hmm . . . so that means it's not making love that's the danger, just that we get pregnant by the men we're destined to marry."

"Then what happened to me?"

Camry shrugged. "Who knows? The upset Matt caused to the continuum might have messed up the magic enough to stop the curse. Anyway, come on," she said, standing up. "Dinner's ready."

Megan turned back to the computer. "I'm not hungry."

"You have to face Kenzie sometime, Meg. He's not going away."

"No, but I am. Look! There's an opening for a field biologist right here in Maine."

Camry leaned over her shoulder and read the posting. "It's for the Pine Lake watershed." She straightened with a frown. "What are the chances of that?"

"Slim to none."

"Exactly. And it's not state or federal, but private money backing the grant. I don't think you should apply, Meg. You remember what happened to Aunt Sadie, don't you? She thought she'd been hired by a development corporation, but it turned out to be a front for some guy looking for a nonexistent gold mine."

"This has to be legit." Megan pointed at the bottom of the screen. "It's a preliminary impact study for a new resort being built at the north end of the lake. A guy named Mark Collins is looking for an assistant to do the actual fieldwork. I prefer fieldwork to running the show, so it's perfect for me."

"It's spooky, I tell you," Cam countered. "The magic's been so screwed up lately, there's no telling why this job showed up here, much less now."

"But it would mean I could move out of Gù Brath and find a rental in town. I can handle Mom and Dad in small doses if I have a place to escape to. I need to get my life back."

"In Pine Creek?" Camry asked, obviously still doubtful.

"The watershed covers hundreds of square miles. I'll look for a rental a little farther out."

"There's nothing farther out but bears and trees."

"And blessed peace."

Camry shook her head. "I still say it's too much of a coincidence."

"Maybe Providence is trying to make amends for screwing up my life," Megan suggested, suddenly feeling more cheerful. "Let's go eat, I'm starved. But don't mention this to anyone," she said, turning off the lights. "Promise me you won't bring it up."

"You don't even know if you'll get the job."

"Are you kidding? The magic owes me big-time. But I don't want to tell Mom and Dad until after I've found a rental and moved in."

"Dad's going to throw a fit."

"I'll survive. Hey, *you've* survived his complaints that you're still a spinster at the ripe old age of thirty-one."

"I'm not ready for hearth and husband. I have galaxies to explore."

"Mom found a way to do both."

"But she forgot to hand down her multitasking gene to me. I can't focus on more than one thing at a time."

Megan hooked her arm through Cam's and headed upstairs. "Yeah, but you got the looks in the family. Sit next to me at dinner and steer the conversation away from anything awkward, would you?"

Camry gave an exaggerated sigh. "See why I'm scared of getting pregnant? In only five months, you've gone from being the family brat to the family mouse."

"Oh, I might still have a few pranks up my sleeve," Megan said with a laugh.

Megan's fears about dinner were soon put to rest, as the main topic of conversation was last night's break-in at the Bakery & Bistro.

That, and the town's sexy new police chief.

Well, the men weren't referring to Jack Stone as sexy, but Megan's twin sister, Chelsea, certainly was—much to her husband's dismay. "He's not very tall, but he sure does fill out a police jacket nicely," Chelsea said to Camry. "And he's got a bit of a swagger. You should ask him out."

"I'm leaving in four days," Cam reminded her. "So what would be the point?"

"A couple of fun dates?" Chelsea offered. "You need to start dating again, and you could practice on Jack Stone."

"Exactly how does one practice dating?" Cam asked with a laugh. "Besides, my life is full enough without adding a man to the mix." She glanced at Megan, who sat between them. "Meg's available. Fix *her* up with swaggering Jack Stone."

Megan side-kicked Cam in the leg.

"There's no reason you can't date," Cam muttered, reaching under the table to rub her shin.

"So," Grace MacKeage piped up. "Do they have any idea who broke into the bakery? Or why? Marge never leaves cash in the shop overnight. And who'd want to steal day-old doughnuts?"

"I spoke with Simon Pratt when I was in town this afternoon," Chelsea said. "Did any of you know he'd gone to the police academy?"

Megan's younger sister, Elizabeth, shook her head. "I had him in school, and he's the last person I expected to see in law enforcement. Simon spent more time in the principal's office than he did in class. The selectmen must have hired him because he's a local, since Chief Stone is from away."

"That's another thing Simon told me," Chelsea added. "He said his boss doesn't like being called *chief* because he's half Canadian Cree."

"Is it significant that Stone is a Canadian Cree?" Greylen MacKeage asked from the head of the table. "If he's an Indian chief, he should be proud of that fact. And if he's our chief of police, it's only respectful that we use his title."

Grace covered her husband's hand. "*Chief* can sometimes be taken in a derogatory context, Grey," she explained. "It's a sensitive area for First Nation People, as they're called in Canada. Maybe you should just call him Mr. Stone when you meet him. Or Jack."

Greylen got a twinkle in his eye. "Maybe I'll introduce myself as Laird MacKeage."

Camry snorted. "Oh, that'll help Megan get a date with him. Men just *beg* to go out with us when you're acting the laird." She pointed her fork at him. "You scared off half my boyfriends in high school with that act."

Greylen nodded solemnly, though the twinkle remained in his eyes. "You may thank me later, daughter, for making sure you made it to college."

"So what was stolen from the bakery?" Matt Gregor asked.

"Nothing but day-old doughnuts and some pies, according to Simon," Chelsea said. "But they trashed the place in the process."

"I told ye to gather some men and root out those nogoods," Father Daar said, looking at Greylen. "Ye should have done it last month, when they strung those Christmas lights all over your old snowcat. Didn't I warn ye their pranks would get worse?" He drove his fork into his potatoes. "They'll be coming up to my place next, I tell ye. An old man living alone makes a good target."

"That's a good point, Father," Kenzie said. "Which is why I've been thinking to move in with you. Ye no longer have the magic to help make things easy, and I'm needing a place to live. I can chop your wood and lug your water. It could work out well for both of us."

Daar glared at Greylen. "I don't need a babysitter—especially a pagan from the Gregor clan. Just catch the vandals so we'll be safe again."

"We now have policemen to keep us safe," Grey returned. "We no longer can take matters into our own hands. And I think it's a good idea for Kenzie to move in with you." He looked at Kenzie. "You're sure you wish to do this? Ye know you're welcome to stay here. And Daar is our obligation, not yours."

"I'm not having that black devil in my home!" Daar

banged his fork on the table. "I don't want anyone living with me."

"Father," Grace interjected, touching his arm. "You can't continue to live alone. You could fall and break a leg, and it might be hours or days before someone showed up. This is a wise move, and it's very kind of Kenzie to offer." She gave Kenzie a crooked smile. "Especially considering how well he knows you."

"I believe Daar and I will get along fine," Kenzie said, grinning at the scowling priest. "Besides, I've a need to feel the forest around me again."

"Can ye cook, Gregor?" Daar asked.

Kenzie nodded.

"Then ye best be providing your own food. I'm a priest, ye know, and have taken a vow of poverty. I can't have ye eating me out of house and home."

"I will provide for both of us, Father." Kenzie turned to his brother. "Have you sensed anything different in the air lately?"

"Like what?" Matt asked in surprise. His eyes narrowed. "You can feel something?"

Kenzie shrugged. "It's more of a smell, but nothing I recognize. It's . . . unnatural. Pungent."

"I've felt nothing," Matt said. "Have you, Winter?"

"Nope. The only thing I've been feeling lately is tired. I had no idea growing a baby was so hard." She looked at her mother. "How did you survive five pregnancies, especially two sets of twins?"

"I wasn't running an art gallery, getting married, building a house, and saving the world while carrying any of you girls," Grace said with a laugh. "You'll start feeling better now that you're into your second trimester." She looked at Megan. "You seem to have gotten your energy back all of a sudden. And from the glow on your face, I'd say trouble's brewing. What are you up to now?"

Megan gave her an innocent look. "I'm five months' pregnant. I'm supposed to glow."

"What's up, daughter?" Greylen demanded. "I've also noticed that look in your eyes that ye get whenever you're scheming."

"Maybe I'm just thinking about Cam's suggestion that I ask Jack Stone on a date."

Cam choked on her food and Megan reached over and slapped her on the back.

"You don't have to jump out of the frying pan into the fire," Cam said. "And you *do* realize the man carries a gun for a living?"

Ignoring her, Meg looked at Chelsea. "How tall is Jack Stone?"

"A couple inches under six feet, I guess. Simon pointed him out as he was walking to his cruiser."

Megan went back to eating, satisfied that she'd turned her parents' scrutiny away from her.

But Cam, apparently, wasn't done causing trouble. "Then let's double-date," she suggested. "You can ask out Jack Stone, and Kenzie, you can be my date. We could all go to dinner in Greenville tomorrow night."

Several bites of food got stuck in several windpipes at that announcement.

"It's been awhile since I've gone on a . . . a date," Kenzie said into the silence. "I'm not sure what's expected of me in this century."

"You don't have to do any thing," Cam drawled. "Just leave your sword home and be your big, handsome self."

Megan glared at Cam. "For all we know, Jack Stone is married."

"No, he's not," Chelsea piped up. "Simon told me he helped Stone move into the Watson place on the lake, and that he's definitely a bachelor. He doesn't own enough stuff to fill a pickup."

Megan wanted to strangle *both* of her sisters.

"I think it's a wonderful idea, Megan," Grace said. "You should wear that new maternity outfit Winter gave you for Christmas."

"I can't go out tomorrow night," she said, quickly backtracking. "I'm driving to Augusta to apply for a position that just opened up."

"I didn't know you were looking for a job," Grace said.

"Meg found a posting for a field biologist right here on Pine Lake," Cam said. "But I think there's something strange about it. What are the chances of a job suddenly opening up right here, right now?"

"Why is that strange?" Greylen asked.

"It's being privately funded. You remember what happened to Aunt Sadie, don't you? This could also be a scam."

"It isn't," Megan countered. "A freelance biologist named Mark Collins is heading up an impact study of the wildlife in this watershed. It's required, to build a new resort."

"We didn't have to do an impact study when we built our ski resort," Grey pointed out.

"That was thirty-six years ago, Daddy. Today you can't build anything without first studying the consequences."

"But why do you want this job? You're going to be

very busy in four more months." He cradled his arms as if he were rocking a baby.

Megan smiled. "I'll get one of those baby backpacks." She looked at her mother. "That's how you carried Robbie when you brought him home from Virginia, and you told us Daddy carried all us girls in a pack until we could walk. I can't think of a better way to spend my first summer with my child—out in the field doing what I love."

"It sounds like a wonderful idea," Grace said.

"And you'll still be able to live here at Gù Brath," her father added.

Megan shook her head. "I'm going to look for my own place."

"Why?" Elizabeth asked.

"Because I'm too old to be living at home with my parents. And because I need to start building a nest in which to raise my child."

No one disputed that reasoning, though her father looked like she'd just kicked *him* in the shin.

"We will discuss your moving out tomorrow night, when you return from speaking with Mark Collins," he said.

Megan sighed and nodded. She might be twenty-nine and living on her own for ten years, but there was nothing like running back home to Daddy to make a girl feel nine years old again.

Chapter Four

*B*eing the chief of police had its perks, Jack realized as he walked around Pine Creek PowerSports. He couldn't remember the last time someone had let him shop after-hours. Then again, thinking Jack was about to drop ten grand on a snowmobile might be the real reason Paul Dempsey didn't mind missing dinner.

"If you're looking for speed, this is the baby you want," Dempsey said, patting the dark cherry cowling of a snowmobile that looked as if it belonged in a *Star Wars* movie. "Don't let the fact that it's a four-stroke scare you off. She's got plenty of get-up-and-go, and her top end is one hundred and nine miles per hour right out of the crate."

Get-up-and-go sounded good. Apparently this machine could live up to its looks. "I don't see a hitch for a fishing sled." Jack bent over to study the mess of wires and engine parts exposed when Dempsey lifted the cowling.

"This baby isn't for fishing!" Paul said. "It's designed for trail riding."

"So I can't ride trails *and* fish with it?"

Paul looked wounded. "Well, you could. But it'd be a sin to hitch a sled behind this beauty." He gently closed the cowling with a sigh and crossed the crowded show-room. "If you're looking mostly to fish, you'll want this one," he said, stopping beside a bigger and definitely less aerodynamic snowmobile. "It's got a longer track, the clutch is geared lower for towing, and it's a two-stroke. This is the workhorse of the fleet."

It was also three grand cheaper.

Jack looked back at the dark cherry snowmobile.

Dempsey immediately returned to the expensive machine. "People sit up and take notice when a man shows up on a sled like this one." He pulled a rag from his back pocket and he started to caress the hood, more than polish it. "Ain't nothing on this lake that can catch it. And being a four-stroke, it'll give you better gas mileage, as well as run quieter and cleaner."

Jack looked back at the fishing machine. Damn, it was ugly. "If I buy one tonight, can you deliver it to my house tomorrow? I'm renting the Watson place in Frog Cove, out on the end of the point."

Dempsey shook his head. "Don't gotta deliver it. You can just drive it home."

"It's got to be ten miles out to my place."

"Don't matter. You just go down the side of this road here, cut through the center of town to the lake, and head up the western shoreline. It'll take you twenty minutes, tops."

"It's legal for snowmobiles to travel on plowed roads?"

"Not really, but no one will bother you. We do it all

the time." Paul's face suddenly reddened. "Leastwise, no one used to bother us. You gonna start enforcing that ordinance? 'Cause I gotta tell you, that would kill business downtown. Snowmobilers make up half of Pine Creek's winter sales, especially at the restaurants."

Jack gave him an easy smile. "I've only been here a week. I'm not sure yet which ordinances I'm supposed to enforce and which ones I'm not."

Dempsey relaxed and started polishing the snowmobile again. "I've got a helmet that perfectly matches this paint. You show up in that and a black leather suit, and you'll have to beat the snow bunnies off with a stick."

Jack gave one last look at the ugly black workhorse, then held out his hand to Paul. "I'll take this one," he said, closing the deal with a handshake, "and I'll pick it up tomorrow afternoon." He reached inside his jacket for his wallet. "Is a check drawn on a Canadian bank okay? I haven't set up with a bank account here yet."

"I take credit cards."

Jack shook his head. "I don't use them. I'll open an account tomorrow, get some money transferred, and bring you cash."

Paul chuckled as he headed for the counter. "Don't bother. I'll take your check. I can't imagine our police chief would try passing bad paper around town." He started writing up the sales slip. "Say, what happened down at Marge's bakery, anyway? Is it true the little bastards trashed the place?"

"Pretty much. Any little bastards in particular you referring to?"

Paul looked up with a frown. "Hell, everyone knows Tommy Cleary and his brothers are behind all our missing stuff."

"Nothing of value was taken," Jack told him. "Just a couple of pies and day-old doughnuts."

"They swiped a snowblower off my lot about a month ago. Found it sitting on Main Street the next day, right in front of the Pine Creek Art Gallery."

"Would that be Winter MacKeage's place?" Jack asked as he took out his pen and began writing the check.

"She's the owner and artist, though she's a Gregor now. She married some rich bastard from away. They're living in a cottage on the lake right across the cove from you, while they build a huge house up on Bear Mountain. Winter's sister, Megan, has been running the gallery most of the fall." Dempsey shook his head when Jack looked up. "Too bad about Megan."

"How's that?"

"She's pregnant. Came home a little over four months ago, looking like a whipped puppy. Word is the bastard sent her packing when she told him she was having his kid."

"A woman named Libby MacBain and an elderly lady were running the art gallery when I stopped in to introduce myself," Jack said.

"The old lady would be Gram Katie, Libby's mom. They're minding the store because the MacKeages have a big shindig up at their place every Christmas. Old Greylen had seven daughters, the poor bastard, but he managed to get five of them married off. I think that leaves only the scientist who works down at NASA, and Megan." He snorted. "I'm surprised Greylen didn't go after the guy with a shotgun."

"That his style, is it?"

Dempsey started writing some very large numbers on the sales slip. "The MacKeages are nice enough folks, but a bit strange. They're like an old-fashioned clan from Scotland, and the MacBains are related to them somehow. If it weren't for the lovely women they married, they'd be a bunch of cranky old hermits, living off in the woods someplace."

"I've met Michael MacBain."

"That would be Libby's husband. He owns a Christmas tree farm just outside of town. You and Simon ever come into more trouble than you can handle, you call his son, Robbie. He was in the Special Forces for a while. He's a good man to have on your side in a fight."

"Thanks for the tip. So, what's the damage?" Jack asked, peering down at the sales slip.

"That depends on if I have a leather suit that fits you," Paul said, sizing him up. He walked over to a rack of black leather jackets. "You wear a large?"

"Yup. And medium pants." Jack slipped on the jacket Paul held out to him and flexed his arms. "Feels good."

"You might want a bigger size to cover that gun."

Jack looked down at the revolver on his belt. "I'm going to have to do something about this damn thing. It's been driving me crazy all week." He took off the jacket. "This is fine. Medium on the helmet, too." He walked back to the counter, set the jacket down, then walked over and sat on the snowmobile he'd just bought.

Yup, if this baby didn't make him one of the locals, nothing would.

Megan came into the living room and plopped down in an overstuffed chair by the hearth, opposite her mother. "You are looking at a woman who is once again gainfully employed."

"That quickly?" Grace asked in surprise. "Was it your

credentials that got you the job, or was Mark Collins bowled over by your smile?"

Megan laughed. "It must have been my credentials, since Mark wasn't even there. A secretary faxed him my résumé, he called back in twenty minutes, and we had a phone interview."

"So is the position what you expected?" Camry asked from the couch, where she was coloring with Elizabeth's almost-three-year-old son, Joel.

"Even better: I'll be my own boss. Mark said he only expects to make it into the field a couple of times this spring and summer. Using the state's criteria, I'm to design the survey—which Mark has to approve—then do the work and hand in the results next September."

"What university is he affiliated with?" Grace asked.

"None. He owns a freelance environmental consulting firm that services large corporations worldwide, including paper and chemical mills, oil companies, mineral mines, and such. If a company wants to expand, they call Mark to do an impact study to meet governmental requirements. He called from his office in Rio de Janeiro, Brazil."

"And he's got an office in Maine?" Cam asked.

"No. It turned out the address listed in the posting was the resort developer in Augusta. It was their secretary who put me in touch with Mark."

"And he hired you without even bothering to check your references?" Grace asked.

"He remembered seeing my name affiliated with that pipeline oil spill study I headed up in Alaska four years ago," Megan explained. "And I could hear a keyboard tapping over the phone, so he was probably doing an Internet search on me as we spoke. Mark said he prefers contracting with regional engineers and biologists when he can, because we're familiar with the local regulations."

"But you haven't lived in Maine for ten years," Grace pointed out.

Megan shrugged. "I listed Maine as my current residence."

"Speaking of which," Cam said, setting Joel on the couch so she could stand up. "Beth and I found you a place to live today. A couple she teaches with is moving, and they're planning to rent out their house in Frog Cove with the option to buy. Beth and Chelsea are over there right now, negotiating your lease."

Megan sat up straighter. "Where in Frog Cove? Is it on the lake?"

Cam nodded. "Out on the point. So if you buy a boat, you can travel to most of your work by water this summer. It's perfect, Meg. There are two bedrooms downstairs and two more upstairs, it's got a beautiful woodstove in the living room, and it has a great view of Bear Mountain. You can even see Winter and Matt's cottage directly across the cove." Cam batted her eyelashes. "And Jack Stone lives just three houses down."

"I should warn you that your father isn't happy about this," Grace said, going to Joel, who had decided eating a crayon was more fun than coloring with it. "No matter how much I reasoned with him last night, I couldn't convince Grey that going back to your fieldwork is exactly what you need right now."

"Why is he so upset?" Megan asked. "It's not like I'm moving to Siberia. I'll only be eight or nine miles away."

Grace sat on the couch with Joel on her lap. "He doesn't like the idea of you living alone with a brand-new baby. He claims that back in the twelfth century, a man his age no longer had to worry about his daughters; he'd have married them off by sixteen and turned the worrying over to their husbands." She chuckled softly. "He thinks society never should have done away with arranged marriages. He'll eventually calm down, once he sees you're able to manage everything—which I know you will." She shot Meg a crooked smile. "But you'll probably have to move back to Gù Brath when you get near your due date. Your father will camp on your doorstep if you don't, ready to rush you to the hospital at your first contraction."

"But you had us girls at home. And Beth had a midwife for Kadin and Joel. I'm using the same woman for my delivery."

Grace sighed. "Let's not mention that to your father just yet, okay? Let's let him get used to your moving out, first."

Camry plucked Joel off Grace's lap. "Come on, Meg, let's go see your new place. Beth and Chelsea and the owner are waiting for us." She shot Meg a grin as she carried Joel out the front door. "Maybe we'll even catch a glimpse of your sexy neighbor."

"Did it ever occur to any of you that I might want to pick out my own place?" Meg asked as they crossed the bridge out front.

Cam led the way to Megan's SUV. "Of course not. We know your tastes. Besides, we figured Dad couldn't argue it's not safe for you to live on a half-deserted camp road when you're only three houses down from the police chief."

Meg snorted. "Great. You've just moved me out of one macho-man environment into another."

* * *

Megan gazed at the house her sisters had decided she should rent. "Okay," she conceded to Camry, "you guys do know my tastes. It's totally adorable."

A couple of porch lights lit up what certainly appeared to be a perfect house on the outside. The shingles were stained gray, the shutters painted a dark green, and the front door—set inside a porch that ran the width of the house—was a deep, rich red. It stood nestled in a stand of old maple, birch, and hemlock on a spacious lot, its cottage-style architecture giving it a cozy, welcoming feel.

"I'll have to buy a snowblower to keep the driveway neat, like it is now," she said. "Plows make such a mess of everything."

Cam arched an eyebrow. "Moved in already, have we?"

Elizabeth came out of the house, and Megan opened the back door of her truck to release Joel from his car seat. "Will someone please explain why they make these buckles so hard to open?" she grumbled, fighting the buckles.

Elizabeth pulled Megan out of the way and reached inside. "So the *kids* can't unfasten them. Hey, big boy," she said with a laugh, straightening with her son in her arms. "Has Auntie Cam been feeding you crayons again?"

"Go potty," Joel said, wiggling to get down.

"Inside, not in the snowbank!" Beth said, rushing to catch him, then steering him toward the house.

"What is it with little boys and yellow snow?" Megan called after her.

"That's his father's doing!" Beth called back, scooping up her son to carry him up the steps. "Walter's been teaching Joel to write his name in the snow."

"*You're* having a girl," Camry declared as they walked up the path to the house. "You can teach her all about your plants and animals, and I'll teach her to drive a spaceship."

"Before or after she's potty trained?" Megan asked—only to go utterly still the moment she stepped into the home of her dreams. "Oh my God," she whispered, trying to take it all in. "It's perfect."

The interior had an open floor plan, the kitchen and living area combined into one large room divided by a counter peninsula. The walls were time-mellowed knotty pine, the hearth supporting the red enamel woodstove was made of river stone, and the floor, except for a small slate area at the entrance, was rock maple.

There wasn't any furniture and no curtains covered the expansive windows facing the lake, which made the place feel amazingly large—despite the fact that the entire house would probably fit in Gù Brath's living room.

"I guess you like it," a woman said. "I'm Joan Quimby. I taught class across the hall from Beth," she explained, holding out her hand.

"Why are you leaving this beautiful place?" Megan asked, returning the handshake.

"Bob and I are moving to Germany. I'm going to teach English to third graders and Bob will teach high school math. Come on, I'll show you the rest of the house." She headed toward a door on the left side of the living room. "There are two bedrooms down here with a shared bath, and two more upstairs with another full bath." Joan stopped inside the lakeside bedroom and smiled apologetically. "The ones downstairs are a bit small, but I like having the larger living area."

"Is there a deck facing the lake?" Megan asked, walking to the French doors on the back wall of the bedroom.

Joan flicked a switch and light flooded a snow-covered deck running the width of the house, as well as a large yard studded with old-growth trees.

"I see a dock pulled up on shore," Megan said. "Do you have a boat?"

"Yes, a pontoon boat. It's parked on the other side of the house, covered in snow."

"Are you planning to sell it?"

"In the spring. Paul Dempsey over at PowerSports is going to come get it once the snow melts, and put it on his lot on consignment."

"Tell him not to bother," Megan said, walking back into the living room to find Chelsea and Camry, at the counter, reading what must be the lease.

Meg walked up and took the paper from them. "I'm not renting this house," she said, smiling at their startled expressions. "I'm buying it." She looked at Joan. "When are you and Bob leaving?"

Joan seemed even more shocked. "Um, we're driving to Boston tomorrow and flying out the day after that." She waved at the empty house. "You want to *buy* it? But you haven't even seen the upstairs."

"I've seen enough. Anything more is just a bonus. I'll write you a check right now for your asking price, if you throw in the boat."

"Meg," Camry said, "what are you doing? Your job is going to last less than a year."

"It doesn't matter where my work might eventually take me; I still need a home base. I'll sell my condo in Boston and move up here permanently."

"Meg, you need to think about this," Chelsea inter-jected. "You can't just walk into a house and buy it in five minutes."

"Why not?"

Nobody had a good answer to that.

"Then it's settled," Meg said, holding out her hand to Joan.

Joan pumped Megan's arm excitedly. "Bob will be thrilled! We never thought we'd sell this place in the middle of the winter." She took the lease and tore it up with a laugh. "You're going to love it here, Megan. The sunrises are beautiful."

The muted whine of a high-performance engine echoed off the bare walls, and the four women followed Joel over to the lakeside windows. A snowmobile shot out from the end of the point, and went zooming past the front of the house in a cloud of snow colored white and red from the head- and taillights.

"That must be our new police chief," Joan said. "He moved into the Watson place about a week ago. I saw him driving what looked like a fancy new snowmobile when he came home just before dark."

"Snow-bile!" Joel shouted, jumping up and down.

Chelsea nudged Megan with her elbow. "Maybe he'll give you a ride if you ask him real nice."

Megan walked back to the counter to dig through her purse for her checkbook. "You can deposit this to-morrow," she said to Joan as she started to fill out the check. "It's from my money market account. Um . . . how much?"

Her face turning a bit pink, Joan named a figure that made Megan suck in her breath. "I guess I haven't been paying much attention to the real estate market lately.

Ah, how about I make this out, but you give me three or four days to transfer some funds?"

"Good grief, Meg, this isn't like buying a toaster," Chelsea said, walking up to the counter. "Make the check out to my law firm in Bangor, and we'll hold the money in escrow while the paperwork is being done. A deed has to be drawn up, and clear title to the property needs to be researched." She looked at Joan. "Do you and Bob have a lawyer?"

"No. We were going to hire a real estate broker and let them take care of that stuff."

"Then if you don't mind, my law firm can act on both Megan's and your behalf."

"Is that legal?" Beth asked, bending down to pick up Joel.

"It's sort of a gray area," Chelsea said. "But this is a simple transaction, since Meg won't have to obtain financing. Why don't you and Bob stop in my office on your way through Bangor tomorrow, Joan? I'll call them in the morning and have someone start the paper-work for you." Chelsea took the check from Megan and handed it to Joan. "Give them this, and you may con-sider your house sold."

"When can I move in?" Megan asked.

"You should probably wait until the deed is signed," Chelsea said. "But it's up to Joan and Bob."

Joan picked up the keys on the counter and handed them to Megan. "After twenty-eight years of marriage, I know what Bob's going to say. Welcome home, Megan and baby," she said, lightly patting Megan's belly. "This is a wonderful place to raise children."

Chapter Five

𝒠ven though there were disadvantages to having a large, overprotective family, there were also some very nice perks when one was five months' pregnant and moving into a new house. While everyone had an opinion on what she needed to do and how she should do it, no one would let her lift anything heavier than her laptop. The only responsibility she'd had was to direct traffic when she and four large MacBain and MacKeage cousins went down to Boston and emptied her condo, and then stand back and watch them unload the truck in Maine.

Camry had decided that what was happening in Frog Cove was much more interesting than her work in Florida right now, considering that her latest attempt to harness ion propulsion had failed. Her job was somewhat an independent position; NASA supplied the lab and Camry contributed the brainpower. So Cam had called whomever she answered to and told them she was extending her vacation another week.

Great. It had been only three days since Megan had purchased her cozy little cottage, and she was ready to strangle her sister. Camry kept insisting she climb right back on the horse she'd fallen off when Wayne Ferris had broken her heart.

"I am not going over there with a pie you baked, to ask for a date," Megan told her for the fourth time in as many minutes. Camry had actually baked an apple pie for Meg to present to her neighbor! Megan plopped into a chair in front of her still curtainless window facing the lake and glared at her sister. "And besides, what do you suppose his reaction will be when he sees my belly? He's going to wonder what sort of woman gets knocked up by one man, then starts looking for a replacement before the kid's even born."

"I'm not asking you to propose to the guy," Cam countered. "I'm only following up on Chelsea's suggestion to use him for practice."

"She made that suggestion to *you*."

"Camry, leave your sister alone," Grace said, walking out of the bedroom, her arms full of packing material. "Meg doesn't want to date anyone. She wants Wayne."

"Good God," Cam said in a strangled voice, jumping to her feet. "You're hoping Ferris will come after her. You think he's going to show up here any day now, hat in hand, and beg her to take him back."

Megan also jumped up, horrified. "Mom! Is that true?"

"It's been *four* months," Camry said. "He's not coming."

"Is it true?" Megan repeated. "All this time, you've been thinking Wayne's going to suddenly show up here?"

"Would you take him back if he did?" Grace asked softly.

"No!" Cam said before Megan could. "The bastard broke her heart!"

Grace continued looking at Megan.

Megan shook her head.

"But what if Wayne realizes he made a mistake?" Grace asked. "You two had only known each other a little over a month, camping in tents out on the tundra in an isolated corner of the world." She set the packing material down and walked up to Megan. "What if once Wayne got back to his empty home, he realized he needs you in his life? What if he's been as miserable as you've been?"

"You have no idea of the things he said to me that day." Megan took a shuddering breath. "Wayne made it perfectly clear that he wanted nothing to do with me or our child. I *begged* him, Mama, to give us a chance, but it was like he suddenly turned into a completely different person. I—I actually became afraid of him," she whispered. "I couldn't pack my bags and get out of there fast enough."

"What do ye mean, you were afraid of him?" Her father came out of the bedroom carrying several collapsed boxes. He dropped them by the door and walked up to Megan, taking hold of her shoulders. "Did he hurt you, daughter?"

"No, Daddy. He just . . ." She wrapped her arms around his waist and leaned against his chest with a sigh. "He just turned into somebody I didn't like anymore."

*   *   *

Jack sat on his snowmobile and sipped hot cocoa from his Thermos. He was parked on the lake about a hundred yards from shore, the moonless night making him nearly invisible while offering him a perfect view of what was going on inside his neighbor's living room.

He'd finally figured out how to approach her, but he was no closer to catching Megan alone than he was to catching whoever had broken into the bakery. He could accept not making any headway on the vandals, considering that every doughnut addict within fifty miles of Pine Creek had left their fingerprints in that bakery, and forensics still hadn't identified that foul-smelling slime.

As for Megan, Jack couldn't believe his luck when Bob and Joan Quimby had come over to say good-bye and told him that a lovely woman named Megan MacKeage had *purchased* their house. And by the way, she was five months' pregnant and single, so could he maybe keep an eye on her?

But she was always surrounded by people. Megan had enough aunts and uncles and cousins and in-laws to populate a small city; he'd been tripping over MacBains and MacKeages in town for the last two weeks. And her only unmarried sister, Camry, was staying at her house at night.

Jack figured his legendary patience would survive only two or three more days before he got desperate enough to kidnap the woman. He really hated it when a hunt ended that way; things had a tendency to get messy, and he always felt he'd somehow failed. He snorted. Catching their new police chief with a local lady bound and gagged in his cruiser would certainly go over well with the fine folks who'd hired him.

Assuming Greylen MacKeage didn't kill him on sight.

* * *

"What year was Wayne born, and where?" Cam asked.

Megan added a handful of marshmallows to her cocoa, then turned to look at her sister sitting on the couch. Their parents had left twenty minutes ago, and Megan and Camry had declared a truce—for now. "Why?"

"I'm Googling him, but apparently Wayne Ferris is a popular name." Cam continued typing on the laptop sitting on the coffee table. "It would help if I knew when and where he was born."

Megan walked over and sat down to look at the screen, intrigued despite herself. "Why are you searching Wayne?"

Cam shrugged. "Just curious. Where's he from?"

"Alberta, Canada. He lives a couple hundred miles northeast of Edmonton . . . in Medicine Lake, I think he said."

"Oohhh, he likes it cold and remote, does he? Maybe that's where he buries the bodies," Cam said, making a frightened face as she hit a few more buttons.

"When did Wayne graduate to being a serial killer? I told you, he isn't violent."

"Most serial killers aren't, outwardly. Haven't you seen those interviews with neighbors saying how they can't believe it, that 'he was such a nice, quiet man'?" Cam turned to Megan. "I understand why you wouldn't have said anything to Mom and Dad, but it's just you and me now. So when Wayne suddenly changed into a different person, did he get rough with you?"

"He got . . . At first he just stared in disbelief when I told him I was pregnant, then he hugged me, and then he turned around and walked out without saying a word. I have no idea where he slept that night. The next morning he showed up at the kitchen, led me by the hand to his tent, and told me to pack up my stuff and get the hell out of there before sunset."

"With no explanation?"

"None." Megan blew on her cocoa, staring off into space. "He refused to even talk about the baby that morning. He was so frighteningly soft-spoken. You know, like how Dad gets when he's really mad at one of us and is trying not to explode?"

"He only gets like that when we do something dumb that he thinks is dangerous. He's reacting out of fear."

"Exactly. I think Wayne was scared to death, once he realized what having a baby meant. Mom was right; we were in an isolated little world of our own for those six weeks. And when he thought about us returning to civilization, he panicked."

"So the weasel showed his true colors." Camry started typing again. "I know it doesn't feel like it right now, Meg, but you're better off without the jerk. You still didn't say if he hit you or not."

"He didn't hit me." Megan stood and walked to the window. "But he sure as hell scared me." She turned back to Cam. "And you know I don't scare easy. But there had been an accident two days before I discovered I was pregnant, and the tension in camp was high for everyone. One of the Canadian government workers who was monitoring our study died."

"How? You were counting geese and caribou, for Pete's sake. What could possibly happen in the middle of the tundra?"

"We don't know how it happened. Somebody found the guy lying facedown in a small pond. He had apparently drowned during the night."

"And you're thinking that's why Wayne reacted the way he did?"

Megan shrugged. "If so, it doesn't explain why I haven't heard from him since."

"Exactly," Cam said, looking back at the screen.

"Hey, how are you getting on the Internet, anyway? I haven't had a phone installed yet."

"The whole house is wi-fi. Joan and Bob had a high-speed cable connection, and they must have forgotten to shut it off. So you've got cable TV, too." Camry made a sound of disgust. "I've found your Wayne Ferris, but the info on him only goes back five years."

Megan returned to the couch, studying what Cam had found. "That's him. He went to undergraduate school in British Columbia and got his master's degree in Toronto." She reached over and scrolled down the page, reading what little was there. "I wonder why there's nothing else?"

"Maybe because Wayne Ferris didn't exist until five years ago?" Cam said. "You knew him what, six weeks? Did he ever talk about his childhood?"

"Not much, now that you mention it. He had this way of always turning the conversation back to me."

Cam rolled her eyes. "Every woman's dream guy, and you fell for him hook, line, and sinker."

"I do know he was raised by his grandfather," Meg defended. "Or maybe his great-grandfather? His parents were killed in a car accident when he was nine. I think he was in it, because he's got burn scars on his hands, but I could never get him to talk about it. I do remember him saying something about inheriting the house in Medicine Lake."

Megan noticed the headlights of a fast-moving sled

racing back to shore. "Jack Stone sure likes his new snowmobile," she said, "He's been out riding again."

"Good. Come on," Camry said, leading Megan to the counter. "It's time you got Wayne Ferris out of your head once and for all." She picked up the pie she'd baked and shoved it in Megan's hands. "We are going over to Jack Stone's house right now, and you're asking him out."

Megan shoved the pie back at her. "No."

"Yes, you are," Camry said. Then she sighed. "Okay, you don't have to ask him out. But we're going over there to introduce ourselves. You really need to see that nice guys still exist, Meg."

"We don't know that Jack Stone is a nice guy."

"Chelsea liked him."

Megan rolled her eyes. "She only saw him walking to his cruiser. For all we know, he's a womanizing, chest-beating caveman who thinks women should stay at home, barefoot and pregnant."

Camry laughed as she put on her coat and boots. "Then he should *love* your belly." She walked over and took the pie while giving Megan a critical inspection. "When was the last time you had a haircut?"

"Never mind my hair," Meg said, tucking a loose curl behind her ear. Dammit, when Camry got like this, the only way to shut her up was to play along to make her think she'd won. "Okay, I'll go. But I'm not asking him out, and we're telling him *you* made the pie."

"But if he knows I baked it, that'll defeat its purpose."

"Not if he gets food poisoning, it won't."

"Fine, then," Camry said, storming out the door. "If he really is as cute as Chelsea said, *I'll* ask him out."

Chapter Six

Jack was just stepping in the shower when he heard a knock on his kitchen door. He didn't know anyone well enough who would drop by for a beer, and he was off duty; Simon needed to quit running to him with inane questions.

The knock sounded again, a bit louder.

With a growl of defeat, Jack wrapped a towel around his waist and strode out to the kitchen. "Dammit, Pratt, you better be here to tell me you caught the bastards."

But as the door swung fully open, Jack found himself staring into the startled, bright green eyes of a woman holding a pie. He also saw Megan MacKeage as still as a stone slightly behind her, her complexion pale in the porch light.

"W-Wayne?" Megan whispered.

"Shit," Jack growled at the exact same time.

"*Wayne*?" echoed the woman in front.

"Megan, sweetheart," Jack said, stepping outside. He

slipped on the ice-glazed snow covering the porch, and grabbed the railing to keep from falling.

Megan stepped back, turned, and bolted into the night.

"Dammit, no! Megan! Don't run!" Jack shouted, taking a better grip on his towel to go after her.

But the other woman grabbed his arm. "Wayne *Ferris*?" She drew back and hurled her pie directly at his face. "You no-good, rotten bastard! You stay away from my sister!" She turned and ran after Megan—but first snatched the towel off his hips, tossing it in the snowbank as she disappeared into the darkness.

The attack sent Jack flailing backward, and he landed on his naked ass on the snowy porch. Scrambling to his feet with a curse, he stumbled into the house and slammed the door so hard, the windows rattled. Groping for something to wipe his eyes, he found a shirt hanging on the peg. "Dammit to hell! Four months of waiting and planning, and she walks up and knocks on my door! And what do you do? You stand there like a mindless idiot and curse at her!"

Talk about being caught off guard. He knew she was five months pregnant, but actually *seeing* her rounded little belly pushing out past her jacket had still been a hell of a shock. Jack strode back to the bathroom, stepped into the shower, and scrubbed his hands over his face and through his hair to wash away the pie. He hung his head with a snort.

Recklessness obviously ran in the family; Megan's sister certainly spoke her mind and backed it up with whatever weapon she had handy. She was a quick thinker, too, snatching his towel so he wouldn't pursue them.

Megan had acted just as recklessly during their stay on the tundra. Once he'd had to stop her from heading into a fistfight between two rugged and nearly out-of-control young men. Armed with only a hiking stick, she hadn't seemed to realize that stick wouldn't have fazed the combatants, much less have protected her. It was as if she didn't even notice their size; she had simply been determined to box in their ears.

Having spent the last two weeks in Pine Creek, Jack was beginning to understand why Megan didn't equate size with danger. He hadn't met one MacKeage or MacBain male under six feet tall. And their women walked around like they didn't have a fear in the world. Of course, what woman wouldn't feel safe and secure being shadowed by a Sasquatch of a husband?

Jack shut off the water and stepped out of the shower. Her utterly fearless approach to life was the first thing that had attracted him to Megan. She was passion personified. Megan brought an energy to her work that was almost spiritual in the way she interacted with the students, the animals they were counting, and the environment she was determined to protect.

He'd been caught completely off guard when she had suddenly turned that amazing energy on him. Megan had cranked her smile to full wattage and asked if she could buy him dinner as thanks for intervening in the student battle. He'd felt as if he were being trampled by a herd of caribou.

Reeling from her smile—not to mention her startling, vivid green eyes focused directly on him—he had stammered out something inane, like it would be his pleasure. So they'd walked to the mess tent, and she had cheekily told him to pick out whatever he desired from the food provided by the university sponsoring the study. From that moment on, that herd of caribou had taken up residence in Jack's gut, turned his mind to mush, and infused every fiber of his being with hope.

Until the *real* reason he was there had suddenly reared its ugly head.

Camry leaned against the inside of Megan's front door and fought to catch her breath. "Oh my God. That was *Wayne*?" she gasped. "What's he doing at Stone's house?" She slapped a hand to her chest. "Oh my God, he *is* Jack Stone!"

"He can't be." Megan leaned against the counter, breathing equally hard and hugging her belly. "Wayne's a biologist, not a law officer. There must be some other reason he's at Jack Stone's house."

Camry pushed away from the door, walking to Megan and wrapping an arm around her shoulders. "If Jack was there, he'd have answered the door. The man who greeted us was obviously just getting in the shower," she pointed out, leading her sister over to the couch.

"Not in front of the window," Megan said, taking a steadying breath. "The chair in the corner. Turn out some of these lights, will you?"

Cam settled her sister in the chair by the woodstove, then snapped off the overhead lights, leaving on only a table lamp by the window and one over the sink. "I'll reheat your cocoa," she said, grabbing the mug and putting it in the microwave. She turned to look at Megan, who was silent, her complexion ashen. "Do you suppose Mom was right?" she asked. "That Wayne is here because he does want you back?"

Megan shook her head.

"Then what's he doing here? If he is Jack Stone, that means he's planning on staying for a while. If he just came here to win you back, he wouldn't have taken a job."

The microwave dinged and Cam pulled out the mug and gave the cocoa a stir. She carried it over to Megan but had to wrap her sister's fingers around it. "Don't get all crazy on me, sis," she said, hunching down to look her in the eye. "He can't make you do anything you don't want to."

"But why is he *here*?"

Cam walked back to the counter and started digging in her purse for her cell phone. "Who knows? Maybe . . ." She shrugged, unable to come up with a plausible answer.

"Who are you calling?"

"Mom and Dad."

"No! We can't call them!"

Cam stopped pushing buttons and looked at her sister. "We have to, Meg. They need to know about this."

"No, they don't," Megan said, standing up. "Dad will rush over here, drag Wayne out of that house, and . . . and . . ."

"And beat him to a bloody pulp?" Cam finished. "You're right. I'll call Robbie, then."

"Same problem," Megan said, taking the phone and dropping it back in Cam's purse.

Camry was glad to see the color coming back in her sister's cheeks. "So we're just going to sit here with the lights out?" she asked, looking toward the stark, black windows.

"If Wayne is Jack, he's been in Pine Creek over a

week," Meg pointed out. "And he hasn't tried contacting me in all that time. Tonight was a fluke. We obviously surprised him."

Cam sat down on the edge of the hearth. "What are the chances you'd buy a house three doors down from your ex-boyfriend?"

"Slim to none," Meg said. She sucked in a shuddering breath. "What am I going to do?"

Camry snorted. "There's not much you can do. It's a free country. The man has a right to be here."

"But if Wayne and Jack Stone are the same person, I have to tell someone! He's a biologist posing as our chief of police."

"Maybe he also has a degree in law enforcement."

"And two names?"

Cam went back to the coffee table. "Let's Google Jack Stone and see what we come up with."

Megan came over and sat down beside her. "Look for a site that might have his picture." Her cheeks suddenly flushed. "He certainly looked different tonight. His hair's a lot shorter, he shaved his beard, and he wasn't wearing glasses."

Cam started typing. "Are you sure that was Wayne, and not someone who just looks like him? Maybe a brother?"

"It was Wayne. And he definitely knew who I was."

"That's right, he called you sweetheart." Cam scrolled down the list Google had come up with, and clicked on one of the sites. "Hmm, the plot thickens," she said dramatically, hoping to ease the tension. "There's no more here than we found on Wayne Ferris. What do you make of this site? It's an ad, and it's sort of cryptic." She gasped.

"Wait, I know what this is. Some guys at work were showing me sites put up by soldiers for hire. Jack Stone is a mercenary!"

Megan was shaking her head before Cam could finish. "That couldn't be Wayne. I told you, he's not rough and tough and . . . and . . ." She sighed. "You picked the wrong site. There isn't even a picture."

Camry clicked back to the Google list, but Meg reached out and shut off the computer. "I've had enough for one day." She dropped her head back against the couch. "I'll deal with Wayne, or Jack, or whoever the hell he is, tomorrow."

"Then let's go to Gù Brath, in case he decides he wants to talk to you."

Meg shook her head. "You were right. I *have* been acting like a wimp for the last four months, and I am utterly disgusted with myself." She cradled her belly in her hands. "What kind of example have I been setting for my baby?"

"It's not born yet, Meg," Cam said, patting her niece or nephew. "It doesn't know you've been a wimp."

"It knows I've been crying for the last four months." She stood up with determination. "We're going to stay right here and figure out what I'm going to do about this." Her eyes snapped with resolve. "It was a hell of a shock seeing him tonight, but it certainly didn't kill me. I've been such an idiot, letting him have that kind of power over me." She headed for the door. "We are marching right back to that house, and I'm giving that jerk a piece of my mind!"

"Wait!" Cam yelped, chasing after her and catching her sleeve. "You need to think this through, Meg. I know you're angry he beat you to the punch, but maybe this isn't the best time to confront him."

"What are you talking about? Beat me to what punch?"

Camry crossed her arms under her breasts. "You told me you intended to go to Canada and throw the fact that you've gotten on with your life in Wayne's face—but he beat you to the punch by showing up here first. I agree that you should confront him, but not tonight. He . . . ah . . . he's probably not in the mood to have anything else . . . ah . . . thrown in his face right now."

"What are you talking about?"

"I threw the pie at him. Hit him square in the face."

Megan blinked, then suddenly laughed. "Oh, I wish I'd seen that. No, I wished I'd *done* that."

"Then you'll love it that I swiped his towel and threw it in the snowbank."

"You what!" Megan laughed even harder.

"I was afraid he'd chase after us. I didn't see anything, though; I was too busy running for my life."

Megan sighed, then shook her head. "Okay, so tonight isn't the best time to confront him. But I don't care that he beat me to the punch, because *I'm* going to have the last word—right before I send him packing."

Megan walked into the Pine Creek Art Gallery, smiling as she headed toward the counter.

Winter was dusting a picture on the back wall. "What are you doing here?" she asked in surprise.

"I'm reporting to work. I still have a job, don't I?"

Winter eyed her suspiciously. "You look different. Sort of excited. Or maybe eager is more like it." She wrinkled her brow. "And you just got a new job. What about your watershed project?"

Megan took off her coat and carried it into the back office. "It'll take two months for me to design the survey, and I can do that in the evening."

Winter followed, obviously still suspicious. "I thought you weren't speaking to me."

"Really? Since when?"

"Since I didn't tell you about Kenzie."

"Ah, that. How is our ancient warrior, anyway? I haven't seen him around lately."

Winter shrugged. "No one's seen Kenzie since he went to live with Father Daar."

"Maybe they've killed each other already."

Winter eyed her closely again. "So what are you really doing here this morning?"

"I'm *really* going to work for you. Cam is driving me crazy. Somebody needs to tell her that she's not an interior decorator. You should see the curtains she bought for my living room windows—they're heavy red velvet! I left her to put them up by herself."

"Speaking of which, when is she going back to Florida?"

"She said something about not going back until the end of the month."

"But that's four weeks away! She'll lose her position at NASA."

Megan shrugged. "Talk to Mom. She knows what it's like to be stuck in the middle of a project and keep hitting a brick wall, no matter what you try. Cam said she needs to give her left brain a rest for a few weeks. I think she's really just too damn nosy to leave right now."

"Nosy about what?"

"Can you keep a secret?" Megan slapped her forehead dramatically. "What am I saying? You kept Kenzie a secret from me since Thanksgiving."

"Are you going to keep making me apologize for that?"

"You bet I am. Okay, listen up: Jack Stone is actually Wayne Ferris."

"What!"

"Wayne is here. Camry and I met him last night, when we took him a pie. Wayne Ferris answered the door."

"Oh my God." Winter groped behind her for a chair, then sat down and stared at Megan, her expression horrified. "What did you do?"

"I ran. Cam threw the pie in his face."

Winter didn't laugh. "I'm still confused. You're saying Wayne Ferris and Jack Stone are the same man?"

"That's what we figure. Why else would Wayne be answering Jack's door—wearing only a towel, late at night?"

"But what's he doing here?"

"Who knows? Cam said it can't be to make amends, because he wouldn't have taken a job if that were the case. He would have walked up to Gù Brath, knocked on the door, and dropped to his knees to beg my forgiveness."

"And are you going to forgive him?"

Megan shook her head.

"Then is there any particular reason you're so chipper the morning after finding out he's in town?"

"Sure is," Megan said, going back into the gallery. "For the first time in months, I'm free."

"Free?" Winter echoed, following her. "The father of your baby—the man who broke your heart—all of a sudden shows back up in your life, and that makes you *free*?"

Megan walked to the door and flipped the sign to Open. "When I was hiding in shock in my kitchen last night, it suddenly dawned on me that I hadn't dropped dead at the sight of him. You know how mad I get at myself for being scared of something? Well, for the last four months I had built Wayne up to be this scary, fire-breathing dragon. And last night I was reminded that he's only a man." She shrugged. "I've done more damage to myself than he ever could."

Winter gaped at her, utterly speechless for once.

"So," Megan said, rubbing her hands together. "Do you want me to continue dusting or should I start filling out the yearly inventory sheets?"

"Do Mom and Dad know he's here?"

"No, and I don't want you telling them, either. I'll tell them once I find out what he wants."

"Maybe Matt should be the one to have a talk with him. Or Robbie."

"Un-uh. I don't need either of them interfering. Wayne is *my* mess."

Winter suddenly jumped up and dragged Megan into the back office. "He just walked by," she whispered, reaching over and snapping the lock on the back door that joined her shop to Dolan's Outfitter Store. "I think he's heading to Rose's next door. Somebody stole her antlers again last night, and this time they also took the bulletin board right off the building."

Megan pulled free, smoothed down the front of her sweater, tucked her hair behind her ears, and walked back out to the counter. "I am not hiding from Wayne. If we bump into each other in town, that's his problem."

"Okay," Winter said, her cheeks flushed. "But promise me you'll have your talk with him in a public place."

"Why? You think he'll try to run off with me or something? I gave him that chance up in Canada, and he tossed my offer back in my face. I'm not about to give him the chance to do it again."

Chapter Seven

*E*very muscle Jack owned ached, his left hand wouldn't stop bleeding, and if he had the strength, he'd kick himself in the ass for breaking his rule of not working in law enforcement. He'd *known* better, but had that stopped him from taking this job to be near Megan? Nope. And today he'd gotten an up-close-and-personal reminder that every sleepy town, anywhere in the world, had a dark underbelly of abuse and oppression.

He'd nearly had John Bracket calmed down enough to get him handcuffed and in the cruiser when that damn dog had come out of nowhere. The melee that had followed would certainly be etched in Simon Pratt's psyche for a while, and it would take a month of Sundays before Jack's gut unknotted.

He'd nearly drawn his gun and shot the dog, when it had finished chewing on his hand and gone after Simon. Bracket's powerful right uppercut was the only thing that had stopped him. And Mrs. Bracket hadn't helped matters, screaming bloody murder as she'd scrambled after the dog despite her bleeding lip, black eye, and sprained wrist.

He should have added the charge of assaulting an officer when he'd booked Bracket into the county jail. But remembering the two children who'd peered wide-eyed out the window, and knowing Bracket was their only means of support, Jack had persuaded Simon to overlook the incident by promising they'd keep a close watch on Bracket when he returned home. Which was another problem with small towns; *not* getting personally involved was nearly impossible.

With a groan that was as much frustrated as tired, Jack got out of his truck and limped up his porch steps. He didn't know which made him madder: that Mrs. Bracket would undoubtedly bail her husband out tomorrow morning, or that now he wouldn't be able to talk to Megan like he'd been planning all day. He wasn't about to show up on her doorstep looking as if he'd just lost a fight to a dog.

Jack opened his storm door with a sigh of regret, and was just slipping his key in the lock when he noticed the envelope taped to the door. He opened the door and stepped inside, snapped on the kitchen light, then tore open the envelope.

YOU'RE INVITED TO DINNER AT MY HOUSE AT
EIGHT O'CLOCK. LEAVE YOUR GUN HOME.

So she'd decided to make the first move again, had she? Jack smiled despite himself. He limped into the bathroom carrying the note with him, turned on the shower, then gazed down at her invitation. The wording was succinct, the handwriting bold, precise, and energetic. It also said, between the lines, that she was once again taking charge of their . . . relationship.

Just like she had on the tundra.

O-kay, then. Beat up or not, tonight they would talk.

"You have to leave *now*," Megan said, pushing Camry toward the door. "It's almost eight o'clock."

"He just got home twenty minutes ago," Camry protested, her hand on the doorknob. "He'll be late."

"Just go, will you? I need some peace and quiet before he arrives."

Camry opened the door but didn't step outside. "Tell me again why you have to confront him at all? If you'd just ignore him, he might go away."

"And that's why you can't keep a boyfriend more than six months. Go!" she said with one last shove. "Tell Mom and Dad I said hi," she called out sweetly as Camry slowly walked to her car, "and don't forget my alibi. I'm staying in Bangor late tonight to do some research, and you didn't feel like spending the evening alone."

Cam opened her car door and looked back at Megan. "You only have butter knives to use tonight. I hid all the sharp ones."

"I told you, Wayne is not violent."

"It wasn't *your* throat I was worried about getting slit," she drawled. "You hold the upper hand tonight, sis. Don't let him sweet-talk his way back into your life. I don't care how good he looks naked."

Megan closed the door, then sucked in a calming breath and slowly exhaled. What *was* she doing, inviting the man who broke her heart over to dinner?

Even worse, what if he didn't come?

Megan pushed away from the door to check on the

chicken roasting in the oven. She was simply determined to clear the air between them once and for all. It was important for Wayne to see that she was utterly, completely, and positively over him. Tonight she was ending things on her terms, not his. She wouldn't be the one packing her bags and running away—*he* would.

Megan jumped at the sound of the doorbell chiming. She pulled off her apron and tossed it on the counter, then opened the door with the brightest smile she could muster.

"Hello, Wayne."

"Ah . . . hi."

"Or should I call you Jack?"

His clean-shaven face turned a dull red. "Jack is the right choice. This is for you," he said, holding out a six-pack of Canadian lager. "I'm pretty sure beer isn't a proper hostess gift, but it's all I had."

Megan's heart fluttered. For one insane minute, she flashed back to him sprawled comfortably in front of a campfire, enjoying a bottle of beer after a long day of wrestling the geese they'd been banding.

"Aw hell, I didn't think. You can't have alcohol," he said, his gaze on her belly. He set the six-pack on the porch, then stepped inside, looking around the room as if expecting an ambush. "Is your sister joining us?"

"No, she's at Gù Brath for the evening. What happened to your jaw? Did Camry do that when she hit you with the pie?"

Wayne—no, Jack touched the side of his face.

Megan gasped at the thick bandage on his left hand, then gave him an accusing glare. "You were in a fight."

"And I eventually won, too."

Megan spun on her heel and marched to the oven,

stuffed her hands in her mitts, and pulled out the roaster—all while being acutely aware of Wayne—no, Jack prowling around her living room.

"This is a nice place you have here," he said, stopping at the woodstove. "The fire's low. Want me to add some wood?"

Megan caught herself just before she told him to make himself at home. "Sure. The large lever on the right is the draft."

Realizing she was calmer when she wasn't actually looking at him, she pulled out a platter for the chicken and casually asked, "So what are you doing in Pine Creek, calling yourself Jack Stone and pretending to be the chief of police?"

"I'm not pretending and I have the wounds to prove it," he said. She looked over and he held up his bandaged hand. "Pine Creek advertised for a police chief, I needed a job, and Jack Stone is my real name."

"Then who is Wayne Ferris?"

"A figment of my imagination that helped me get a position on your environmental study."

She stopped in the middle of lifting the chicken out of the pan. "So you're a cop, not a biologist?"

"I don't have a degree in either field. I just read a few books on the tundra's ecosystem so I could sound like I knew what I was talking about."

"But why? What were you doing there?"

He closed the damper on the stove, walked over, and took the utensils from her, then lifted the chicken out of the pan, his back to her as he spoke. "My name is Jack Stone, I own a house in Medicine Lake, and I'm a highly specialized hunter."

"You *hunt* the animals we were counting?"

"No—people." He set the chicken on the platter, licked one of his fingers, then leaned back on the counter to look at her. "Specifically, I hunt runaways."

"What kind of runaways?"

"Anyone who needs finding, but mostly teenagers. Worried parents contact me to find their kids and bring them back home."

Megan gaped at him. He tracked down runaway kids? "Why don't they just call the police?"

He led her to the chair by the woodstove, then sat on the ottoman facing her. "Because the ones I go after are usually out of the reach of law enforcement. They've disappeared in a large city like Toronto or New York, run off to join a cult, or else they've deliberately jumped off the face of the earth."

"And you find them and bring them to their parents?"

He shrugged. "That depends on their age and how they're doing when I find them. Under sixteen, I usually bring them home. But even then, if they're surviving just fine and I have a good idea what they're running from, I only report back to the parents that they're alive and well and doing okay."

Megan leaned back in her chair. "*You* decide if life on the street is better than living at home with their families? How wise you are, to know what's best for those kids."

He stared at her in silence for a moment. "You come from a close-knit community, Megan, and a large, loving, intact family," he said softly. "Some kids aren't so lucky. And if it's wrong to judge their circumstances by my own set of standards, then so be it. Better me than no one at all."

Megan's face flushed with heat. "I'm sorry. Yes, that's

better than no one going after them." She stood and went back to the kitchen to finish getting dinner on the table. "Who were you . . . um, hunting when we met?"

"Billy Grumman, though his real name is Billy Wellington. His parents had been searching for him for four years. I was their last hope."

She turned in surprise. "But he's only nineteen or twenty!"

"He ran away from home at sixteen, kicked around New York City for a year, then got drafted into some sort of cult."

Megan was intrigued. "It's hard to believe Billy's a runaway. He seemed just like the others."

"After four years, I doubt he considered himself a runaway any longer."

"Yet he found a way to get an education, and his schoolwork was exemplary enough that he was a team leader."

Jack walked to the kitchen and started opening drawers. "He's very well educated because the cult he belonged to was paying for it. Where are your knives, so I can carve the bird?"

"Camry hid them before she left."

Jack stilled. "Your sister thinks I'm *dangerous*?"

"No, she thinks I am." Megan spooned the potatoes into a bowl, then carried it to the table. "What kind of cult pays for college?"

"A very sophisticated organization with an environmental agenda, apparently," Jack said, setting the chicken down and taking a seat across from her. "I don't mess with the organizations I'm infiltrating," he said, driving his fork into the bird and pulling off a large chunk of breast meat. "I try to approach my target when they're alone, to talk with them."

Target. Infiltrate. Well, spit—Jack Stone was a damn *warrior*.

"So did you talk Billy into contacting his parents?"

He rested his arms on the table and looked her directly in the eye. "No, I stuffed him in a small plane and smuggled him back across the border to his parents in Kansas."

"You didn't give him a choice?"

"Sure I did. He just didn't like either choice I offered."

"And they were?"

"That I would take him home to his parents, or to the Royal Canadian Mounted Police."

"The police? Why?"

"You remember the government worker who died?"

She nodded.

"I'm pretty sure Billy knows something about his death."

"Were they drinking together, and the man fell in the pond and Billy was too intoxicated to help him?"

Jack shook his head. "The guy wasn't drunk, and it wasn't an accident, Megan. He was murdered—which is why I wanted you out of there."

Megan leaned back with a gasp. "And you think Billy did it?"

"No. But I think he might know who did." He shifted in his seat, clearly uncomfortable. "It's my guess the organization paying for Billy's education wanted him there for their own reasons."

"What was going on?"

"I wasn't able to find out, and Billy's not talking. He

was definitely shaken by the guy's death, but apparently he was more scared of his benefactor than he was of facing murder charges. So I dragged him back to his parents and suggested they help their son disappear for a little while."

Megan crossed her arms over her belly and stared silently at the man sitting across from her. It all sounded plausible—even his suggestion that he'd ditched her in some half-assed attempt to protect her. But then, he made his living by persuading people into doing what he wanted, didn't he?

"I don't believe you," she said flatly. "I was there for two months, and I didn't see anything odd happening. I think that *you* realized you were a jackass four months ago, and that an apology won't cut it, so you made up this fantastical story about a murder to make it seem like you gave me the boot for my own good." She pushed her chair back and stood, pointing a finger at him. "I know exactly how you think, because I grew up surrounded by men just like you."

He looked angry—and confused. "Your father and cousins and uncles are no-good liars, who make up stories to . . . to what? Control their women?"

"No, they're warriors whose first thought is survival by any means, fair or foul. They act first and deal with the consequences later. When I told you I was pregnant, your instinct was to fight your way free. And now you've come up with this elaborate story to make me think you acted like a jerk that day for my own good."

Jack also stood up, his jaw clenched. "You can't compare me to the men in your family. You don't even *know* me."

Megan glared at him across the table. "I knew

someone named Wayne Ferris. He was a sweet, gentle scientist who could soothe a frightened gosling we were banding, but he couldn't talk a girl out of her clothes to save his soul."

"That *is* me," he said, thumping his chest. "I *am* a good guy—and it's not a crime to want to take things slow."

"*You* are a warrior clear down to your DNA, Jack Stone—if that's even your real name. I'm giving you the boot." She pointed at the door. "Good-bye Wayne, Jack, or whoever the hell you really are."

He stood staring at her in disbelief.

Good! She hoped he realized he'd blown his chance four months ago, and that his heart was breaking just like hers had.

She went over and opened the door, and waited.

He finally set his napkin on the table and silently walked out, grabbing the six-pack of beer on his way by.

Megan closed the door behind him, fighting back tears. She had done the right thing—the *sensible* thing—for her and her baby. If she couldn't trust him with her own heart, how could she risk the innocent heart of her child?

She had been smart to see him again, if only to learn that the man she'd fallen in love with didn't exist. The man who'd sat across the table from her tonight, thinking she was gullible enough to believe such a story, was a complete stranger.

Chapter Eight

Jack set down his third bottle of beer, still burning at Megan's little tirade. She thought *he* had a fantastical imagination? Halfway through his explanation of why he'd sent her packing four months ago, the woman suddenly decides he's lying through his teeth, he's some sort of warrior, and that he definitely isn't anyone she wants anything to do with.

Couldn't talk the clothes off a woman to save his soul, could he? And just when had rushing headlong into a relationship become a good thing? Maybe he'd gotten a little too caught up in playing Wayne Ferris the shy nerd, but Megan had seemed especially attracted to his nerdiness.

She sure as hell wasn't attracted to warriors—she'd said the word in a way that implied it was a bad thing.

Which was weird. Jack had met a lot of her extended family now, quietly gleaning information from them about the woman who had charged into his life like a fast-moving storm. Having seen how protective the men were, he understood why Megan could have decided he'd sent her packing for her own safety.

But as hard as it had been on her that day, it had been even harder for him to watch her expression change from disbelief to shock to anger, then see her cringe away when he'd had to get tough. Her silence had been the worst, as she'd packed up all her belongings that had slowly accumulated in his tent over the previous weeks. And Megan sitting on her suitcase by the makeshift airstrip, looking totally dazed and brokenhearted as she waited for the supply plane to arrive was an image Jack would carry to his grave.

He gave a start when the cell phone in his pocket suddenly started vibrating. Who in hell was calling him at eleven-thirty at night?

"Hello?"

"Frank Blaisdell, who owns the restaurant on Main Street, said he heard a noise coming from the direction of the bakery when he was walking to his car. He said it sounded like someone was inside."

"Ethel? Are you at the office?"

"No, I'm home in bed."

"Then how do you know what Frank Blaisdell heard?"

"He called me, because he didn't know your number."

"He's supposed to call 911, not any of us personally."

"I told him that, but Frank thought 911 would get him the county sheriff instead of you or Simon. He tried Simon first, but the boy's not home tonight. Are you going to go investigate or not?" she asked impatiently.

"I'm going, I'm going," Jack said, striding to the bedroom to get his gear.

"You want me to call Simon's cell phone? He mentioned

going to Greenville tonight. It'll take him an hour to get back here."

"No, I'll handle this," Jack told her. "Go back to sleep, and tomorrow we'll figure out how to get word to everyone to call 911 so this doesn't happen again. See you in the morning." He strapped on his gun belt as he strode back into the kitchen, then quickly laced up his boots and grabbed his jacket on the way out the door.

This was his chance to catch the little bastards red-handed!

Jack spun out of his driveway and headed to town, nearly colliding with Megan's sister as she came speeding up the camp road. He spun into a snowbank to avoid her car, then backed out of it, snapped on his lights and siren, and raced toward town with a feral smile. If her look of horror was any indication, Camry MacKeage would think better of it the next time she felt the urge to throw a pie in his face.

Turning onto the main road, Jack quickly brought his attention back to his mission. He sure hoped he didn't have to shoot his gun tonight. It might be hard to convince the state police that even though he had three beers in his system, he was stone cold sober and quite capable of confronting Pine Creek's criminal element.

Camry stormed into Megan's house. "That maniac nearly ran into me! He went tearing out the camp road like a charging bull moose."

"And you were just crawling in, I suppose?"

"He didn't even have his siren or strobes on." She snorted. "He turned them on *after* he nearly smashed into me." She sat down on the ottoman, sliding Megan's feet over to make room. "So out with it, sis. What did you say that sent him tearing into the night like that?"

"I have no idea why he tore out of here, since he left my house over two hours ago. He must have gotten a police call." Megan dropped her feet to the floor and sat up. "Maybe those brats are at it again. Last night they took the F off Farley's store across the street and nailed it on Winter's sign, so that it read Pine Creek Fart Gallery."

"At least they have an imagination," Cam said with a laugh, unbuttoning her coat. "Which makes me think the bakery break-in was somebody else. The kids have been sticking to harmless pranks."

Megan stood up with a yawn. "Or they really like day-old doughnuts. I'm going to bed."

"Wait, you didn't tell me how tonight went."

"He claims Jack Stone is his real name, and that he hunts down runaway kids."

"He's not a biologist?"

Megan shook her head.

"Then that must be what the Internet ad was for. He hires out to parents looking for their children." Camry brightened. "That's a noble profession."

Megan rolled her eyes. "It's a lie, Cam."

"It is?"

"Of course it is. He claims he was working undercover to get close to one of the students so he could talk him into returning home to his parents. He said Billy had run away when he was sixteen, four years ago."

"Then how was the kid paying for school?"

"Some cult he belonged to was footing the bill." At Camry's look of confusion, Megan tossed her hands up. "See what I mean? Wayne made it all up."

"But why? If he doesn't hunt runaways, then why was he in Canada on your study?"

"Who knows and who cares? I showed him the door the moment I realized what he was doing."

"So what *was* he doing?" Cam asked. "Did he tell you why he's here?"

Megan flushed. "I didn't give him the chance," she admitted. "I kicked him out before dinner was over."

Camry gaped at her. "But that was the whole point of this evening! He was supposed to beg you to take him back, and you were supposed to throw his offer in his face. Come on," she said, grabbing Megan's hand and walking to the door.

Megan took the coat she shoved at her. "Where are we going?"

"To town. Let's go see what your boyfriend is doing."

"Are you nuts?" Megan said, hanging her coat back on the peg. "Jack Stone is not my boyfriend, and we are not chasing after him."

"Okay," Cam said, handing her back her coat. "Then we'll go check on Winter's shop, just to make sure nobody broke into it."

"You need to go back to work, Cam," Megan muttered as her sister led her outside. "Before I strangle you."

"Oh, come on, loosen up," Camry said as she opened the driver's door. "When was the last time we snuck out of the house on an adventure together?"

"It's not sneaking out if I *own* the house." Megan climbed in the passenger seat and fastened her seat belt. "And spying on an ex-boyfriend is not an adventure. What if we mess up his police work?"

"We'll park on the edge of town and sneak down to Winter's fart gallery on foot. We'll watch from inside, out of the way."

"Winter will strangle you if she ever hears you refer to

her shop as the fart gallery. She was not amused by that prank."

Camry started the car and headed toward town. "So what are you going to do if Jack stays on as our police chief?" she asked. "You *are* carrying his child."

"*If* he stays, and *if* he wants to be part of my baby's life, then we'll come up with some sort of arrangement."

"He'll want visitation rights, Meg. Are you willing to let him take your baby for the day?"

Megan looked down at her belly. "I'll cross that bridge when I get there, if it comes to that. But once he realizes it's over between us, he'll give up and leave."

Camry reached over and patted Megan's knee. "And if he doesn't, we'll just have Winter turn him into a toad."

Being careful not to let his feet crunch on the snow, Jack crept along the edge of the buildings on the lake side of Main Street, using the shadows to conceal his progress. He slowly made his way toward the bakery at the end of the street, his ears tuned to sounds of activity and his eyes alert for movement. He was just passing Dolan's Outfitter Store when a muffled crash came from inside.

He pressed against the side of the building, his eyes locked on the slightly ajar door as he pulled his billy club from his belt. Another crash sounded, followed by an angry growl of surprise, then an even louder crash, as if a shelf of heavy pots and pans had been cleaned off in one swipe.

Dammit, the little bastards were trashing the place.

Jack scanned the lakefront park to make sure no one else was lurking about, then quietly walked up the steps and used his billy club to push open the broken door— only to rear back from the stench.

Their stinky doughnut thief was at it again.

Another violent crash came from inside, sounding as if an entire shelving unit fell over. Jack froze with his foot on the threshold when a deep, wounded scream unlike anything he'd ever heard before reverberated off the interior walls. The entire building began to shake as whatever had made that sound started toward him at a run.

Jack turned to scramble down the steps just as it burst through the door. Realizing he was about to be trampled, he dived to the side and rolled out of the way. He immediately started to rise, but froze when a huge, dark, screaming shadow went tearing past him toward the lake.

What the *hell*?

Jack jumped up to get a better look but was suddenly grabbed from behind by a large arm of solid muscle wrapping around his throat. He lashed back with his billy club, making his attacker grunt and the arm around his neck tighten. He reared up to butt the guy in the head, but the man simply fell backward to the ground, pulling Jack with him. Powerful legs wrapped around his thighs, effectively keeping him still long enough for his attacker to squeeze the breath right out of him.

As the world went black, Jack's last thought was that *little bastards* was a misnomer—because the apparition *flying* out over the lake had to be seven feet tall, and the guy choking him to death weighed at least two hundred pounds.

Jack woke to whispered conversation but didn't open his eyes when he realized he not only knew one of the speakers, but that he was equally familiar with the lap his head was resting on—though it was a little rounder than the last time he'd been in this position. Since he no longer seemed to be in imminent danger, he decided to play possum and learn what in hell all these people were doing at the scene of his crime. Besides, the concern in Megan's voice gave him hope.

"I don't know why you insisted we bring him to the gallery, Robbie. We need to take him to Aunt Libby, so she can check him over," Megan whispered urgently, feeling Jack's head for lumps. "He should be awake by now. He might have a concussion."

"He's only had the wind knocked out of him," said a rich-timbered voice that Jack recognized as Robbie MacBain's. "He'll come around soon."

A feminine snort sounded nearby. "He really is a nerd, isn't he?" a familiar voice said far too cheerily. "He didn't put up much of a fight when that guy attacked him, and now I see what you mean about his size, Meg. Robbie tossed him over his shoulder like a sack of grain."

So the pie-hurling sister was here, too. Wonderful.

Megan gently patted his face. "Come on, Wayne, wake up," she petitioned, patting a bit harder.

"Wayne?" Robbie repeated, his tone suspicious.

"Wayne Ferris," Camry chirped, again much too cheerily. "The bastard who broke Megan's heart. Only now he's calling himself Jack Stone and pretending to be our chief of police."

Megan clutched him protectively against her. By God, she *did* still love him. Jack slit open his eyes and saw MacBain looking at Megan, obviously not pleased.

"Jack Stone is Wayne Ferris? Your biologist from Canada?" the towering Scot asked.

"Sort of," Megan said. "But he's not a biologist, and he's not mine anymore."

Camry snorted again. "You're acting like he's still yours."

Damn skippy, he was hers. And the protruding belly he was nestled against proved it.

"So who the hell is he?" Robbie asked impatiently.

"He told me his real name is Jack Stone, that he hunts down runaway kids, and that he was posing as a biologist because he was after one of the students on the study," Megan explained.

"But Meg decided that's probably a lie," Camry added. "And I'm beginning to agree with her. He's not a very competent hunter, is he? He can't even catch a bunch of brats."

Not liking the direction the conversation was taking, Jack was about to fake a miraculous recovery when MacBain said, "That was no kid who brought him down. The man was my size."

"Did you recognize him?" Megan asked, her hand lightly rubbing Jack's chest, making him feel warm and fuzzy and a little bit dizzy.

"No, he ran into the woods when I shouted. Who else knows that Stone is Wayne Ferris?"

"Just Cam and Winter, and now you."

"You haven't told Greylen?"

Megan cuddled Jack closer. "I'm afraid of what Daddy might do."

"The bastard deserves a good beating," Robbie growled.

Camry laughed. "It seems the townsfolk are doing that for us. The man's a mess. What happened to his hand?"

Again, Jack was just about to groan and open his eyes when MacBain said, "Maybe you should ask him. He's been awake for the last ten minutes."

Jack's head hit the floor with a thud when Megan

suddenly scrambled out from under him. He sat up, rubbing the back of his head, and glared at her. "Police work is not a spectator sport. You had no business chasing my siren into town."

"I told you we should have left him in the snowbank," Camry said.

Jack turned his glare on her. "I'm writing you up for speeding on the camp road."

She smiled sweetly. "How was the pie, by the way? Were the apples cooked through?"

"What are you all doing here?" he asked, specifically looking at MacBain.

Robbie shrugged. "I often take walks in the evening."

"Six or seven miles in the dead of winter? Don't you live up on the west side of TarStone Mountain?"

Robbie nodded. "Did you get a look at your attacker?"

Jack shook his head and tried to get up, only his right knee wouldn't cooperate and he fell back to the floor with a hiss of pain. MacBain grabbed him by the shoulders and lifted him to his feet before Jack could yelp in surprise.

"You must have banged your knee when you fell running away from the brats," Camry said. "But it was thoughtful of them to stop and bandage your hand while you were passed out."

"The hand is from earlier today, when a pit bull decided I looked like lunch," Jack said as he leaned on the counter. His knee felt the size of a soccer ball. He tried putting his weight on it and quickly decided that wasn't a good idea.

"Damn," he muttered, reaching in his pocket for his cell phone, then sitting down when MacBain slid a chair up beside him. He punched the speed dial. "Pratt, where are you?" he asked the moment the line connected. "Then get dressed and get down to Main Street ASAP. We've had another break-in. I'm inside the art gallery. What? No, they trashed the outfitter store this time. Hey, you got any crutches at your house from your football days? Good, bring them along, would you?"

"The closest hospital is in Greenville," Megan said when he slipped the phone in his pocket. "Cam and I will drive you."

Jack shook his head. "I need to help Simon. I'll drive myself in once we get the scene secure." He looked at Robbie. "I hear you were in Special Forces, and that you might be willing to lend a hand if I need it."

MacBain nodded.

"Are you up to following the tracks that guy made to see where they lead?"

Robbie gave a slight nod, then looked at Camry and Megan. "I believe you've had enough entertainment for one night, ladies. Time for you to go home."

Camry started to say something, but Robbie softly said, "Now" under his breath, and she immediately closed her mouth and stood up. Megan gave a resigned sigh, and Jack watched, amazed, as the two women buttoned their coats and walked out the front door. The overhead bell jingled cheerfully in the stark silence as they disappeared into the night without so much as a backward glance.

Jack looked at Robbie MacBain. "How did you do that? More importantly, can you teach me to do it?"

Robbie lifted one brow. "It took me years to perfect that trick, so I suppose teaching you would depend on how long you intend to stick around."

"I'm here for however long it takes," Jack said,

standing up on his good leg and squaring his shoulders. "I love her."

"You have a strange way of showing it."

"I sent her home for her own good. A man was murdered on the tundra, and Megan has a habit of jumping in the middle of something first and asking questions later. It was the only way I could think to keep her safe."

A slight grin softened MacBain's mouth. "She takes after her father, that one does." He just as quickly sobered. "You have your work cut out for you, Stone. Megan was devastated when she came home, and it's been my experience that women don't recover from broken hearts very quickly—if ever."

"I'll eventually wear her down. Any suggestions on how I approach Greylen MacKeage?"

Robbie headed for the front door. "I'd wait until you're healed, if I were you." He opened the door. "And then prove you're man enough for his daughter by taking whatever he dishes out."

"Wait!" Jack said as Robbie stepped outside. "What has Megan got against warriors?"

Robbie snorted. "She's made no secret of not wanting to fall in love with one, though I doubt even she understands why."

"And your theory is?"

"Isn't obvious, Stone? Megan *is* the very thing she's running from."

Jack stared at the closed door. Holy hell. He'd been planning a courtship when he should have been preparing for battle!

Chapter Nine

With a yawn that nearly wrenched her jaw, Megan slipped on her robe and trudged into the kitchen. "Who were you talking to?" she asked Cam, yawning again.

Camry dropped her cell phone back in her purse. "Rose Brewer. Those brats made a mess of her store, so I'm going over to help her clean up."

"What time is it?"

"Almost eleven."

"Good heavens, I slept the morning away. Give me ten minutes and I'll go with you."

"Un-uh. You shouldn't be lifting stuff, and we don't need a supervisor."

Megan didn't argue, since she was feeling a bit lazy this morning anyway. Besides, with Cam gone all afternoon, she could curl up next to the woodstove and finally start working on her survey. Megan picked up a piece of toast Cam had left on her plate. "Did Rose say if anything was stolen?"

"She can't tell yet because of the mess. She said the candy rack was definitely a target, and that they must have been inside for quite some time because the place is littered with empty wrappers."

"They broke in for candy?" Megan asked in surprise. "Then they must be younger than everyone thinks. Older kids would have gone after cigarettes and beer."

Camry straightened from lacing her boots. "Great. Pine Creek's street gang is a bunch of ten-year-olds. Rose also said the store reeks of stagnant mud and rotting vegetation, and she doesn't know if she'll ever get rid of the smell. Where do you suppose they found mud this time of—"

The doorbell chimed, and since she was standing right beside it, Camry opened the door and just as quickly closed it again.

"Cam! Who's here?" Megan asked, opening the door back up. "Wayne."

"Jack." He straightened on his crutches and hobbled inside. "I have some questions about what you two may have seen last night."

"I saw you running as if the hounds of hell were on your heels," Cam said, hanging her coat back on the peg. "You fell, the brats escaped, and then a man stepped out of the shadows and would have squeezed you to death if Robbie hadn't shown up. Shouldn't you be writing this down?" she asked, pointing at the notebook sticking out of his pocket.

"Thanks for your statement, Ms. MacKeage. I see you were just headed out, so don't let me keep you," he said, opening the door for her.

"I've changed my mind. I'm staying."

"No, you're not," Megan said, handing Camry her coat. "Rose is waiting for you."

"If you're helping Rose Brewer clean up," Jack said, "keep a list of anything else that was taken, would you?"

"Why, certainly, Officer Stone," Cam purred, slipping back into her coat. "Anything to help Pine Creek's finest catch the bad guys."

"You'll be helping Rose more than me," he growled, clearly nearing the end of his patience. "She'll need that list for her insurance claim."

Cam started another scathing remark, but Megan quickly intervened. "Would you just get going?" She shoved her sister out the door.

Cam stopped on the porch and turned back to her. "Don't you dare cook him breakfast. And get dressed," she hissed in a whisper.

Megan closed the door, turned to find her unwelcome guest staring at her belly, and promptly blushed. "I—um—I'll get dressed," she said, holding her robe closed as she all but ran to her bedroom.

The moment she shut her bedroom door, Megan slapped her hands to her cheeks with a groan. That short haircut, angular jaw, and smooth, weather-tanned skin made him even more handsome. And God help her, those deep, sexy, intense blue eyes still had the power to turn her mind to mush.

No, turn her mind to lust.

He may have been a bit slow leaving the starting gate, but once he'd gotten going, Wayne had certainly brought magic to their lovemaking. He had been so intensely focused on her that the entire world had ceased to exist. They could have been a speck of dust floating through the cosmos, so immersed she'd been in the sensations he elicited.

She had innocently gone to Wayne's tent that evening

to ask him about something, but when she'd caught him staring intensely at her mouth as she spoke . . . Well, the next thing she knew, her lips were pressed against his and she was attacking the buttons on his shirt. She'd gotten them both down to their underwear in five minutes. She could have done it in two, but she kept stopping to kiss each spot of his flesh she exposed. He had the most beautiful body . . .

Once he recovered from the shock of her attack, he'd lowered her to his sleeping bag, pinned her exploring hands over her head, and proceeded to make maddeningly slow, tender love to her.

Megan shivered at the image of their naked bodies twined together, jerking herself back to the present. Okay. Even though the man in her living room was a no-good lying heartbreaker, she couldn't turn away anyone who looked as pathetic as he did. The guy was a battered and obviously tired mess. She dressed in slacks and a sweater, ran her shaking fingers through her hair, and returned to the kitchen to find Jack sprawled on the couch, his right leg resting on the coffee table, and his notebook in his hand.

"Did you ladies really see anything, or do I get to arrest your sister for lying to a police officer?"

Megan pulled out the frying pan and set it on a burner. "We heard a god-awful scream come from the back of Rose's store just as we stepped into Winter's gallery. We ran to the back window and saw the kids nearly plow you over when they came running out. That's when the man stepped out of the shadows and grabbed you from behind." She went to the fridge and took out a carton of eggs, a stick of butter, and a bowl of diced ham. "What did you and Robbie talk about after we left?"

"You, mostly. After the guy brought me down, what did he do then?"

"He ran into the woods when Robbie shouted at him."

"In which direction?"

"Up the eastern shoreline of the lake. What specifically did you and Robbie talk about, about me?"

"I was impressed at how well you and your sister obeyed him. I asked him to teach me how to do that."

Megan broke the eggs in the frying pan with a snort. "In your dreams. What else?"

"I asked him what to expect when you introduce me to your father."

"That's not going to happen, either. What else?"

When he didn't immediately answer, she turned to look at him.

"I'm not going away, Megan. It doesn't matter how big a family you have to hide behind, or how large your cousins are."

She lifted her chin. "I am not hiding behind anyone."

"Good," he said with a nod. "Is it a boy or a girl?"

"What?"

"Are we having a son or daughter?" he asked, his gaze dropping to her belly. "Did you have one of those tests that determine the gender?"

She turned back to the stove and dumped the diced ham over the eggs. "I don't know what sex it is."

"Don't know? Or aren't saying?"

She eyed him over her shoulder. "I want to be surprised."

"Good. Me, too." He looked down at the notebook in his hand. "You said you saw a bunch of kids run out of the store. Did you see how many there were?"

She shrugged, turned back to the stove, and shut off the burner. "They were in a tight pack, so I couldn't tell."

"Did you see where they went?"

She frowned, opened her mouth, then shut it again.

"Or did you hear anything? Maybe an engine starting, like a snowmobile? Or . . . a small plane? Did you see something *flying* out over the lake?" he quietly asked.

"I didn't hear an engine. But I might have seen something flying." She looked away, opening a cupboard and taking down a plate. "It might have been a flock of geese."

"In the dead of winter?"

She filled the plate with most of the omelet she'd made, set a fork on it, and carried it over to the couch. "Okay, I have no idea what I saw flying out over the lake. Maybe Camry got a better look."

"Not that she'd give me a straight answer," he muttered, then smiled in gratitude as he took the plate from her. "Thanks. I'm starved."

"After you eat, I'll drive you to the hospital," she offered as she returned to the stove, resigned to losing her peaceful afternoon.

"I don't need a doctor," he said around a mouthful of food. "Give me a couple of aspirins and a soft bed, and I'll be good to go by tomorrow morning."

Megan scoffed up her own eggs directly out of the pan, the silence stretching awkwardly between them. It was disconcerting having him in her house, talking as if they were old friends.

Are we having a son or daughter? By God, he'd had his chance to know his child, and he'd tossed it away. She didn't care if he threatened to hang around until hell froze over, he was *not* waltzing back into her life.

She swallowed the last bite of egg. "Why did you really come to Pine Creek?"

She turned around and saw that he didn't answer her because he was sound asleep. His empty plate was balanced on his belly, his arms had fallen to the side, and he was softly snoring.

Megan walked over to the couch, set the plate on the coffee table, then unlaced and took off his boots. Careful not to bang his injured knee, she slid his legs around until he was sprawled lengthwise on the couch, propped a pillow under his head and another one under his knee, then grabbed the blanket off the back and covered him up. She tucked the blanket under his chin, her fingers brushing the rough stubble on his cheek, and without stopping to think, leaned down and kissed his forehead. Her lips somehow decided to linger on his warm skin, and he snuggled deeper into the pillow with a sigh.

She jerked upright, then stalked back to the kitchen. Damn the man! She didn't care *what* wonderful memories his being here evoked, she was not letting him off the hook that easy. He wanted to be part of her life, he was going to have to earn her love all over again!

Waking up to whispered conversations was fast becoming a bad habit—though an enlightening one. This time Jack didn't recognize the male who was speaking. He carefully slit open his eyes and the soft glow of interior lights told him he'd slept the day away. He frowned at the empty house. He was still on Megan's couch, though he was sprawled lengthwise now; his boots were off, there was a pillow under his swollen knee, and he was snuggled toe to chin under a soft blanket.

The conversation was coming from outside. He saw two people standing under the porch light, but the sheer curtain covering the door window made it impossible to identify the man. He was another Sasquatch though, towering over Megan as she rested a delicate hand on his arms folded across his chest.

Something about their postures tickled a memory at the back of Jack's mind. Where had he seen Megan looking up at a man just like that?

"Matt told me Jack Stone is the father of your child," the guy said, his voice menacing as it came through the slightly open door. "And that Wayne Ferris was an alias Stone was using in Canada, when he seduced ye."

Jack snorted. *He* hadn't seduced anyone; it had been the other way around.

"And yet ye have him sleeping on your couch, after ye told me ye hoped the bastard rotted in hell," the Sasquatch finished in a heavily accented growl.

Jack winced. Megan had actually said that?

"And just who told Matt about Wayne?" Megan stepped away from the man. "I bet Winter told him, and of course your brother told you. Which means my sister can keep *your* secret for months, but she blabs *mine* the first chance she gets."

"Husbands and wives don't keep secrets from each other. You'll do well to remember that, lass, when ye find yourself married."

Jack smiled. No wonder Megan preferred nerds; the men around here were either issuing orders or lecturing her. Wayne Ferris must have seemed like a breath of fresh air. She had both hands on her hips now, and was looking up at the giant as if she could slice him to shreds with her glare.

"I'm not *ever* getting married," she said, the growl in her own voice loud and clear. "I don't need a man messing up my life or that of my baby's. All we need is each other."

"That's telling him, sweetheart." Jack closed his eyes and snuggled back under the blanket with a smile. If Megan didn't think she wanted to get married, that was okay with him—for now. He would eventually wear her down.

"As for the favor you want," she continued, "I still say Elizabeth is your best bet, but if you insist on me, then I'll do it. The first time you get all macho, though, it's over."

Jack opened his eyes to see the man pull Megan against his chest in a way that was anything but familial. What in hell had she just promised, that the Sasquatch felt compelled to thank her with a hug? And what was his relation to Megan? A brother-in-law? He was Winter's husband's brother, if Jack had heard right.

And that made Megan fair game in anyone's book.

He was the man on TarStone Mountain! That's where Jack had seen him before. He'd love to have the poaching bastard in the crosshairs of his rifle scope again and send him scurrying behind a rock. A rival for Megan's affection was the last thing he needed right now.

Maybe his knee wouldn't be better in the morning. Maybe he'd be so helpless for the next several days, Megan wouldn't have the heart to send him home.

He just had to figure out how to get rid of Camry.

As if conjuring the devil herself, Jack heard a car speed into the driveway and skid to a stop. A door slammed, and a feminine voice called out, "Kenzie! You've come for a visit. How nice."

So the hugging poacher was Kenzie Gregor. Jack tossed off his blanket, sat up, and gingerly lowered his feet to the floor. Now that he knew whom he was up against, all he had to do was figure out what the bastard was up to.

"Shhh," Megan hissed, lifting her finger to her lips as she moved to block the door. "Wayne's sleeping."

Jack rubbed his face with a heavy sigh. Was she ever going to call him Jack, or was he going to have to change his name?

"Don't tell me he's still here," Camry said, not even trying to lower her voice. "Kenzie, did you bring your sword?"

Jack froze in the act of standing up. *Sword?*

Gregor gave a belly laugh. "Sorry, I left it at home." He looked down at Megan, and Jack saw the bastard smile. "Should I run up the mountain and fetch it, lass, and rid ye of your troublesome boyfriend once and for all?"

"He's not my boyfriend," Megan snapped. "And he's only on the couch because I couldn't carry him home."

Time to end this farce, he supposed. "I'm awake," Jack called out. "And I don't know which hurts more, my knee or my wounded feelings."

Megan swung open the door and stepped inside but was quickly herded out of the way by Camry. "Liars don't have feelings," Camry said, walking directly up to the coffee table, presumably so Jack could better see her scowl. "Game's up, lover boy. Kenzie's going to help you home."

Jack formed a T with his hands. "Truce. I've had less

than five hours sleep in the last two days, and every damn one of my muscles ache. And since you're not the sort of woman who kicks a man when he's down, could we please stop the salvos until I'm back on my feet?"

"That's the sign for time-out, not truce," Camry said, though her face did redden. "You wave a white flag for a truce." She set her hands on her hips, not unlike the way Megan often did. "And what makes you think I wouldn't kick a man when he's down?"

Jack gave her his sincerest smile. "Because you're the sister who's most like Megan, she told me, even more than her twin, Chelsea."

Camry opened her mouth but closed it again without uttering a word. She simply turned and walked away.

"Kenzie?" Megan said, peering out the still open door. She turned to Camry. "Where'd he go?"

"Who knows," Camry said with a negligent wave. "Likely back to his hidey-hole in the forest. Have you ever noticed how uncomfortable he gets indoors?"

Jack perked up. Kenzie Gregor was a forest hermit?

How interesting.

Unless he was a warrior like most of the other men around here, and a shell-shocked veteran who couldn't handle civilized society anymore. Jack had dealt with a few such lost souls growing up in Medicine Lake. Did Gregor have hopes that Megan would help him come in from the cold?

Not on my watch, she won't. Jack leaned back on the couch with a moan and rubbed his knee.

"Oh, no, you don't," Camry said, pointing at the door Megan was closing. "You are hobbling home right now."

"Those crutches are worse than ice skates on the packed snow. I nearly broke my neck getting up the walkway." He turned a pleading gaze on Megan. "I'll be as quiet as a church mouse. You won't even know I'm here."

Megan looked at her sister. "What can it hurt to let him spend the night, Cam? We'd do no less for a complete stranger."

"But he's not a stranger. He's the bastard who broke your heart."

"To keep her safe," Jack growled.

Camry spun toward him. "Safe from what?"

"Megan didn't tell you? A man was murdered on the tundra a couple of days before your sister told me she was pregnant. Breaking her heart was the only way I could think of to make her leave."

Camry turned to a suddenly silent Megan. "Is that true, Meg?" Not waiting for an answer, she spun back to face Jack. "You didn't have to crush her heart. You only had to explain your concern."

Jack arched an eyebrow. "And knowing your sister, you think she would have just packed up and come home?"

Camry turned to Megan again, holding her arms out in question. "How come this is the first I'm hearing about this?"

Megan went to the woodstove and dropped a piece of wood inside. "I didn't know the man had been murdered. I thought he'd gotten drunk, fallen in a pond, and drowned." She faced them both, her expression defensive. "And for all we know, that's exactly what happened. Wayne's the only one saying he was murdered."

Man-o-man, she really wanted him to be Wayne, didn't she?

"*Jack* has proof," he told Camry. "You can call the

Royal Canadian Mounted Police in Edmonton and check it out. They investigated, and they shut down the study the very next week."

"It was already shutting down when I left," Megan defended.

Camry threw up her hands. "Sorry, sis. If what he's saying is true, you're not going to find anyone around here who'd be willing to beat him up for you. Hell, Dad will probably give him a pat on the back."

Jack found himself torn between wanting to jump for joy that Greylen MacKeage would take his side, and wanting to run over and hug Megan when he saw her shoulders slump in defeat. But he stayed right were he was, not willing to chance being sent home. Maybe he should work on Camry a bit more, since she seemed to be softening.

"Did Rose Brewer notice if anything else had been stolen?" he asked while looking around for his crutches.

"Nothing that she could see. But they must have eaten four cases of candy." Camry shook her head in amazement. "That's a lot of sugar for a couple of kids to put down."

"How many kids did you actually see running out of the store?" Jack asked. "Megan, where are my crutches?"

"Under the couch," she said from the sink, where she was suddenly very busy washing dishes.

Camry walked to the staircase. "I couldn't really tell. I just saw them running past you toward the lake. They stayed in a tight pack."

"And where did they go then?" he asked.

Camry shrugged. "Beats me. That's when the guy stepped out of the shadows and grabbed you from behind."

"Did you get a look at him?"

"No, it was too dark. He was big, though." She eyed him speculatively. "About the size of our cousin, Robbie MacBain."

"Robbie isn't the man who attacked me."

"How come you're so sure?"

"The guy who jumped me had the same smell that was all through Rose's store, only not quite as strong. MacBain smells sort of like pine pitch."

Camry wrinkled her nose. "I swear I'll never get that foul odor out of my nose hairs. And the slime . . ." She shuddered, then walked over to Megan. "You're a biologist. What does this smell like to you?"

Megan leaned close to take a whiff of Camry's sleeve, then jerked away. "*Eewww*, that's awful," she said, wiping her nose on her own sleeve.

"But do you recognize it?"

If Jack hadn't been watching carefully, he might have missed Megan's reaction. But when she stilled with her face buried in her sleeve, and her eyes widened before she suddenly turned back to the sink, he was certain she *did* recognize the odor.

"I can't say what it is, exactly," she said, her back to them. She started washing the dishes again. "It's definitely organic, though."

Jack remained silent, but Camry, bless her pushy heart, was like a dog with a bone. "Take another whiff," she suggest, lifting her arm again. "You're sure you don't recognize it? It's sort of pungent. And stagnant."

Megan wiped her hands on a towel, then walked to the oven and opened it. "One whiff was enough. Let me think about it; maybe it will come to me later."

Camry seemed puzzled by Megan's unwillingness to

even hazard a guess. She walked to the stairs again, and looked back at Jack. "Rose said Simon told her the bakery break-in had the same slimy goo all over the place, and that the state forensics lab hasn't been able to identify it."

"Not yet," Jack confirmed.

She cast a sidelong glance at her sister, then told Jack, "I think it's reptilian."

"Reptiles aren't slimy," Megan interjected. "It's more likely from an amphibian, like a frog or salamander."

Camry gave Jack a smug smile, obviously proud of herself for finally getting Megan to comment. "Rose's store was covered with it," she said. "That's an awful lot of frogs."

Megan became very busy again.

Camry shrugged at Jack and ran up the stairs. "I'm taking a shower," she called as she disappeared.

Jack studied Megan. What could she possibly know about the break-ins?

Or had she recognized the smell from hermit boy?

So what secret was the bastard hiding? No, make that *Secrets* with an S, to include the favor he'd asked from Megan. Hermit boy had hugged her, and that's what Megan had just noticed on her own sweater. Kenzie Gregor smelled like a bog.

He was the right size to be Jack's attacker, too.

Jack pulled his crutches out from under the couch and slowly got to his feet. "Thank you for letting me stay, Megan. I can't imagine how I'd lug firewood to keep the stove going. It's all I have for heat."

She twirled to face him, her hands on her hips and her beautiful green eyes snapping fire. "Just don't get the wrong idea. I'd do the same for a stranger I found on the side of the road. Understand?"

"Yes, ma'am."

"And if you so much as allude to us getting back together, you're out of here. Got that?"

"Got it."

"And no talking about the baby."

"Come on, Meg. You can't ask me to ignore our baby."

"It's not *our* baby, it's mine. You blew any chance of it being *ours* four months ago."

Jack felt his neck heat up. "I didn't have any choice. You were in danger."

"Did it ever once occur to you to simply tell me about the danger, instead of treating me like a mindless idiot?"

"Of course it did," he snapped. "And it also occurred to me that you'd dig in your heels and try to get to the bottom of it yourself."

As suddenly as the tension had built, it disappeared. Megan gave Jack a speculative look. "So let me get this straight. I had to leave because it was dangerous, but it was okay for you to stay?"

"I was in the middle of a job."

"So was I."

"But I wasn't pregnant. Look, I'm sorry if you don't care for double standards, but those with wombs are to be protected by those without. Especially if that womb happens to be occupied."

"So if I hadn't been pregnant, you wouldn't have sent me away?"

Jack wiped a hand over his face. Dammit, he was digging this hole deeper and deeper, and she was about to start throwing dirt on top of him.

"Unfair. That's one of those questions women ask like, 'Do these pants make my butt look fat?' If I say yes, I'm still in the doghouse, and if I say no, you're going to assume I'm lying."

"There are towels in the bathroom closet," she said, nodding toward the downstairs hall. "And there's a bed set up in the room on the left. You can sleep there tonight." She turned and walked to the fridge. "Dinner's in an hour."

Jack hobbled through the hall door, entered the tiny bedroom on the left, and nearly dropped to his knees. The place was packed full of baby things. A crank-up swing, a car seat, toys, tiny clothes, and colorful little blankets were stacked to the ceiling on one side of the room, the single bed teeming with more baby stuff on the other.

Jack broke into a cold sweat. Holy hell, he was going to be a *daddy*.

Chapter Ten

Camry didn't even try hiding her smile as she approached Jack's bandaged hand with the sewing shears. She was beginning to understand why Megan had fallen for the guy. He was sort of endearing, she decided, her smile widening when she took a large snip of the shower-soaked gauze and Jack flinched.

"I really can do this myself," he said, trying to take the scissors from her with his good hand.

Camry firmed her grip on his wrist and took another snip. "I can see what a great job you've been doing. Those are some mean-looking scars on your hands and wrists. They look like burn marks." She stopped snipping and arched an inquiring brow. "Are they reminders not to tug on the devil's tail?"

Jack turned his uninjured palm up to look at it, then slowly closed his hand into a fist and dropped it to his lap under the table. "No, they're to remind me why I became a pacifist."

She snorted. "How's that been working for you?" She loosened the wet bandage. "So tell me, Jack, are you really half Canadian Cree?"

Camry looked up again to meet Jack's assessing gaze. She had to agree with Megan that his size did make him approachable. Not that he was wimpy by any means. Jack Stone was compact, sculpted with obvious strength, and had sharp, intelligent, compelling blue eyes. Maybe Robbie could give him a couple of lessons in basic self-defense.

"My mother was a woodland Cree from Medicine Lake, Alberta."

"And your father?"

"He was American, from Montana. They met at a Greenpeace rally in Vancouver." He held up his good hand when she started to ask him another question. "Mom was a conservation agent working to get large logging concerns to practice sustainable harvesting, and Dad was a biochemist who was fed up with chemical farming practices," he continued. "It was love at first sight for my father, but it took him three years to convince my mother that she couldn't live without him."

"Do they still live in Medicine Lake?"

He shook his head. "They died in an auto accident when I was nine."

"Oh. Sorry," she muttered, turning her attention back to his hand. "So who raised you after that?"

"My maternal great-grandfather, for the most part. We lived just outside of Medicine Lake until he died when I was fifteen."

Camry looked up. "Then where did you go?"

"I finished raising myself. When I was twenty I joined the Canadian Air Force, but after four years I decided

I wasn't warrior material," he said, darting a glance toward the kitchen where Megan was putting the finishing touches on dinner. "I kicked around Ottawa, Toronto, and Montreal for another couple of years, working different jobs. Then one summer when I was visiting Medicine Lake, I found out that a friend's sixteen-year-old daughter had run away from home, and I offered to find her."

"Did you?"

Jack nodded, his eyes lighting with satisfaction. "Had her back home in less than three weeks."

Intrigued, Camry also glanced toward the kitchen to see if her sister was listening—which she obviously was. Megan had her back to them, but she was perfectly still.

"Where'd you find the girl?" Cam asked.

"In Vancouver, living with a young man she'd run off with."

"And you talked her into going home?"

"She had realized her mistake within days of landing in Vancouver; her boyfriend was a jerk and they were living in a crack house. She didn't know how to call her parents and ask if she could come home." He shot Camry a crooked grin. "Curiosity might get a person in trouble, but it's usually pride that keeps them there."

"So you found out you had a knack for tracking down runaways, and you turned it into a profession?"

"Something like that."

"How do you go about finding those kids?"

"Personal experience," he said evenly. "I ran away from half a dozen foster homes before I went to live with my great-grandfather."

"When you were only nine?"

Jack finished unwrapping the bandage himself. "I was

trying to get to Grand-père in Medicine Lake. I didn't know he was fighting the courts for custody for me."

"Why wouldn't they give him custody? He was family."

"He was also eighty years old at the time."

"But he eventually won?"

"Only because after a year of arguing with the courts, he up and stole me from the foster home I was staying at. He took me to live deep in the forest until he died. When I came walking out of the woods alone, social services got their hands on me again and took me back to Edmonton. Not that I stayed long; I simply disappeared again."

Camry gaped at him. He'd been running away since he was nine years old? She flinched when the oven door suddenly slammed shut. Jack grabbed his crutches, stood up and scooped the tape and gauze off the table, then hobbled into the downstairs bedroom without saying another word.

Camry turned in her seat to find her sister glaring at her. "What?" she asked quietly.

"Please tell me you don't believe one word of that," Megan hissed.

"Nobody could make something like that up, Meg. It's too heart-wrenching."

"You can't honestly believe that a nine-year-old child would run off on his own like that."

"But what if he did? Can you imagine what he went through, and how scared he was? And then his great-grandfather died. He must have had to bury him all by himself. And then he walked out of the woods, alone again."

"He made it up, Cam. He's trying to gain our sympathy."

"What if it's true?"

"Okay, what if it is?" Megan raised her chin defensively. "What does his childhood have to do with anything?"

Cam stood up and walked over to the counter in order to look her sister directly in the eye. "You and your baby are it, Meg. The two of you are the only family he's got."

Megan cringed away. "Whose side are you on?"

Cam took hold of her shoulders. "Yours. I'm on *your* side, sis. But can't you see why he's come here? He's looking for a family of his own."

"But how can I trust him?" Megan whispered. "He's done nothing but lie to me since we met."

"You do what any smart woman does," Cam said. "You have him investigated. And if Jack's story doesn't check out, *then* you get Winter to turn him into a toad."

"And if it does check out?"

Camry sighed. "That's your call. But you heard the man; our pride is what usually keeps us in trouble. You and the baby are the ones who will have to live with your decision."

Jack was unsure whether he was helping his cause or hurting it. The abbreviated version of his childhood had bothered Megan for some reason, yet it may have nudged her sister closer to his camp.

He pushed his empty plate away and leaned back in his chair with satisfaction. Who knew Megan could cook? The university funding the tundra study had provided a meal tent, and it had never occurred to him that she might have a domestic side. Not that he'd been thinking of hearth and home when he'd met her; he had

been focused only on experiencing that passion she ex-
uded like an elixir.

Thank God she'd been thinking along those same
lines, albeit light-years ahead of him. Now, though, she
was acting as if she wished the ground would open up
and swallow him whole. She had spoken maybe three
sentences toward him during the entire meal, delivered
with an aloof politeness.

He did learn that she was conducting an environmental study for a man named Mark Collins, whom neither
woman appeared to know much about. The majority
of the conversation had been about Camry's work. Ion
propulsion was going to put Earth on the cosmic map,
apparently, once Camry figured out how to stabilize the
stuff.

What must the MacKeage household be like when
all seven daughters and their scientist mother got together? Jack was gaining a whole new respect for Greylen
MacKeage, considering his own head was still spinning
from a conversation that had quite literally been out of
this world.

"We should hurry up, Meg. I'll clear the table and
pack the dishwasher," Camry offered, gathering up the
plates. "You go to the baby's room and decide how you
want to arrange it before everyone gets here."

"You have company coming?" Jack asked, also getting
to his feet.

"Just Mom and Elizabeth and Chelsea," Camry told
him, her eyes sparkling with mischief. "And Daddy."

Jack froze as he was reached for his crutches.

"Actually, it's good that you're here," she continued,
rinsing the plates in the sink. "You can entertain Daddy
while we work on the baby's room."

Holy hell! "Maybe I should head over to my house. I don't want to be in the way."

Camry straightened from putting the plates in the dishwasher. "You won't be in the way, Jack. Besides, when I ran over to get you some clean clothes, your house was cold. It can't be more than fifty degrees in there."

The perfect excuse! "Then I should go start a fire so the pipes don't freeze." At the sound of a giggle, Jack turned and found Megan with her hand over her mouth, her eyes shining with amusement. "What?" he snapped, forgetting he was trying to get back in her good graces.

"Nothing," she said, making a futile attempt to stifle her smile. "I'm just remembering a conversation my family had over Christmas vacation. Your great-grandfather didn't happen to be a Cree chief, did he?"

"Because our father is probably going to call you Chief," Camry stated, also laughing at their little joke, which he seemed to be the brunt of. "To show his respect."

"Grand-père wasn't a chief," he growled. "He was a shaman."

Jack wanted to kick himself the moment he saw Megan's reaction. She went perfectly still, her face blanching to the color of new snow.

Hell. What woman *wouldn't* love hearing the child she was carrying descended from shamans?

"He—he practiced the magic?" Camry squeaked.

Jack turned toward the kitchen and saw that Camry was as pale as her sister. Wonderful. Now they both thought he was weird.

"He was a medicine man," he growled. "He used herbs and prayers to heal people."

"Did you, ah . . . inherit his gift?" Megan asked.

"No."

"How do you know for sure?" Camry asked.

Jack held his crutches away from his body. "I'm thirty-four years old. Don't you think I'd know something like that by now, and would heal myself if I could?"

"That's not how the magic works," Megan blurted out, then looked just as surprised at what she'd said as he was.

The magic? What was going on here? These two woman—scientists, for Pete's sake—appeared both fascinated and horrified that his great-grandfather had been a shaman.

"Exactly how does *the magic* work, then?" he asked. "And what good would it do me, if I can't heal myself?"

Megan narrowed her eyes, and there went her hands to her hips again. "Could your grandfather heal himself?"

"Great-grandfather," he reminded her. "He used his medicinal herbs and sweat lodge whenever he was ill. You didn't answer my question. How does the magic work?"

"How should I know? I'm a biologist, not a wizard."

Wizard? Where had that come from?

"They're here!" Camry said, rushing to the door and opening it to look outside.

Jack didn't hear any vehicle driving in, no car doors shutting, nobody talking.

"Oh, I thought I heard something," Camry said, closing the door. She then rushed across the room to the stairs. "I'll be back in a minute. Let them in when they get here, will you, Jack?" she called out.

Jack turned to Megan, but she had disappeared, too. "Guess that ended that conversation," he muttered to the empty room, only to realize this was his own chance to escape. He tucked his crutches under one arm and limped out onto the porch, then carefully made his way down the shadowed driveway.

A dark Suburban rounded the corner and pulled into the driveway, bathing Jack in blinding light just as he hit a patch of ice and his feet headed in two different directions. He fought to keep his balance for several seconds, realized it wasn't going to happen, and threw himself toward the nearest snowbank.

His crutches landed on top of him, driving his face into the snow. Jack gave a pained sigh of defeat. He might as well stay here until he froze to death, rather than continue to be beaten up by everyone—including himself.

He could swear he heard Grand-père laughing his head off. For five years, Forest Dreamwalker had tried to persuade Jack that his brother's gift had passed down to him, always ending each lecture with a warning that the longer Jack continued to deny his calling, the louder it would become.

Apparently destiny had resorted to shouting.

"Are you all right?" came a male voice. "You needn't have jumped out of the way. I wouldn't have hit ye."

Wonderful. Jack couldn't think of a better first meeting with his future father-in-law. He spit out a mouthful of snow. "I'm fine."

"Let me help ye up."

"No, thanks. I think I'll stay right here for a while."

"Jack?" Camry said, rushing off the porch and over to them. When she tried to stop, she also slipped on the ice, and skidded into Jack with enough force to make him grunt. She would have landed on top of him if her father hadn't caught her. "Jack, what are you doing out here?"

"Taking a snow bath."

"This is Jack Stone?" Greylen MacKeage said in surprise. He reached down, grabbed Jack by the shoulders, and lifted him to his feet. "I've been looking forward to meeting you, Chief Stone," the towering Scot said, grabbing Jack's right hand and giving it a firm shake. The man looked like he was pushing seventy judging by his graying hair, but he had the grip of a bear. "I am Laird Greylen MacKeage, Megan's father."

Laird? Did that title even exist anymore?

"And I'm Grace MacKeage," a petite, beautiful woman said as she appeared beside her husband. Her eyes shone a startling blue in the porch light. "You gave us a fright, Mr. Stone. Are you sure you're okay?"

"Yes, ma'am, I'm fine," he said, taking the hand she extended. "I just slipped on the ice."

"Are these yours?" another woman said, bending to pick up his crutches. She held them out with a smile, and Jack found himself staring into Megan's eyes but not Megan's face. "I'm Chelsea," she said. "Megan's twin sister."

"The lawyer from Bangor," Jack acknowledged with a nod, taking the crutches from her. "Megan's told me about you."

Another woman crowded Chelsea out of the way. "I'm Elizabeth Sprague, Megan's younger sister. I teach third grade here in town."

Jack nodded. "I've met your husband. Walter, isn't it? He's the high school principal?"

"Yes. He mentioned you stopped by his school a few days ago, to speak to him about our pranksters."

Pranksters was a cute name for the little bastards, Jack supposed. But then, Elizabeth Sprague was a teacher, and no teacher wanted to believe any child was a criminal.

"It's freezing out here," Megan called from the door. "What are you all doing standing outside?"

"We're coming in," Greylen MacKeage said, herding the women toward the house. He turned back to Jack. "Need any help getting in? I've been looking forward to speaking with you, Chief Stone. I have some ideas on how ye might capture your young hoodlums."

"I was just headed home."

"Then I'll walk with ye, to make sure you don't fall again. You don't happen to have any cold ale at your house, do you, Chief?"

Chief? Did that mean he supposed to call the man laird? "I have some Canadian lager," he offered, tucking his crutches under his armpits and carefully making his way out the driveway.

"Wayne? Where are you going?" Megan called from the porch.

Jack kept walking.

"I mean *Jack*. Jack, you can't fend for yourself yet."

He finally stopped and turned to her, acutely aware that the man standing beside him had gone perfectly still, and that his hands were balled into fists at his sides. "I'll be okay," Jack assured her. "Your father can build me a fire." He looked at Greylen and shrugged. "She calls me Wayne sometimes."

"I'd give my right arm for five minutes alone with Wayne Ferris," Greylen growled. "He's the bastard who got her with child and then discarded her like trash."

Jack started for home again. O-kay, then. When they reached the driveway, he asked, "You wouldn't happen to prefer something a bit stronger than beer, would you, laird?"

"I never turn down scotch, Chief."

"Then what say we build a nice crackling fire, I'll dig out my good scotch, and then I'll tell you an interesting story?"

Greylen shot him a curious look, then nodded curtly, going up Jack's porch stairs ahead of him.

"The key's under the mat," Jack told him, following at a more labored pace.

Greylen peeled back the mat and picked up the key. "Ye haven't much sense for security, for a policeman."

Jack merely shrugged. Greylen opened the door and snapped on the light. "What is your story about, Chief?" he asked, walking to the woodstove in the middle of the back wall.

"Oh, it has a little of everything," Jack told him, limping to the cupboard that held the scotch. He took down the unopened bottle and two tumblers, then filled both glasses three-quarters full. "There's a mystery, a murder, and even some romance."

Greylen placed paper and kindling in the firebox. "And I will be interested because?"

Jack carried both drinks over, handed one to Greylen, then touched their glasses together. He took a long gulp, letting the liquid fire slide down his throat as he hobbled back to the counter to put some distance between them. "I believe you'll be interested because it's about me and Megan and our child, and the fact that the mystery and murder I was trying to protect her from may have followed her home."

Chapter Eleven

"*J*ack Stone is Wayne Ferris?" Grace whispered, plopping down on the single bed in shock.

Camry's announcement brought utter silence to the tiny bedroom. Megan also froze in surprise, torn between wanting to strangle her sister and wanting to hug her for taking the burden off her shoulders—though she probably wouldn't have been quite so blunt about it.

Camry straightened with a box of baby clothes in her hands. "And he's claiming he broke Megan's heart so that she *would* come running home, because he thought she was in danger." She shot Megan a frown. "Seems Meg forgot to mention that a man was murdered in camp just before she realized she was pregnant."

Grace looked from Camry to Megan. "But why was he calling himself Wayne Ferris?"

"It was an alias," Camry said. "He claims he was working undercover to get close to one of the students; that the kid was a runaway, and his parents had hired Jack to find him."

"Is this true, Meg?" Grace asked. "A man was murdered on your study? And Wayne—Jack—was trying to protect you?"

"That's the story *he's* telling."

"Meg's just angry because Jack came to Pine Creek to win her back before she could go after him herself," Camry continued, as if Megan hadn't spoken. "Jack's here because Meg and the baby are all the family he's got left. His parents died in a car crash when he was nine, and his great-grandfather raised him. But then *he* died when Jack was fifteen."

"Oh my God," Elizabeth said, hugging a bundle of baby blankets to her chest. "He broke your heart to save your life, Meg. He really does love you."

"And he's taken a job here," Chelsea interjected. "So you can raise your baby in Pine Creek after all."

"Hell-oo!" Megan said, waving her arms vigorously. "Are you all forgetting that not only did he break my heart, but that he's all but admitted he's a liar?"

"He'll fix your heart," Grace said, her smile warm and motherly as she stood to take hold of Megan's shoulders. "And he has to lie for a living, if it helps him find runaway kids. The important thing, Meg, is that he's here. I told you he would come for you, didn't I?"

"Damn," Camry said with a groan, dropping her box on the bed. "I just realized this means the curse is still intact. There goes my love life again."

Megan stepped out of her mother's embrace and scowled at her sister. "No, the curse is *not* intact, because I am *not* marrying Wayne."

"Right. You're marrying Jack."

"I am not! He lied to me four months ago, and for all we know, he's lying now."

Camry looked at Chelsea. "You must know a good private investigator. Let's get Jack checked out, and if he is lying, then we get Winter to turn him into a toad."

"And if he's telling the truth?" Grace asked, directing her question to Megan.

"Do you honestly expect me to simply forget what he did, and *how* he did it? You have no idea what he said to me that day. He nearly killed me."

"But he didn't," Grace said softly. "And if he really does love you, and only said what he did to protect you, then yes, you have to forgive him." She smiled sadly. "But if your heart says Jack Stone is not the man you want to spend the rest of your life with, your father and I will respect your decision."

Grace turned to Camry, giving her a warning glare. "Winter is not turning anyone into anything. The magic's been messed with enough lately. Let's just let Providence get used to our new resident wizard for a while, shall we?"

"Speaking of Winter, why isn't she here tonight?" Camry asked, obviously anxious to change the subject.

"Matt had to fly to his New York office this afternoon, and she went with him." Grace turned and surveyed the bedroom, shaking her head. "I think we've overdone it with the hand-me-downs. This poor baby won't have anything new to call its own."

"Chelsea, could you come upstairs with me?" Megan asked, heading into the hallway. "I have a box up there I need to go through. You can carry it down for me." She stopped in the door and looked back at the others. "The closet has built-ins and the bureau is empty, so you can put everything away as you sort. We'll be back in a few minutes."

The moment they reached the top of the stairs, Megan looked down to make sure no one had followed, then turned to her twin sister. "I'm going to do as Camry suggested and have Wayne checked out. Your law firm must use private investigators. Can you give me the name of a good one?"

"Are you sure you want to do that, Meg? It's been my experience that their reports never tell the whole story."

"You know the saying 'fool me once, shame on you, but fool me twice, shame on me'? Well, regardless of what Mom says about following my heart, this time around I'm listening to my left brain. I don't care what it costs, just find me an investigator who can travel all the way to Medicine Lake if he has to. I want more than a report filled with public documents; I want pictures and personal interviews, right down to what Jack Stone's favorite food was when he was five years old."

"Holy smokes, you really are angry, aren't you?"

"I'm so angry I bet I could turn him into a toad without any help from the magic."

Greylen MacKeage was no saint, nor did he have any desire to become one. He was wise enough, however, to know he shouldn't be entertaining thoughts of violence when he was getting so close to meeting his Maker. But God help him, he really wanted to beat Jack Stone to a bloody pulp for what the bastard had put his little girl through. Then again, his warrior's heart made him wonder if he might have behaved just as badly toward Grace thirty-six years ago, when she had been in danger.

"You're saying ye have no idea why the man was

murdered," Grey reiterated. "Only that you suspect it had something to do with the study being conducted on the tundra. May I ask why ye never bothered to find out?"

"Because it wasn't any of my business," Jack told him. "Once Megan was safely out of the way, I focused only on getting the boy back to his parents in one piece. The murder, and whoever did it, is the Canadian police's problem."

"Yet you're thinking now that the problem has followed my daughter home."

"Yes." Jack Stone shifted in his chair beside the woodstove, opposite Grey. "I did discover who headed the organization funding the boy's education. It's the man Megan is working for now, Mark Collins. And I find that a bit too much of a coincidence."

Grey suddenly stood up, hiding his smile when Jack flinched. Good. If he couldn't beat him up, by God, at least he could enjoy watching the bastard squirm. Grey walked to the counter, grabbed the bottle of scotch, and refilled Jack's empty glass before sitting back down and filling his own. "I'll tell Megan she has to resign her position immediately."

Jack took a gulp of the scotch. "That's not going to make the problem go away. Collins will simply find another way to get to her."

Grey nodded. "You're right. If he went to the trouble of fabricating this project and she resigns, he may come at her directly. Any idea why, Chief?"

"Nope," Jack said, frowning down at his glass. "Until Collins's name came up at dinner an hour ago, I thought the problem had stayed in Canada." He looked toward the woodstove, staring at the fire lapping the glass. "I need to think about the connection."

"I'll have Megan move back to Gù Brath until this matter is cleared up."

Jack looked up in alarm. "You can't mean to tell her."

Greylen lifted one brow. "Are you not a man who learns from his mistakes?"

"She'll throw a fit when she finds out it was Collins who planted that kid on her study, to watch over whatever he was doing on the tundra. She might confront him herself."

Grey leaned back in his chair. "I see you've come to know my daughter quite well." He shook his head. "I can control her. And if not, then I'll ask her cousin Robbie MacBain to have a talk with her."

Jack Stone's face darkened, and Grey once again stifled a smile. "No offense, MacKeage," Jack said in a growl, "but Megan is my responsibility now. She is carrying my child."

Grey made a point of letting his gaze travel over Jack's battered body. "No offense, Stone," he growled back. "But ye seem to be having trouble defending *yourself*."

"I am aware of my track record here in Pine Creek, but maybe you shouldn't be so quick to judge me. I can be surprisingly effective when I put my mind to it."

"Can ye, now?"

Jack's eyes darkened to the color of tempered steel. "Pacifism is not the same as defenselessness, MacKeage. When push comes to shove, I am more than capable of protecting what's mine."

With his door closed and a request that Ethel send his phone calls to Simon, Jack sat in his office tucked in the back corner of the police station. The citizens of Pine Creek, Frog Cove, and Lost Gore had spared no expense in remodeling the hundred-year-old storefront on Main Street. They reasoned that by putting an impressive face on law and order, criminals would think twice about targeting their tiny resort communities.

Too bad their plan wasn't working.

Not that his own plan was doing any better. In winning back Megan, he had gone from being optimistically hopeful to suddenly desperate last night at dinner. What in hell was Mark Collins up to on the tundra, and what was his connection to Megan?

Jack laced his fingers behind his head and leaned back in his plush leather chair as he stared at the four yellow pads of paper lined up on his desk. Each pad represented a problem he was dealing with; four seemingly unconnected issues occurring simultaneously.

Why, then, was his gut telling him a common thread held them together?

Lord, he hated puzzles. He didn't care how hard his military superiors had tried to persuade him that he belonged in covert intelligence; Jack had no patience with puzzles as a kid, and he hadn't grown any fonder of them since. And despite having a sixth sense, as they'd called it, for seeing threads running through the information he'd gathered for them, puzzles still drove him crazy.

Jack studied the first pad, where he'd written LITTLE BASTARDS in bold letters across the top. This was the problem that had gotten him hired, and likely the only one that wasn't connected to the others.

Pad two, THE BREAK-INS, denoted much more serious offenses. Definitely criminal. Though nothing of great value was ever stolen, the last break-in had resulted in physical contact. Jack wondered just how far his attacker would have gone if MacBain hadn't shown up. As for whatever the hell had run out of that store, he'd swear it had flown off into the night.

And that's where the first thread appeared, linking pad number two with pad number three, which he had titled MEGAN. Topping Megan's list was Kenzie Gregor, sublisted by secrets, designs on Megan, hermit boy, right size for attacker, and possible odor link to break-ins.

Next was MacBain: why had he been in town that night?

Camry: how to ditch her long enough to get Megan alone again.

Win over Megan's family: he was making progress there.

Turn some of Megan's anger back into some of that mind-blowing passion. Yeah, like that was going to happen anytime soon.

And then there was the thread linking Megan to pad number four, MARK COLLINS. Collins headed some sort of environmental organization that attracted runaways with the promise of an education, possibly brainwashing their altruistic young minds to help him . . . do what? Then there was the murder, which was tied to Billy Wellington, who was tied to Collins.

But what did any of it have to do with Megan? Had she seen or done something that might have interfered with whatever Collins was doing on the tundra? Could she have something he wanted? Data? Notes? Samples of . . . whatever?

Jack looked back at the other three pads. There was something else linking everything together. Something he was overlooking. His gaze moved from pad two to pad three, and his mind's eye saw another thread slowly weaving between them.

Well, hell. Jack grabbed a pen and flipped the page on Megan's pad, where he added *magic* to the list, followed by a question mark. Under that he wrote *shaman,* then *wizard* . . . and then he hesitated. Finally he wrote *baby,* followed by another question mark.

He set down his pen, closed his eyes, and rubbed his face with a tired sigh.

His office door suddenly burst open, and Megan stormed right up to his desk and planted her hands on her hips. Jack casually piled the legal pads on top of each other and folded his hands over them with a smile. "It's okay, Ethel," he called. "Beautiful women can disturb me anytime."

Ethel snorted and closed the door.

Megan's gaze narrowed. "What did you and my father talk about last night?"

"You, mostly."

"You told him you're Wayne."

"Wasn't I supposed to? Sweetheart, you've got to give me a plan book to follow if you don't want me making things up as I go along."

"Then how come you're still alive?"

"Because your father is rather old-fashioned. He seems to think parenthood is a team effort." Jack smoothed down the front of his uniform. "And he thinks being a police officer is a noble profession, and he's pleased that I want to settle down here in Pine Creek."

Her scowl deepened. "What other lies did you tell him?"

"Not a one," he said, placing a hand over his heart and holding the other one up in a scout's salute.

Megan set her palms on the desk and leaned closer. "Then why, when I stopped into Gù Brath to let him know that I'm heading up the lake to start my survey tomorrow, did he insist that I had to speak with you first?" she asked with lethal softness. "And that if you say no, I can't go?"

"That's why you're breathing fire? Because your father told you to come ask my permission?" Jack leaned back in his chair with a whistle. "How do he and MacBain do it?"

"I am *not* asking permission for anything," she growled. "I'm here to find out what *important thing* you have to tell me."

"It appears there's a connection between Collins and Billy Wellington, which now seems to be connected to you. Mark Collins was paying for Wellington's education."

She straightened and crossed her arms under her breasts, over her bulging belly. "My, my, you just keep embellishing your little tale, don't you? You've even managed to tie in my new job to make my father believe I'm *still* in some sort of danger."

Jack knew that on some level she actually believed his "tale," but apparently her pride—and obvious need to indulge in a bit of revenge—was stronger than her desire to forgive him. He stood up. "Yeah, like I'm foolish enough to lie to your father." Just to rile her further, Jack mimicked her stance by crossing his own arms over his chest. It was time to bury the nerd. "How are you planning to get up the lake tomorrow?"

She was momentarily caught off guard by his question, but quickly recovered and lifted her chin defiantly. "By snowmobile. There's a state ITS trail that runs up the east side of the lake, and a local spur at the north end that goes right through the area I'm studying."

Jack knew she was expecting him to argue that she

shouldn't be snowmobiling when she was five months' pregnant. Instead he asked, "How long a trip is it?"

She eyed him suspiciously. "Two hours up and two back, and a few hours to look around the north end of the lake."

He nodded. "We should leave no later than nine, then, so we can be back before dark."

Her arms fell to her sides. "We?"

Jack rubbed his hands together excitedly. "I've been dying to try my new sled on the trails around here. And since this is your turf, you can be my guide. It's a win-win opportunity for both of us."

"I do not need a babysitter."

"But I do. I've only ridden on the lake so far, because I don't know the trails."

"Then join one of the local snowmobile clubs. They have maps, and they organize trail rides every weekend. You are *not* going with me."

"Why not?"

"Because . . ." She tossed up her hands in frustration. "Oh, okay! But you'd better not interfere in my work or slow me down."

"Slow you down?" He eyed her suspiciously. "What do you have for a sled?"

"I'm using one of the ski resort's snowmobiles. It's not a speed demon like yours; it's a working sled. By 'slow me down,' I mean you'd better not start complaining that I'm going too fast for my condition."

He gave a negligent shrug. "Riding on groomed trails is no more strenuous than driving a car. So," he said, walking around the desk and opening his door. "Are you packing our lunch, or should I have the restaurant throw us something together?"

Megan reluctantly followed, then stepped directly in front of him. "I'm in charge of tomorrow's ride."

"Of course you are."

"*I'll* bring a gun."

"Expecting trouble?"

"No. But only an idiot heads into the deep woods unarmed. And I'll bring lunch. I have leftovers that need to be used up."

"Great. I love cold roast beef sandwiches, especially with mustard and cheese."

"And I'm bringing snowshoes, because I want to check out a deer yard I think is up there. What about your knee?"

"It's much better, thanks. But in the interest of not slowing you down, I'll just find a sunny spot and take a nap while you hunt for your herd of deer. If you bring the leftover gravy, I can build a fire to heat it up. You want me to make the cocoa?"

She again eyed him suspiciously, apparently wondering why he was being so cooperative. "Um . . . okay. But I—"

She was interrupted when someone cleared his throat nearby. Jack looked over to see Robbie MacBain standing there, Ethel hovering behind their newest guest. She shrugged when Jack didn't say anything, then went back to the front desk.

"You two sound like you're planning a trip to the backcountry," MacBain said, frowning at Megan. "Have you spoken with your father today?"

"Apparently you have," Megan snapped. She suddenly shot her cousin a smug smile. "I'm going, and Wayne's going with me."

Robbie's glare returned to Jack. "This is your idea of keeping her safe?"

"I'll be right behind her the whole way. If a moose tries messing with her, I'll run it over with my sled."

He thought MacBain was going to punch him, and bit back a grin.

Megan snorted. "I'll most likely be saving *him*," she said, doing exactly that by stepping between them.

She was his little warrior, all right, giving him hell one minute and protecting him the next. Jack wondered if she even realized what she was doing.

"We'll be on the snowmobile trails, Robbie," she continued. "What can possibly be dangerous about that? Tomorrow's a weekday, so there won't be much sled traffic, and I'll have the satellite phone if we run into trouble."

"Did you follow that guy's tracks the other night?" Jack asked Robbie.

"That's what I've come to talk to you about," he said, walking past Megan into the office.

By the scowl Megan gave his back, she apparently didn't like her cousin's dismissing her any more than she liked Jack doing it.

So Jack did it again. "I'll meet you in front of your house at nine tomorrow morning," he told her, stepping back into his office and partially shutting the door. "Don't forget the gravy."

Megan spun on her heel and stormed down the hall. Jack took a moment to admire her lovely backside, then closed the door and turned to Robbie.

"What's your background, Stone?"

Jack walked to his chair. "Covert intelligence."

"You were in the field?"

"And more dark alleyways of European and Middle Eastern cities than I care to recall." He sat down and motioned for Robbie to do the same. "I promised Greylen I would keep his daughter safe, and I will. Tell me about Kenzie Gregor."

"Kenzie? Why?"

"What's his story? And what's his interest in Megan?"

"He's only been in this country a short while, he lives up on TarStone with an old priest named Daar, and he considers Megan a sister. I made some calls this morning to a few of my old military friends, and they're looking into Mark Collins for me."

"Good. The more information we get on Collins, the better. Explain the social structure around here for me—best as I can tell, there are at least three . . . clans? The MacKeages, the MacBains, and the Gregors. Is Greylen really a laird?"

"He's laird of the clan MacKeage. My father is also a laird, though neither man uses the title anymore." His eyes lit with amusement. "Unless they're wanting to flex their muscles at someone."

Jack ignored that last part. "Yet you seem to be the go-to man around here. Megan and Camry respect your authority, as does Greylen."

Robbie settled back in his seat with a smile. "I was the first American born. My mother, Mary, and Grace MacKeage were sisters. Mary died when I was born and Libby is my stepmother. As for my role here, I suppose you could call me a sort of guardian of the families."

"Why do they need you to look out for them?"

"That's the way clans work. Four MacKeage men and my father settled here thirty-nine years ago, and though they readily adapted, they've come to rely on me in most matters because I grew up here. The old priest who lives on TarStone, Father Daar, came with them. He's a strange fellow who usually keeps to himself. If you happen to meet him, don't take too seriously what he might say. He's getting on in years and becomes confused sometimes."

"And the Gregors?"

"Matt owns a jet engine company in Utah. He arrived in Pine Creek last September, and owns Bear Mountain. Winter, Grey's youngest daughter, married Matt at Christmas. His brother Kenzie has been here since the wedding."

"And Kenzie Gregor lives with the priest."

Robbie nodded. "He looks out for the old man. Why are you interested in Kenzie?"

"Because he's interested in Megan."

Robbie shook his head. "Not in that way."

"And I believe he's the man who attacked me two nights ago."

"What makes you think that?"

Jack shrugged. "Where did the tracks lead?"

"I followed them to a bog about three miles up the east side of the lake, at the base of Bear Mountain. Then they simply vanished into thin air."

"Tracks don't just vanish."

"Bear Creek enters the lake through that bog, and the flow has covered nearly thirty acres in glaze ice." Robbie also shrugged. "That's where I lost him. The man may have had a snowmobile parked on one of the nearby trails, and could have gone in any direction after that. Have you considered that maybe the connection to Collins is with you, not Megan?"

"I've considered it, but why go to the trouble of hiring Megan if it's me he's after?"

"To use her to get to you? After all, you're the one who directly interfered in whatever he was doing in Canada, according to what Greylen told me."

"I see your point," Jack said, shuffling through his pads until he found the one marked MARK COLLINS. "But the thread I'm seeing is linking Megan to him, not me."

"Thread?" Robbie repeated, peering down at the pad.

Jack wrote his own name on the page, followed by a question mark. "Covert intelligence, remember?" He looked up. "I was good at my job because I could see threads linking what appeared to be unconnected information together." He shrugged. "You would likely call them gut instincts. I call them threads." He stood up, walked to his office door, and opened it. "Thanks for following those tracks the other night. I appreciate your effort."

Robbie stepped into the hallway. "I hope you're able to keep your promise to protect Megan."

"I have a feeling you'll be watching my back."

The tall Scot smiled tightly. "Aye, Stone, I will." He started walking away, but stopped at the end of the hall and looked back. "Good luck tomorrow, my friend. Mind that my cousin doesn't run you in circles and leave you in the woods. She can get creative when she's wanting to prove a point."

"Thanks for the warning," Jack said, stepping back into his office and softly closing the door. O-kay. Another thread had just connected; MacBain knew Jack's attacker and was covering for the bastard. Obviously *guardian* wasn't a hollow title.

Nor was *laird*, apparently.

Megan's family was nearly as weird as his own.

Chapter Twelve

$\mathscr{J}$ack sat on his snowmobile on the lake in front of Megan's house, sipping coffee from his Thermos as he watched the MacKeage family in action. Greylen had arrived on a snowmobile laden with equipment about twenty minutes ago, and Grace MacKeage had pulled into the driveway in their SUV shortly after. Camry, in a coat thrown over her pajamas and unlaced boots on her feet, was battling the cold by dancing in place as she added her own two cents to the send-off.

When Grace wasn't playing the buffer between Megan and Grey, she was eyeing Jack, apparently trying to assimilate what she knew about Wayne Ferris with the man her daughter was heading into the woods with this morning.

Jack shot her a wink.

Grace immediately left the group and walked over to him. "May I offer you a word of advice, Mr. Stone?" she asked, her expression congenial.

"I only take advice from people who call me Jack."
He pulled out a cup and large Thermos from his
saddlebag, poured out some hot cocoa, and handed it
to her.

"Thank you, Jack," she said, taking the steaming cup.
She looked back at the scene near shore and shook her
head. "My husband raised our girls to be very comfortable in the woods, yet every time one of them heads
out, he feels compelled to remind them of everything he
taught them."

"It's a father-daughter thing. He wouldn't be lecturing
a grown son, would he?"

Grace blew on her cocoa. "No, he wouldn't. That's
why you only got a nod from him this morning."

Jack chuckled softly. "A man can say a lot with a nod.
This morning, it said that if I don't bring his daughter
back safe and sound, not to bother coming back myself."

Grace gave a soft laugh. "Are you a patient man, Jack?"

"It so happens my patience is legendary. Why, am I
going to need it?"

"Oh, yes." She moved closer and lowered her voice.
"Camry said you don't have any family. Is that true?"

"It's been just me and my shadow for the last twenty
years."

"Then promise me you won't let the size of our family
scare you off."

"Exactly which size would that be? The height, or
your sheer numbers?"

Megan's beautiful mother laughed. "Both, I suppose."
She grew serious again. "At times you might feel like
you're running a gauntlet, I'm afraid. They're going to

test you repeatedly, and I suspect Megan will be leading the pack."

"My great-grandfather used to call me Coyote," Jack told her. "And coyotes are very resilient animals, Mrs. MacKeage."

"Call me Grace, Jack. And *please*, stop calling Grey laird," she asked, rolling her eyes. She turned thoughtful. "If I remember correctly, isn't having a coyote for a totem a good thing? Aren't they considered uncommonly cunning?"

"A rocket scientist who knows Native American lore?"

"You'd be surprised how open-minded scientists are about the unexplainable. You might want to remember that when you're dealing with Megan. Camry said your great-grandfather was a shaman."

Jack sighed. "Forest Dreamwalker was the last of a dying breed, which lost its appeal with modern medicine." He gave her a crooked smile. "Don't worry. Your grandchild will have ten fingers and toes and won't be born with a feather in its hair."

She gave him a sharp look. "We will love that baby if it has twelve toes and two heads. We are not prejudiced people, Mr. Stone."

"I'm sorry. I had no call to imply that you are," he said, feeling his face flush. "It's just that when most people hear the word *shaman*, they start thinking of campfire rituals and mystical trances."

She remained silent, and Jack wanted to kick himself. "At the risk of shooting myself in the foot, Megan and Camry seemed alarmed when they learned about my great-grandfather."

Grace looked down at her cocoa. "They've been

fascinated with the magic since they were little girls." She looked up. "So, Jack. Can you explain to me why you couldn't have kept my daughter safe without completely devastating her?"

"When Megan told me she was pregnant, I simply panicked. I didn't know what in heck was going on, other than that a man had been murdered. I just wanted her off that tundra so I could concentrate on getting Billy Wellington out of harm's way."

"Do you have any idea what it does to a woman when she gives herself to a man that completely, and he throws it back in her face?"

"No, ma'am. I only know what it did to me."

"Do you love her?"

"More than I ever thought possible."

"And have you told her that?"

Jack stilled in surprise. "Not lately," he admitted.

Grace gave a feminine snort. "Don't you think you should?"

"She won't believe me."

"*I* believe you, Jack."

"You do? Why?"

"Because you've let yourself get beaten up all week."

"You think that's been on purpose?"

"Are you incapable of defending yourself, then?"

Damn, she was perceptive. "But what would my getting beaten up prove to Megan?"

"Maybe that you need her as much as she needs you?"

"Are we leaving today, or what?" Megan called out. "You're slowing me down, Jack."

She'd finally called him Jack! "I'm ready when you are," he called back, quickly stashing his Thermos and picking up his helmet. He looked at Grace. "You think it's as simple as me telling her that I love her?"

"No—I think it's that complicated."

Megan pulled up beside them on her sled. "What are you two talking about?" she asked through the open visor of her helmet.

"You, mostly." Jack slid on his own helmet, then reached out and started his sled. Megan zoomed off, heading up the cove, and Jack looked at Grace again. "Thanks for the advice." He slapped down his visor and gave his sled the gas, aiming for the cloud of snow dust already half a mile up the lake.

Megan zoomed up the lake with abandon, every fiber of her being humming in joy. *Finally* she was back doing what she knew and loved. How had she strayed so far from herself? She didn't belong behind some counter selling her sister's paintings; she belonged outdoors with the cold wind nipping her nose and the crisp air sharpening her senses.

She felt so exhilarated, she didn't even mind that Jack was tagging along. It rankled that her father had so quickly decided that he liked him on some man-to-man level, but that didn't mean she couldn't enjoy today's outing—and maybe even have a bit of fun at Jack's expense.

Megan checked her mirror and saw that Jack had caught up and fallen in line behind her, and she stifled a snort. Did he think she was falling for his act? She was on to him now; under that defenseless-appearing exterior, Jack Stone was as hard as his last name implied.

Megan continued across the lake as fast as she dared,

considering every little bump bounced her baby down on her bladder. Damn. She hadn't thought about having to stop for bathroom breaks with Jack along. She'd borrowed Elizabeth's suit from when her sister had been pregnant, but she was going to have to take off the damn thing completely to pee in the woods—which was going to be chilly and time-consuming.

She sure hoped Jack was a patient man.

Megan frowned. Those had definitely been angry bees, not butterflies, fluttering around in her stomach when she'd stood nose to chin with him yesterday, jostling for position. And she didn't care how stressed he had looked, or that any fool could see he needed a day in the woods as much as she did. Why had she capitulated so quickly and agreed to let him come along?

Because she was a softhearted sap, that's why.

Megan zoomed past a lone ice fisherman tending his traps, gave him a wave, and aimed her sled toward a well-traveled path leading to shore. She slowed down to maneuver over the rough transition from lake to solid ground, then glided up the winding spur to the ITS trail.

Maine had an amazing Interstate Trail System that took advantage of many of the unused logging roads in the winter. These virtual highways were proudly maintained by local clubs, to the point that they were nearly as wide and often smoother than their automobile counterparts.

They were definitely faster.

Megan stopped at an intersection, looked for sled traffic before turning north onto the ITS trail, and accelerated to thirty-five miles per hour. She noted Jack still in her mirror, and wondered how he liked taking second place. When a man owned a snowmobile engineered to attack the trails at speeds in excess of ninety miles per hour, that usually meant he had a lead dog mentality. Did Jack?

Of course he did. He'd bought that chick magnet, hadn't he?

Good Lord! Did he see her as some fluffy snow bunny who would swoon over a man riding a cherry red rocket?

Naw. Jack knew her better than that.

Was he afflicted with little-man syndrome, then?

Megan snorted. Jack might be several inches shorter than the men in her family, but he sure as heck didn't appear to be trying to prove anything to anyone. Getting beaten up three days in a row—including Camry's pie in his face!—wasn't exactly impressive.

Megan caught herself gaining speed and realized her sense of urgency was coming from her bladder. Darn. Only half an hour into their trip, and already she had to pee. She drove until she found a little-used spur going off to the right, went up it a few hundred yards, then pulled to the edge of the trail and shut off her machine.

Jack pulled up directly behind her. Megan took off her helmet, climbed off her sled, and walked back to his. "I have to go to the bathroom," she said. "Shut off your engine so we can hear if anyone is coming down the trail."

He took off his helmet, frowned at her, and said, "How come you didn't take care of that before we left?"

"I did. You try riding around with a baby sitting on your bladder."

His eyes dropped to her belly and his frown reversed

to a lopsided grin. "Oh. I hadn't thought about that." He reached out to turn the key on his snowmobile, but stopped and looked at her. "Are you sure it's okay to just shut if off? Shouldn't I let the engine idle for a few minutes, so I don't damage something?"

Megan reached over to shut off his sled. "It's the other way around, Jack. If you let a powerful engine like this one idle too long, it can overheat. You grew up in Medicine Lake, so how come you don't know anything about snowmobiles?"

"Grand-père was old school. We snowshoed wherever we wanted to go. I did get a snowmobile when I was sixteen, but it was older than I was and broke down within a month. I think it's still sitting in the woods thirty miles north of Medicine Lake."

"You told Camry and me that your great-grandfather died when you were fifteen, and that you got hauled off by human services after that."

"I also said that I ran away again." He grinned up at her. "Since they hadn't found me the first time around, I headed straight back to where Grand-père and I had been living. The people of Medicine Lake diverted the social workers looking for me, and gave me odd jobs so I could support myself. That's how I got the sled. I bartered it for some doctoring."

Megan narrowed her eyes at him. "You also said you didn't inherit your great-grandfather's gift."

"But I did inherit his herbs. And I'd gone with him whenever he tended the sick, so I knew the drill." He shrugged. "People just assumed his gift had passed down to me. And the way I saw it, having fresh eggs to eat in the middle of winter was damn well worth praying over someone."

"My God, you were a con artist, deceiving sick people."

"No, Megan, I was just a kid trying to survive. Go on, go to the bathroom," he softly told her, waving toward a thick patch of bushes.

Megan turned and walked into the woods, unzipping her suit with a scowl. Confound it! She was not going to feel bad for calling him a con artist, no matter how wounded he'd looked. It was a wonder lightning hadn't shot from the sky and struck him dead. Even idiots knew better than to mess with the magic.

Still, shame washed over her, making her feel like she'd just kicked a puppy. She couldn't imagine not having the security and love of her family. What would she have done, how hard would she have fought to survive, if she had been orphaned at nine, raised by an old man who probably needed more looking after than she did, and then been orphaned again at fifteen?

Heck, Jack literally *had* raised himself.

Safely out of sight of the trail, Megan tramped down a place in the snow. She slid her suit down to her knees, sat down on top of it, and pulled off her boots so she could take the suit completely off. She stuffed her feet back in her boots, dug around in her pocket for a tissue, then dropped her pants and long johns to her knees with a sigh. This was so much easier for men!

"I'm beginning to hope you're a boy," she told her baby, cradling her belly while leaning against a tree to support her back. "And I won't mind if you want to write your name in the snow."

A full five minutes later, huffing and puffing as she wrestled her snowsuit back on over her layers of clothes, she heard Jack call out, "Everything okay back there?"

"Just peachy!" she shouted.

She growled under her breath when she heard him chuckle, and swore out loud when she had to put her foot down in the snow to keep from falling. She plopped down and brushed her sock clean before pulling on her boot with a sigh. It was going to be a long day.

Jack handed her a bottle of water when she returned to the sleds. "I prefer hot cocoa," she told him. "You said you'd bring some."

"In the interest of not slowing us down with bathroom breaks, I thought you should limit your cocoa intake, since it contains caffeine. But you need water so you don't dehydrate, which can happen fast in winter."

"You don't need to lecture me on winter survival," she said, shoving the bottle at him and stomping back to her sled. She picked up her helmet and took a calming breath. "I'm pretty sure this spur circles back onto the ITS trail in three or four miles. We might as well continue on it, since this whole area is part of the watershed I'm studying."

"You're just *pretty sure* it circles back?"

She glared at him. "I won't get us lost."

"Still, I think I'll leave a trail of bread crumbs." He pulled his own helmet down over his head, effectively shutting her out.

Megan sat down on her sled and turned the key, then shot up the narrow spur. The man obviously had no sense of adventure.

She drove eight or nine miles before she started thinking she might have to eat crow. The trail wasn't going in the direction she thought it would; it was taking them northeast.

She came to another intersection and stopped. Should

she go right or left? Even though left was east and she wanted to head west to get back on track, tote roads could be deceiving. Why weren't these stupid trails marked?

Jack walked up to her sled and flipped up his shield. "I vote we go right," he told her loudly, to be heard over their idling engines.

"Why? That's east. We want to go west to get back to the lake."

"Just a hunch."

Megan looked around. Directly in front of them was a small mountain, though she wasn't sure which one. She looked left and right, but both directions showed only a short piece of the trail, since it was winding through dense forest. She looked back at Jack. "And if I think we should go left?"

"Then we'll go left." He shrugged. "Either direction, it's got to come out someplace."

He turned and walked away, and Megan watched in her mirror as he got back on his sled and waited. She looked up the new trail in both directions again, then gave her sled the gas and turned right, having learned long ago that when someone had a hunch and she had nothing, it was smarter to go with the hunch.

Within four miles the knot in her gut began to unwind as the trail slowly curved westward, taking them up and over the mountain, heading back toward the lake. She smiled. Jack might not want to admit it, but some of his great-grandfather's magic must have rubbed off on him.

Then again, maybe he was just lucky.

It was another ten miles before the area began to look familiar. The ridge to their right was the north end of

Scapegoat Mountain, and she was sure the peat bog that she'd glimpsed through an opening in the forest was Beaver Bog. That meant the mountain ahead of them was Springy, and the deer yard she was looking for was . . .

She raised her left hand to warn Jack she was stopping, and brought her sled to a halt. She set the brake and got off, lifting her visor as she walked back to him. "I think the deer yard I'm looking for is just over there," she said, pointing to a nearby ridge. "Let's find a place off the trail to set up camp. If the yard is there, I don't want to spook the herd by getting any closer with the snowmobiles."

"That's fine with me. I'm starved."

"It's ten-thirty."

"I overslept and didn't have time for breakfast. Did you remember the gravy?"

"Did you bring a pot to warm it in?" she asked, eyeing his small saddlebags.

He nodded toward her sled idling in front of them. "I'm sure your father stashed a pot in that pack basket."

"For a man who grew up in the wilderness, you certainly don't carry much survival gear."

He grinned up at her. "Give me a good knife and some rope and I can live like a king."

"Then you can set up camp and cook dinner while I check out the deer yard."

"That'll take you at least a couple of hours."

"So have a nap."

"Sounds like a plan to me. Pick a sunny spot out of the breeze," he said, waving her toward her sled and flipping down the visor.

Once again, Megan found herself stomping back to her snowmobile. She had to stop letting him rile her.

What had happened to Wayne-the-nerd, anyway? She actually missed him. Yet Jack-the-jerk was much more . . . stimulating.

Which was scary, considering she'd sworn off *all* men four months ago. Too bad her hormones hadn't gotten the memo.

Chapter Thirteen

Jack added more twigs to the small fire he had going, gave the remaining gravy a stir, and licked the spoon clean. He then settled back on his leather jacket and ski pants, which he'd taken off and laid over some fir boughs to make a bed. He closed his eyes with a sigh, thinking that if he got any smarter he might scare himself. Being out here alone with Megan was just like when they'd been out on the tundra, only better. This time there weren't any squabbling students to babysit or honking geese trying to peck him for messing with their young; it was just the two and a half of them in the middle of miles of wilderness.

Yup, he sure loved seeing a plan come together. Jack fell asleep with a smile, thinking life didn't get any better than having the little woman off at work while he kept the home fires burning. With that thought warming his heart, he drifted off into dreamland.

His mother visited him first, her radiant smile surrounding Jack with familiar serenity. "I like her family," Sarah Stone said. "Grace MacKeage will make you a wonderful mother-in-law. She's exactly the feminine influence I'd hoped you would find."

"*Maybe* she'll be my mother-in-law," Jack told the childhood vision of his mother. "I need the cooperation of her daughter for that to happen."

"Megan will come around. You heeded your grand-père's warning to send her home, and now you'll simply have to undo the damage."

"But how?"

"By being who you truly are, my son. The longer you deny it, the harder your journey will become."

"You sound like Grand-père."

"Because I am his granddaughter, Coyote."

"Where are Dad and Walker? I want to see them."

"They're fishing with my father. Grand-père's here, though. He has something to show you."

"I'm not in the mood for one of his lectures." Jack's voice rose when his mother began to fade into the shimmering light. "Stay and talk to me about how to fix things with Megan. I need your help, Mama. I miss you."

She stopped disappearing, only a faint image of her radiant beauty remaining. "You can't miss what you've never lost, Coyote. Every breath you take is my breath; every beat of your heart is my heartbeat; every time you hear the wind in the trees, I am singing to you. I walk inside you, my son."

"Stay, Mama."

"I'll be back again soon, but I must go find your father and brother now. Heed your grand-père's words, Coyote, for with the gift he brings you, he also brings wisdom."

"Mama!"

"Coyote! Quit your hollering," Forest Dreamwalker commanded as he appeared out of the ether, the epitome of shamanistic lore from his flowing gray hair down to the wrinkles on his aged face. "You're too old to be crying after your mama."

"I will never outgrow my need for her, old man."

"A father must be strong. Do you wish your son to think you weak?"

"What I wish is for you to stop plaguing my dreams," Jack growled. "My brother was to be your heir, not me. Wait—you said my *son*. Megan's having a boy?"

"Piqued your interest, have I? So now you'll listen to me?"

"What is that under your robe?"

"This?" Forest Dreamwalker lowered the edge of the thick wool robe he wore. "Why, it's an infant!"

"My son?" Jack asked, sitting up.

"According to what I saw when your mama changed his diaper," the old shaman said with a chuckle.

Jack stretched out his hands. "Let me hold him."

"In three and a half months, Coyote. Until then, he's ours to play with."

"Jack. My name is Jack now."

"Only because some fool social worker didn't know the difference between a coyote and a jackal. She had no right changing the name your mother and father gave you."

Jack dropped his outstretched hands with a sigh. This had been a bone of contention with his great-grandfather for nearly twenty-six years. "She changed it because no one would have adopted a kid named Coyote," Jack told him for the thousandth time. "And

I've kept it because it suits me. Move your robe so I can see my son."

The old man peeled back the wool a bit more. "You'll have to trust me that he's got your eyes," he said. "I'm not about to wake him, as he has the scream of a warrior. Which gives me hope that he'll inherit his mother's highlander spirit."

"There's nothing wrong with wanting to travel a peaceful path." Jack reached out again. "Let me hold him."

"If I do, will you agree to listen to me?"

Jack stilled. "You would use an innocent child to bargain?"

"Only because you force me to such extremes."

He really, really wanted to hold his son. "Okay."

The old man hesitated. "Promise me you won't wake him."

"I just want to hold him," Jack said, reaching out again. He took the child, surprised by how little he weighed. "He's not very big," he said, setting his son on his lap so he could study him.

"He will be when he's born," Forest said with a chuckle. "As I'm sure his mama will discover. No, don't unbundle him," he admonished, reaching out and tucking the blanket back around him. "He likes the security of being tightly swaddled."

But the child—his son!—started wiggling, then gave a yawn and stretched his little legs, pushing his feet against Jack's belly with surprising strength. His tiny arms started fighting the blanket, and he suddenly cracked open his eyes.

"Now you've done it," Forest growled.

Jack opened the blanket. The baby went perfectly

still, staring up at Jack with dark, solid navy eyes. Then his little cherub face scrunched up, his arms and legs started to windmill, and he let out a bellow that rocked Jack right down to his soul.

"Soothe him," Forest said frantically. "Hold him up to your chest so he can hear your heartbeat."

Jack pulled his shirttail from his pants high enough to expose his chest and carefully lifted his son, cradling the infant's face against his bare skin. He shuddered at the contact, and closed his eyes on a sigh when the boy started rooting against his skin.

He was holding his son!

Forest Dreamwalker sat beside Jack and shook his head. "Even this young, they know what they want. Give him your little finger to suckle."

Jack did, eyeing his great-grandfather suspiciously. "When did you learn what babies want? You had one son, and I doubt you spent much time with him until he was five or six."

"Ah, but I spent a great deal of time with Sarah from the moment she was born. Your mother was always wanting to be walked, and my son had no patience for pacing in circles to soothe her. That precious chore was mine."

Jack knew his family history by rote, since he'd spent five years alone in the woods with Forest Dreamwalker. Forest's son had found himself the sole parent of a three-month-old daughter when his wife had suddenly decided to move to Vancouver—with no husband or baby to cramp her new lifestyle. Sarah had been raised by her father and grandfather, and to this day Jack wondered how the two men had managed to keep a baby alive, much less raise her to become such an amazing woman.

"Listen up, Coyote," Forest said. "This puzzle you're grappling with is even more dangerous than you think."

"Which one?" Jack asked, looking down at his son.

"Aye, you're right. There are two distinct problems, with two very real dangers. You must tread carefully, Coyote, if you wish to keep your family safe."

"*Aye?*" Jack repeated, looking at Forest in surprise.

The old shaman smiled proudly. "I've added a new word to my vocabulary in honor of your son's Scottish heritage. The child has grown used to Laird MacKeage's voice, and responds favorably when I also say aye to him."

Good Lord, his kid was going to have some interesting dreams, with shamans and Highland warriors for ancestors. "He's *my* son," Jack said. "And I'm going to teach him to solve his problems with cunning, not might."

Forest gave a pained sigh. "Thank the moon Greylen will be around to teach him the ways of a warrior." He glared at Jack. "Are you going to listen to what I have to say or not?"

"I'm listening," Jack said, though he dropped his gaze again, rubbing his thumb over his son's soft cheek.

"Your woman has something Mark Collins wants."

"What is it?" Jack asked, looking up.

"I'm not all-knowing. But I can tell you it's something Megan isn't even aware of."

"Do you at least know what Collins is up to? What sort of business he was conducting out on the tundra?"

"It has to do with energy," Forest said. "Oil or some other sort of fuel."

Jack canted his head in thought. "Maybe she brought back samples or data that would prove there's shale oil under that part of Canada. Collins might be trying to hide that fact from the government, and that's why that man was killed."

"Maybe. But Collins is the least of your worries right now. You need to keep a close eye on that Kenzie Gregor fellow."

Jack looked up sharply. "So he *is* interested in Megan."

"No," Forest said with a shake of his head. "It's not her heart he's wanting."

"Then what?"

"Her knowledge. But that's not what you should be worried about. It's Gregor's connection to your break-ins that you must pay careful attention to."

"So what's the connection?"

Forest leaned closer. "Magic," he whispered. "Ancient Celtic magic, Coyote. A very powerful kind."

Jack gaped at his great-grandfather. "There's more than one kind of magic?"

The old shaman nodded. "The drùidhs have been charged with protecting the trees of life, whereas people and animals are my thing. My duty is to a person's more immediate well-being, so I was given the gift of helping individuals deal with daily life."

"Is Kenzie Gregor a drùidh?"

"No, but his brother Matt is. And Megan's sister Winter also possesses the power."

Jack leaned back, splaying his hand over his son in a protective gesture. "Winter's a drùidh? And Megan knows this?"

Forest nodded. "But you can't let her know that you know. That's something Megan must tell you herself." He smiled. "When she does, you'll know she finally trusts you and has completely forgiven you for what you said to her four months ago."

"I acted on your advice," Jack snapped.

Forest looked affronted. "I told you to send her away. The way you did that was *your* poor choice."

"It was the only thing that would make her leave. I sure as hell didn't mean it."

"I know that, and you know that, but does Megan? What you said, Coyote, is not something a woman easily gets past—no matter how much apologizing you do." Forest reached out to take the child.

Jack leaned away. "Wait. What about this magic business? How do I deal with Kenzie if his brother's a wizard?"

"By staying well away from Matt and Winter Gregor. Catching their interest could prove dangerous. Instead, you need to . . ." Forest dropped his gaze to his lap as his mind turned inward in thought.

Jack knew this could take awhile, so he gave his attention back to his son. He leaned forward to cradle the boy in his hands and lifted him up to kiss his tiny forehead. "Don't you frown at me," he said with a laugh. "It seems like I've been waiting forever to meet you."

The little bundle of joy he was holding stared up at Jack, the wisdom of the universe shining in his deep, dark, bottomless eyes. "Should we tell your mama she's having a son?" Jack asked. "Or keep this our little secret for a while?"

"You can't tell her," Forest suddenly interjected. "How would you explain how you know?"

"The same way I explain everything you tell me— that it's my gut instinct." He grinned down at his son. "It's worked for me for thirty-four years. I'll teach you how to rely on your own gut, baby boy." He looked up at Forest. "So, how do I deal with Kenzie Gregor?"

The old shaman squared his shoulders. "It's not my job to tell you what to do. You must find your own path, Coyote. That's what life is all about."

Jack gave a soft snort. "That never stopped you in the past. At least give me a hint."

Forest remained silent, true to his stoic Cree heritage—which he used only when it worked in his favor.

"Can you at least tell me what ran out of that store the other night and flew away?" Jack asked. "Was it man or beast?"

"It was both."

"Both."

"Aye, though I'd say it was more magical than real."

"What do you mean? Are you saying a figment of everyone's collective imagination is breaking into those buildings?"

"You'll solve that mystery when you discover Kenzie Gregor's secret," Forest told him, raising his voice to be heard when the baby began to cry.

Jack laid his son back on his lap and quickly swaddled him in his blanket. The infant grew even more unhappy, and his crying got louder. Jack stuck his little finger in its mouth, but apparently his son wanted to exercise his lungs and muscles, because he kicked off his blankets and cried even louder. Jack held him up to his chest again, but that didn't help, either.

"What have you done to my great-grandson?" Shadow Dreamwalker demanded as he appeared out of the ether.

Jack smiled up at his grandfather. "Grand-père pinched him." His grin widened when Mark and Walker Stone also appeared. "Hi, guys. How was the fishing?"

"Give me the child," Sarah Stone said, also appearing

from the swirling light surrounding Jack's dream. "Grand-père, how could you?"

"I didn't pinch him! He just started in for no reason."

The moment Jack's mother cradled the baby to her bosom, the boy snuggled down with a contented sigh.

Jack looked around in awe. Five generations of Dreamwalkers were present, and his father and brother. How amazing was that?

Shadow Dreamwalker had died before Jack was born, but Jack had gotten to know his grandfather quite well in his dreams. One big happy family; except that they were all *over there,* and he was over here—alone.

He smiled at his eleven-year-old brother, Walker. It had taken Jack quite a few years to come to terms with feeling responsible for killing his family. It had been Walker who had persuaded him that all siblings engaged in petty fighting, and that their father's stopping the car and making Jack sit under a tree in a time-out . . . Well, no one could have seen the accident coming. Fate, Walker had repeatedly assured Jack, did not lie in the hands of a nine-year-old boy.

Still, it was going to take more than a few imaginary conversations with his very dead brother to convince Jack that pacifism wasn't the better path.

"It's time to go," Sarah said, gently rocking her grandson. "Megan is on her way back." She smiled down at Jack. "I hope you saved her some lunch."

"When will I see you all again?"

"When you need to." Mark Stone leaned down and kissed Jack on the cheek. "You've found yourself a wonderful woman, son. Do whatever you must to keep her, even if it means getting beaten up a few more times."

Forest harrumphed and stood up. "Megan MacKeage is leading you on a merry chase, and you're letting her."

"She earned that right, wouldn't you say?" Jack countered. He lay back down on his jacket, laced his hands together behind his head, and gave his father a nod. "I'll find a way to keep her." He looked at his mother and winked. "Take good care of my son. You'll have him to yourselves only for three and a half more months. Then he's all mine." He looked at his great-grandfather. "And he's going to travel a peaceful path if I have to drag him down it myself."

Forest Dreamwalker swirled his robe around himself with his usual dramatic flair, and vanished into thin air. Everyone else, with waves and cheerful good-byes, slowly turned and walked into the shimmering ether.

Smiling with deep happiness, Jack decided to continue sleeping, hoping to extend the memory of his son's downy-soft skin pressed against his own.

Huffing and puffing with each step, Megan wondered how she'd gotten so out of shape. She was known for snowshoeing the full ten miles up and down TarStone Mountain in less than six hours, but today two miles in three hours was pretty much doing her in. The twenty-four pounds she'd gained in the last five months was obviously the culprit.

She was suddenly glad Jack had tagged along today; she was cold and tired and so hungry she could eat a horse, and the thought of returning to a cozy camp with a roaring fire and hot food was the only thing keeping her going. Though she knew she'd better not get used to it, that didn't mean she couldn't take advantage of Jack's attentiveness for the time being.

She finally trudged into camp, only to find Jack asleep, the fire out, and the basket of food nearly empty. She bent over and scooped up a handful of snow.

"You throw that, you'd best be prepared for the consequences."

"You ate all the food!"

"I saved you some," he said, sitting up with a yawn.

"And you let the fire go out."

"If you're cold, I can warm you up," he offered, patting a spot beside him.

"In your dreams."

"You might enjoy my dreams," he said with a chuckle, leaning forward to lace up his boots. "Did you find the deer yard?"

"No."

"Are you sure this is the right area?" he asked, looking around. "There aren't any cedar groves here."

Megan plopped down on the snow and started unlacing her snowshoes. "There's a large stand of it on the back side of the ridge, but the deer stripped it clean as high as they could reach several years ago. They must have found another yard."

Jack pushed her hands away and finished taking off her snowshoes for her. He then unlaced her boots and took them off, then stood, scooped her up in his arms and plopped her down on his snowmobile suit. Before she could even yelp in surprise, he was already sitting down and putting on her snowshoes. "There's a couple of sandwiches left, some crackers, and a full Thermos of hot cocoa," he told her. "Why don't you eat and then have a little nap?" He scanned the sky, then looked back at her. "We've got a few hours of daylight left. You mind snowmobiling after dark?"

"Why, where are you going?"

"To find your deer yard. You're in no condition to drive without having a nap."

Knowing he was right—though loath to admit it—Megan settled down on his jacket and rubbed her belly. "I don't know what got into the baby a little while ago, but it started kicking something fierce. I actually had to stop and sit down on a log. But just as suddenly as it started, it stopped."

Jack stilled, a funny expression on his face. "Just a short while ago?"

"Yeah. I swear the kid was doing somersaults."

Jack crawled over and placed his hand on her belly, his eyes meeting hers. "Maybe he's going to run away and join the circus when he's ten."

"Or *she* might become a ballerina," she said, feeling disconcerted to have his hand on her belly.

"Will you mind much if we have a boy?"

"I won't mind if we have a puppy as long as it's healthy."

That made him smile. Megan felt her insides flop—and it wasn't the baby doing gymnastics this time.

"Then I vote we have a boy. Would you consider naming him Walker, after my brother?"

"You have a brother?"

Jack gave her belly an affectionate pat, then started stirring the fire, putting on twigs and coaxing it back to life. "I used to."

"What happened to him?"

"It's a long story, best left for another time." He stood up. "Look, if you really are that hungry, I can bring back a rabbit."

Megan stared up at him. Who did he think he was,

Nanook of the North? "I'm not loaning you my gun."

"I don't need a gun," he said with a shrug. "Eat your sandwiches, Megan, and drink a whole bottle of water. I'll be back in less than three hours, I promise. There's enough firewood to last until then." He grabbed the blanket beside the pack basket and tossed it to her. "It'll get chilly as the sun drops. Keep this close."

"You need your jacket," she said as he started to leave.

"I've got enough layers on. Sweet dreams, sweetheart," he called back with a wave, tromping around a thick stand of alders.

Megan blinked at the spot where he'd disappeared, then dropped her gaze to the food basket. For a man trying to win her back her affections, Jack Stone didn't have any more of a clue how to go about it than Wayne Ferris had had. He expected her to survive all day on a box of crackers and two sandwiches? She'd packed five!

Megan stuffed her feet in her boots, tromped over to Jack's sled, and unzipped his tank bag. She pulled out a map, a handheld Global Positioning System receiver, and a mangled candy bar. She pocketed the candy bar and put the other stuff back, then unzipped the right saddlebag.

Four long-neck brown bottles peered up at her, two of them missing their caps and obviously empty. She pulled out a full bottle, and snorted. "Beer. Had yourself quite a little feast, didn't you?" she muttered, shoving it back in the bag. Something crunched in the bottom.

She reached down beside the bottles and pulled out an unopened bag of curly cheese puffs. "You bring beer and junk snacks, yet eat all the healthy food. I'm the one growing a baby here." She turned and tossed the cheese curls toward the bed, then looked back in the saddlebag. Stuffed between the bottles to keep them from breaking were a pair of socks, a thick wool hat, and spare mittens.

Megan moved on to the left saddlebag and found it contained a sturdy rope, a small ax, and two thin Mylar space blankets. She also found three more candy bars—which she pocketed—and a flattened roll of duct tape.

She walked back and fed the fire some twigs, then sat down on Jack's leather suit. The gravy was a lost cause, since lichen and moss had fallen into the open pot, so she ate both sandwiches, the crackers, and all four candy bars, then ripped open the cheese curls. She scoffed down half the bag before she decided she was more tired than hungry. With a sigh of contentment, she finally settled back on the bed Jack had made.

It was surprisingly comfortable. She rolled over and lifted the jacket sleeve, and saw that he'd arranged more than a foot of fir boughs on the ground, which kept her off the cold snow, just as her father had taught her. Apparently Jack had been listening when his great-grandfather had passed down his survival skills.

Which probably explained why he didn't know squat about courting a woman. Being raised by an old man in the middle of the wilderness wasn't exactly conducive to learning about the opposite sex. Still, Jack must have learned *something* once he'd gotten out in the real world. He'd been in the military, for crying out loud. Megan laced her hands together over her belly with a snort. That's probably where he'd acquired his sex education.

Although, once he'd gotten over her surprise attack, he'd certainly . . . *performed* well enough. Oh, okay. He'd done better than merely perform. He'd actually taken her beyond the stars and back, she remembered with a shiver.

And then he'd done it all over again. And again.

"Don't go there, Meg," she growled, snapping her eyes shut. Only that merely made the memory stronger, to the point that she could practically feel his intimate touch.

"Damn," she muttered, rolling onto her side, grabbing the blanket, and balling it up against her belly and chest. "Think of something else," she commanded herself. "Think about your baby."

Megan fell asleep a few minutes later and did dream about her child—of a little boy doing somersaults in the air as he flew from one trapeze to another.

Chapter Fourteen

Jack walked into camp three hours later to find Megan curled up on his suit. He also found four empty candy wrappers and half a bag of cheese curls on the ground beside her—which explained the orange powder all over her face.

"Trust me, playing possum only gets a person in trouble," he said, knowing damn well she was awake. He picked up the bag of cheese curls and stuffed them in the pack basket. "Been snooping, have you? And eating my stash?"

"You ate my lunch," she shot back, as she snuggled deeper into his suit. "What time is it?"

He picked up the candy wrappers and threw them in the basket. "Time to dig out the satellite phone and let Greylen know you won't be back by sunset. The last thing I want are your uncles and cousins coming out to search for us."

She still didn't move. "You call him. He won't lecture you."

"No, he'll just be waiting on my doorstep with a shot-gun."

"Daddy prefers a sword," she mumbled.

Jack straightened with the pot in his hand. "A sword?"

Megan cracked open one eye, and one corner of her mouth lifted in a lopsided grin. "He's pretty good with it, too. I've seen him cut a four-inch sapling clean through in one stroke."

"What's he doing with a sword?"

"It belonged to his father. All my uncles and cousins have swords," she added, finally rolling onto her back and opening both eyes—likely to better gauge his reaction. "They're very skilled with them, too. They clean up at the highland games down on the coast every summer."

Not wanting to disappoint her, Jack looked stricken. "Damn, and I left my bow and arrows in Medicine Lake. They wouldn't come after a defenseless man, would they?"

She finally sat up, stretching her arms over her head with a yawn. "That depends on whether or not I get home in one piece."

"Hit the bushes, then. We're leaving in ten minutes," he told her, plucking the blanket from her lap and fold-ing it.

She stood up with a little giggle and sauntered toward the bushes. "Gù Brath's number is programmed into the phone. You might stand a chance if Mom answers. If Daddy does, you better have a good story ready."

"Are you nuts? I'm not lying to your father."

She stopped and looked back, arching one delicate brow. "It's your funeral."

"I'm telling him our trip is taking longer than we thought because of the baby, and that I didn't realize how out of shape you've let yourself get."

Her eyes narrowed. "Did you find the deer yard?"

Jack bent down to hide his grin and continued packing up camp. "I found a herd of thirty or forty of them holed up about three miles due north." He stopped to look at her. "They seemed healthy. They certainly had plenty of feed. I did come across a yearling moose carcass, though. It looked to me like a mountain lion brought it down."

She had just started into the bushes, but swung back around to face him. "A mountain lion? You're sure? There's never been a documented sighting of one around here that I know of."

"It was definitely a large-cat kill."

Her face beamed. "Do you know what this means?"

"That you were smart to bring your gun?"

"It means that if I can confirm a mountain lion is living in the area, they can't build a resort here."

"Do you think the developers will be as happy with this news as you are?"

"Of course not. But that's why the state requires a study. That way the developers won't put too much money into a project before they find out they can't build."

"And if the developers send someone out here to quietly shoot the cat, will that make their little problem go away?"

"Not if I've already documented it. All I have to prove is that this area has had a mountain lion living here recently. It will then be designated a large-cat habitat, and all development will be banned."

He waved her away. "We can discuss this later. We're burning daylight."

She didn't move but frowned instead. "You said three miles north. You couldn't have covered that much ground in the time you were gone."

"Actually, I zigzagged a lot. I really traveled a total of eight miles."

She eyed him dubiously. "In three hours? That would mean you went . . ." She calculated in her head and then glared at him. "Nobody can do that on snowshoes."

"He can if he thinks a hungry cat is dogging his trail. That kill was over a week old. Will you get going? I'm hungry, and I can't wait to get home and slap a TV dinner in the microwave."

Jack gave a silent chuckle when she stomped off into the bushes. He pulled his revolver from the back of his waist and stashed it in his tank bag, then walked over to Megan's sled and rummaged around in her saddlebag for the phone.

"Greylen," he said when the sword-wielding laird answered. "This is Jack. I just want to let you know that we're still at the north end of the lake. We should be back home in three or four hours."

"What happened? Did ye have sled trouble? Where's Megan? I'd like to speak with her."

"She's in the bushes at the moment. You have seven daughters. Surely you remember what it was like traveling the backcountry with a pregnant woman."

There was a pause on the line, then a soft laugh. "Aye, I remember. So what delayed ye, other than bathroom breaks?"

"A detour down an unmarked trail," Jack told him. "And a couple of naps. The weather's been good, and Megan is thoroughly enjoying herself. I think she's missed being out in the field. She'll call you as soon as she gets home."

"Take your time traveling back, and don't overrun your headlights. The deer and moose like to use the trails at night."

"We'll be careful. Good-bye."

"Good-bye, Chief."

Jack hit the disconnect button with a chuckle. Apparently Greylen wasn't acknowledging they were on a first-name basis. But if Jack was going to run the MacKeage gauntlet, he would do it as an equal. Highlanders had nothing on Cree warriors.

"Was my father very mad?" Megan asked, emerging from the bushes, a bit winded and pink faced.

"Would you be worried if he was?"

"No," she said with a laugh. "He's all bluster. At least with us girls," she clarified. "I've decided to come back up here tomorrow or the next day. If I can document a mountain lion in the area, it will shut down the study before it's even begun."

"And you'll be out of a job."

"That's the way this business goes."

"Megan, did you notice anything . . . oh, I don't know, anything strange when we were on the tundra? Did you see any sign that there might be oil under that section?"

"Oil? You mean like bubbling tar pits that swallow up woolly mammoths and sabertooth tigers?"

Jack shook his head seriously. "I've been thinking about Mark Collins's connection to Billy Wellington, Billy's connection to your study, and your connection to Collins by way of this job. Honestly, don't you find it odd that the common factor here is Collins?"

"It's what he does, Jack. Mark is in the consulting business, and he hires biologists for studies all over the world. Why are you so convinced there's something fishy going on?"

"Because a man was murdered."

She sat down on her sled and looked up at him. "Okay, just for the sake of argument, let's say Mark *was* involved in that man's death. What has it got to do with me?"

Jack sat down on his own sled, which was parked beside hers. "This is just a theory. Call it a hunch if you want, but I think Collins was hired by someone—an energy company, maybe—to make sure your study didn't expose the fact that there's oil or natural gas under that area of tundra. So Collins put Billy Wellington on the study to keep an eye on things."

"But that implies Billy might have killed that man."

Jack shook his head. "There would be too much money involved to trust something like that to a kid. And Billy was really shaken by that guy's death. I think he told Collins that the government worker had discovered something, and Collins sent someone more experienced to deal with the problem."

"That still doesn't connect anything to me."

"Unless you discovered the same thing the government worker did."

"But what? I didn't see anything that pointed to oil."

"What about that dead arctic fox you found, and those half-eaten ptarmigans? Did you ever find out what killed them?"

"No. I took DNA samples, but I gave the carcasses to—" Her eyes widened. "To the government worker! He was supposed to send them to Ottawa." She stood up.

"And remember that dead snowy owl I found three days earlier? I gave him that carcass, too."

"Did he send them out?"

"No. He was waiting for the supply plane to arrive." She sat down again, stunned. "My God, do you think those dead animals are the link?" she whispered. "Could that man have been killed because of what had killed *them*?"

Jack took her hands in his. "It's a good possibility, if those birds ingested oil, and the fox and owl ate them and also died. It's also possible that Collins wants those DNA samples you took."

"But why wait four months to try to get them from me?"

"You've been surrounded by a small army since you've been home, and Gù Brath is a veritable fortress. I suspect Collins did send someone to Pine Creek, but when he realized he wasn't going to get your samples by stealing them, he decided to simply hire you to get close enough to find them."

"I—I suppose that makes sense. Except that I found the job on the Internet. How could he know I'd even be looking?"

"I suspect the job was posted just to make it look legitimate. Chances are if you hadn't seen it, you would have gotten a letter from Collins soon. Then, when you checked it out, you would have believed him because the job had been posted long before he contacted you."

She pulled her hands free and stood up. "Then we need to get going. I want to get home and find those samples."

"Where are they?"

"In my mother's lab. I stashed my trunk there when I came home, and forgot about it."

Jack felt like he was finally making progress. He kicked snow on the fire to put out the last of the dying embers. "First thing tomorrow, you find those samples and bring them to me at the police station."

"But they need to go to a lab."

"I'll get them to one." He strapped the basket on the back of her sled, then looked around to make sure they had everything. "I have connections in the Canadian government. This isn't an academic problem, Megan. It's a government one."

Jack would swear he heard her mutter something about a *nerd* as she climbed onto her sled and pulled on her helmet.

"Wait!" he shouted as she reached to start her engine. "Which trail are we taking back?"

She flipped up her visor, then pointed west toward the lake. "The one we're on should continue to the ITS trail that runs down the east side of Pine Lake."

"Are you sure, or just *pretty* sure?"

She just flipped down her visor, started her sled, and shot off down the trail. Jack waited until the snow dust had settled enough for him to see, then followed.

It was dark by the time they broke out of the forest and onto the lake—*not* the ITS trail. Jack's gut tightened; he did not want to travel the lake in the dark. He pulled up beside Megan, who had stopped and shut off her sled.

"I have no idea where the ITS trail is," she told him. "I don't know how we could have missed it."

Jack unzipped his tank bag and dug out his map. "We're going to have to find it, because we're not traveling the lake at night."

"I bet we're just a few miles north of where we should

be, and I'm pretty sure there's a club trail that runs the length of the lake," she offered. "We just have to find it, follow it south until we pick up the ITS trail, and we'll have a straight shot home."

Jack walked to the front of his sled, bent down in the beam of the headlight, and studied the map. "It's a lot more than a few miles to the ITS trail," he told her when she walked up beside him. "More like ten or twelve. See," he said, pointing out where they were. "This trail brought us out here, and the ITS takes a sharp eastern turn way down there."

He stepped back for the headlights to illuminate the area in front of them, and saw sled marks splaying out in all directions. "We should go back the way we came."

"But that will take all night."

"It's better than taking a cold swim." He folded the map and turned her to face him. "I don't like traveling on ice at night."

"We'll be on the club trail, for crying out loud. The local club will have marked it with small trees. They check it almost daily and set it well away from any dangerous spots. I vote we take the lake. Ten measly miles, Jack. And we've had subfreezing temperatures for nearly two months." She reached out and laid her hand on his chest. "Are you forgetting that I grew up here? I know this lake like the back of my hand."

He didn't point out that she'd gotten them lost twice today, since he suddenly realized this conversation was no longer about getting home. It was a test to see if he was capable of trusting her. And how could he persuade her to trust *him* again if he didn't do the same?

Dammit to hell. "Okay," he growled. "We'll take the lake. But I lead."

Her grin slashed broad in the headlights. Megan patted his chest and practically skipped back to her sled. "Not a problem, Jack. Better your taking a cold swim than me. Don't worry, I'll throw you a rope if you fall through the ice."

Jack climbed on his sled, headed toward the well-marked trail a couple of hundred yards out from shore, and set a comfortable pace down the lake. Megan stayed behind him for exactly ten minutes. Then she pulled up beside him and matched his pace for about a mile, gave him a cheerful wave, and zoomed ahead.

Jack sighed.

They traveled another four miles, and Megan had just shot through a narrow cutting in a peninsula when the . . . *thing* appeared in the beam of her headlights. Jack didn't know who was more surprised—him, Megan, or it.

About the size of a small horse, the startled animal dropped whatever it had been eating, reared up on its hind legs, and let out a bloodcurdling roar just as—holy hell, those were *wings* on its back!

Realizing it was impossible for her to stop in time, Jack watched in horror as Megan veered to the right to avoid hitting it. The beast lashed at her sled with its tail as if trying to slap her away, and flapped its massive wings in an attempt to get airborne.

Jack gave his sled full throttle, shot over the peninsula, and aimed directly for it.

The—honest to God, it looked like a damn *dragon!*—swung around at his approach, gave another deafening roar, and charged toward him. Jack waited until the very last second before turning to the right, barely dodging its lashing tail. He wasn't able to avoid the wildly flapping wings though, and was nearly unseated when one of them slammed into his helmet.

He immediately swung his sled in a circle back toward the beast. Thick, rolling smoke started to billow around him as his snowmobile slowed down, plowing into heavy, sucking slush. The sled ground to a halt, and Jack barely ducked in time when the beast suddenly appeared through the cloud of smoke, flying directly over his head with another bloodcurdling roar.

He turned the key and tore off his helmet, jumped off the sled, and immediately sank up to his knees in slush. The sudden, stark silence was broken only by the soft, rhythmic woosh of the dragon's wings as it flew into the darkness.

Several of the threads suddenly knit together. The slime at the break-ins. The bloodcurdling scream. That . . . that prehistoric throwback was what had flown off over the lake that night!

Jack finally tore his gaze away from the disappearing beast and looked around to see if Megan was just as awestruck as he was.

Only he couldn't see her anywhere. Not even her headlights.

Nor could he hear her sled's engine.

Dammit, she'd literally vanished into thin air!

"Help! Jack, help!"

Cold dread tightened his stomach. She'd broken through the ice!

"I'm coming, Megan!" he shouted, unzipping his saddlebag and grabbing a rope before running toward the sound of her splashing. He was forced to slow down as he approached the black pool of water, the slush sucking at his boots like quicksand. "I'm here, Megan!" he called to her. "Float on your back! Try to get your helmet off!"

He could barely see where she was struggling in the water. He heard her sputtering and coughing as she slapped to stay afloat. The ice beneath him suddenly started to sag, and Jack stopped dead in his tracks.

"You're okay. Don't panic. Try to bring your feet up and float on your back," he called out, uncoiling the rope. "I'm going to toss you a line. Don't try to catch it, just float there and I'll throw it across your chest."

"My suit is dragging me down!"

"No, it's not! It's got enough trapped air to float you. Now, get ready for me to throw the rope. Megan! Are you listening to me!"

"I'm sinking!"

"*No, you're not!*" Jack dropped to his hands and knees and crawled closer. The moment he felt the ice start to buckle he stopped again, though there was still a good twenty feet between him and the pool of dark, frigid water. He inched back several feet, knowing that his getting wet wasn't going to help Megan. "Kick your feet to bring yourself closer to the edge of the ice," he commanded. "I'm throwing the rope. Wait until I tell you to grab it."

He tossed the rope at the blob in the middle of the pool. "Grab it, Megan. Pull off your gloves if you have to."

He could make her out struggling in the water, and then she finally said, "I've got it! Pull me out!"

"Not yet. Wrap it around your waist a couple of times. You won't be able to hold it tight enough."

He watched her struggle some more while he slowly inched closer on his belly to distribute his weight.

"Okay. Pull me out!"

Jack took up the slack in the rope and gave a tentative

pull to see if she would come with it. "Stay on your back," he commanded. "Keep kicking, but gently."

Inch by inch, second by interminably long second, Jack reeled her in. He watched her slowly rise up onto the ice, only to have it break beneath her. "Don't struggle! You'll eventually reach solid ice. Keep kicking softly."

She broke through two more times before the ice held.

"That's it, you're doing great, sweetheart. I've almost got you. Stop kicking now," he told her when she finally came fully out of the water. "I'm going to pull you away from the hole, but I have to keep us apart so we don't stress the ice. Just lie still and let me do the work."

"I-I'm s-so cold," she cried in a whisper, her voice still muffled by her helmet. "I-I can't feel my hands anymore."

"I'll have you warm in just a few minutes, I promise," he said, scooting backward and dragging her with him.

The moment he felt the ice was solid beneath him, Jack stood up and dragged her another fifty feet out onto the lake. Only then did he run to her, drop to his knees, and lift her shoulders up to his chest. She was crying uncontrollably and panting heavily, violent shivers interspersed with heaving coughing. He fumbled with the chin strap on her helmet, pulled it off, and pressed his face against hers.

It felt like he was holding a block of ice, which was fast becoming a reality now that she was out of the water. "I've got you," he whispered, holding her tightly. "You're okay, sweetheart. You're going to be okay. I've got you."

She tried to say something, but her gasping sobs and wracking shivers made her unintelligible.

"Shhh, don't talk," he told her, standing and scooping her up in his arms. He only made it a few yards before he had to stop and strip off her wet boots and snowsuit because they were weighing him down. He continued plodding through the deep snow to the main shoreline, since the peninsula had outcroppings of ledge dotting its length. He needed to get her someplace he could build a fire. He glanced at his snowmobile on the way and saw it was stuck in the slush up to its hood. It was no use to them now; he'd be lucky to get it out of there before spring.

It took him ten minutes to reach shore, and he set Megan down under a spruce tree where the snow wasn't deep. "Can you stand?" he asked, holding her under her arms to keep her steady. "We have to get you out of these wet clothes."

She tried helping, which only made it more difficult for him. He brushed her hands away, pulled her sweater, turtleneck, and long johns off over her head, then took off his leather jacket and wrapped it around her. Keeping one hand on her arm for support, he wrestled out of his own ski pants and set them on the snow.

"Okay, so far so good. I'm going to pull down your pants and set you on my suit. Then I'll pull yours all the way off and slip your legs into my ski pants, okay?"

He wasn't expecting an answer and didn't wait for one. Jack pulled her pants down to her knees, set her on his suit, and then stuffed her legs inside, zipping the bib closed up to her chin. He then stripped off his outer shirt and wrapped it around her wet head several times before hunching down in front of her.

"You're okay now, Megan. The worst is over, sweetheart, and you won't get any colder. I'm going to leave you long enough to get wood to start a fire, okay? Nod if you understand."

Hugging herself and shivering violently, her face ghostly white in the moonlight, she nodded. Jack kissed her cold cheek, then stood up and pulled his knife from the sheath on his belt. He headed into the woods to gather material for a fire, thanking God and his ancestors that he'd gotten her out in time.

He had a roaring bonfire going in less than ten minutes, and five minutes later Megan was showing signs of thawing. Jack took his first painless breath in thirty minutes, and the knot in his gut started to loosen. But only a little. Because they were without transportation in the middle of nowhere, and had no phone, no food or shelter, and only one set of dry clothes between them.

The food and shelter he could deal with readily enough; it was the transportation that bothered him. Though he could keep Megan warm and even comfortable, he would prefer to get her home sooner rather than later.

"Oh my God. The baby," she whispered.

Jack looked up from stoking the fire to see her hugging her stomach. "Are you having cramps?" he asked, unzipping the ski bib. He reached in and splayed his hand across the bare skin of her belly, relieved to discover she was no longer dangerously chilled.

"N-no. But what if . . . what if the cold water hurt the baby?"

He crawled behind her so that she was sitting between his thighs facing the fire, placed his hand on her belly again, and pulled her back against his chest. "The cold didn't hurt the baby, Megan. He's very well insulated, and you weren't in the water long enough to bring your core temperature down that far." He rested his cheek against hers. "Besides," he added with a forced chuckle, "with his genetic heritage, he probably just considered this a refreshing dip in the lake."

"You can't keep calling it a *him*," she said, relaxing against him with a deep sigh. "I don't want to get used to the idea that it might be a boy."

Jack also sighed, knowing she was going to be okay. "Even if I have a hunch that it is?"

"There's a 50 percent chance you'll be disappointed."

"Naw," he whispered against her cheek. "My hunches are at least 90 percent on target."

They fell silent after that, staring into the fire, soaking in its life-sustaining warmth. Jack felt as if it had been a hundred years since he'd held Megan like this. He was loath to move, partly because he was so damned relieved she was going to be okay, and partly because he was in no hurry to head back onto the lake. But they really did need the survival gear in the saddle-bags.

"I have to leave you for a few minutes. Will you be okay?"

She tilted her head back onto his shoulder to look up at him. "Where are you going?"

"To get some of our stuff."

She turned in his embrace to face him. "It's too dangerous. Wait until morning, when you can see what you're doing."

"We're twelve hours away from daylight, and the temperature's going to drop below zero tonight. We need the survival gear on your sled."

She clutched his shoulder. "My sled's under water, Jack!"

"It's probably only nine or ten feet deep next to that ledge. And I noticed that your survival gear is in a dry sack. I'm betting there's at least one sleeping bag in there, some food, and possibly a radio."

"One frozen person is enough for tonight. You can't take care of me if you're a block of ice yourself."

"I'll strip off and be in and out in two minutes flat. I've done it before. If I have dry clothes to put on, I'll be fine."

"No."

Seeing that she was recovered enough to argue with him, Jack peeled himself away from her and stood up. He walked over and pushed the two half-rotted logs he'd dragged from the woods deeper into the fire. "Any other suggestions, then?"

"Yes. We sit right here, keep the fire roaring, and we wait. Trust me, they'll be looking for us before daybreak."

"Not here. We're still four or five miles north of where we should be."

"They'll use a plane to scour the lake, and they'll see our smoke."

"You'll be well on your way to developing pneumonia by morning if I don't get you settled into a sleeping bag in some sort of shelter."

"No."

"And then there's that . . . whatever the hell we saw. We need our guns."

"You can get your gear, but you are *not* going after my stuff."

He stood up. "I'll be back in twenty minutes."

"Jack," she growled, stretching out his name to emphasize her warning. "If something happens to you, then

I'm stuck out here alone. I don't even have boots. If you die, I die, too. Along with our baby," she tacked on for good measure.

"Believe me, I understand the consequences. I'll bring back your boots and suit and get them dried out." He pointed toward where he'd hung her wet clothes on a branch. "As soon as something is dry enough, put it on."

He walked onto the lake. "If an hour goes by and I'm not back," he called, "*then* you may worry. But not before."

"It doesn't take an hour to walk out there and back!"

"I'm going to see if I can free my sled. You just concentrate on keeping warm so our son doesn't catch a cold."

Our son. He liked the sound of that.

Chapter Fifteen

Damn him, he was going after her gear! She knew it because he hadn't actually promised that he wouldn't—apparently thinking that if he didn't lie to her, she might start trusting him again.

He'd obviously forgotten about lies of omission.

Megan settled back on the bed of fir boughs he had made after he'd built the fire, and opened his jacket to feel the heat on her neck and chest. She cupped her belly in her hands. "Oh, baby," she whispered. "I nearly killed us both trying to avoid that . . . that thing. No, make that all three of us, because Jack would have died trying to save you and me."

She scooted closer to the fire. "So what do you think?" she asked her belly. "Is Jack Stone the sort of man we want in our lives? I think he really does love me." She patted her belly. "He definitely loves you. I can't count the times I've caught him staring at my stomach. You'd think he's never seen a pregnant woman before."

She picked up a stick and poked at the fire. "He said he used to have a brother—is he dead, or are they just estranged?" She unzipped the bib of her ski pants, hoping it would help her bra dry. "He must have died, if Jack wants to name you after him. I was planning to name you after my uncle Ian if you're a boy, but maybe we can compromise. Are you feeling cozy in there, baby, like your daddy said?"

Could a fetus even catch a cold, or had Jack only been trying to distract her? Megan leaned to the side and looked out at the lake again. She could just make out the position of his sled because the moon was reflecting off its windshield. She couldn't, however, see any shadow moving around it.

A violent shiver wracked her at the thought of Jack trying to retrieve her gear. That water was so numbingly cold, and she'd come so close to dying. She'd been so surprised when that . . . that . . .

What in hell *was* that creature? It had looked like a dragon. But they were reptilian, not amphibious, weren't they? She snorted, settling back in front of the fire and picking up the stick again. "They aren't either, you crazy woman, because dragons do *not* exist."

Unless . . .

Kenzie! He'd seen the creature, too! Hell, he'd been close enough to catch its odor. She had smelled the same rank odor on his clothes that she'd smelled in the air tonight, just before she'd hit the water. Which meant Kenzie *did* have something to do with whatever was breaking into the shops in town.

And he was probably the man who had attacked Jack that night; the guy Robbie had chased off. Then Robbie had followed his tracks and would have caught up with him—which meant her cousin also knew what was going on.

It was the damn *magic*. It had to be.

Kenzie had been a panther for the last three years, before Winter and Matt had turned him back into a man on the winter solstice. So why couldn't the magic conjure up a dragon? Hell, it could turn the sky green if it had a mind to. Providence—which was the real force behind the magic—was even capable of creating an entirely new tree of life, which it had done by combining Matt's oak and Winter's pine. A dragon was mere child's play!

"Oh God," she groaned. "What am I going to tell Jack?"

The man wasn't blind; he had seen exactly what she had, and eventually he was going to want to talk about it. That creature was breaking into the town shops, so wouldn't Jack want to let the citizens know he was closing in on the culprit?

Speaking of which, why *was* it breaking into the shops? It had only stolen doughnuts and candy bars, according to what Jack and Camry had said. But it had looked like it was eating a fish tonight, when it had suddenly appeared in her headlights. Had it been using the open water next to the ledge as a fishing hole? She'd have to check that out first thing in the morning, before they were rescued.

Okay, she needed a plan. She was going to have to persuade Jack that what they'd seen was some sort of anomaly, like Bigfoot or the Loch Ness monster. Yeah, she'd tell him that Pine Lake was so vast and deep, it had its very own mystery creature.

But she didn't have anything to back up her story. There hadn't been any other reported sightings, and the

Loch Ness monster and Bigfoot were well-established, ongoing legends.

Maybe she could imply the creature was new to the area. She snorted. Yeah, she could just see herself saying, "Isn't this exciting? We're the first ones to sight it! We'll make the national news!"

No, the quieter they kept this, the better. Her father and uncles had managed to keep the magic a secret for nearly forty years, and her generation had to continue keeping it a secret. She'd just have to persuade Jack that they shouldn't speak to anyone about what they saw tonight; not even anyone in her family. It would be *their* little secret.

He might go for that, if he thought sharing a secret would bring the two of them closer together.

Megan checked her clothes on the branches and discovered that her turtleneck and silk top were dry, but that her sweater still had a long way to go. She slipped off her jacket and slid the bib of Jack's pants off her shoulders, then decided to take off her bra since the back elastic wasn't drying. She pulled the two jerseys on over her head, rezipped the bib, and slipped back into the jacket. She'd already taken off the shirt he had wrapped around her head, and she turned it on the branch so the back would dry, sure he would need it when he returned.

She crawled past the fire enough to see the lake again. How long had he been gone? Twenty minutes? Half an hour? And how in hell was she supposed to rescue him without her boots?

Megan sat back and eyed the bottoms of the ski pants she was wearing. They were made of thick leather and were long enough that she could tie the ends closed and walk with her feet inside them. She gazed around camp trying to spot something to tie them with, that wouldn't break after only ten steps.

Her bra! She could use the straps.

She snatched the bra off the branch and tried ripping a strap off one of the cups. That wasn't happening. She looped it over her foot and pulled, but the only thing that ripped was the satin cup. She searched for a couple of rocks, then had to use a stick to free them from the frozen ground. She set the end of the strap on one rock and beat it with the other.

"Come on, you stupid thing," she growled, pounding the double-stitched material. "I have to go save Jack."

It was a good thing she was only a C cup; anything bigger would probably be quadruple-stitched! Figuring she'd mangled the material enough to weaken it, she looped it over her foot again and pulled. It gave with a sudden tear that sent her flying backward.

She scrambled upright and did the same to the other strap, then pounded the tiny metal rings on the back until they broke. She finally dangled the freed straps in front of her. "Am I my father's daughter, or what?" she said proudly. "I should have my own 'Survivor-woman' show on the Discovery Channel!"

She was just leaning forward to tie the bottom of her pants closed when she heard Jack approaching at a hurried pace. Megan shoved the straps in her pocket, grabbed her mangled bra and looked around, then simply tossed it in the fire. She lay down on the bed of fir boughs and closed her eyes, sleepily fluttering them open when he strode into camp.

"That didn't take long," she said, stretching with a fake yawn, watching him drop his heavy load of gear.

He hunched down in front of the fire and held his hands to its warmth, glancing at her out the corner of his eye. Yup, his hair was soaked and had started to freeze, and every inch of visible skin was covered with goose bumps.

"Did you fall in the slush? Your hair's wet," she pointed out, ignoring the fact that his clothes were dry.

He stiffened. "No." He pushed a log deeper into the flames a bit more roughly than necessary.

A blind man couldn't miss her dry sack sitting on the ground, even though he'd tried to hide it by throwing her wet snowsuit on top. Then again, maybe he was grumpy because he was freezing.

"Did you remember the cocoa?"

He gave her a suspicious glance, then reached under her wet snowmobile suit, pulled out the Thermos, and tossed it to her. He picked up several more sticks and shoved them in the fire, only to suddenly stop in mid-shove. He used the stick in his hand to lift something out of the flame, which he held up between them.

Megan realized it was the charred remains of her bra. She snapped her head around to look up at the branch the clothes were hanging on. "Well, jeez," she said in disgust, looking back at her bra with a frown. "It must have fallen into the fire."

Jack eyed the distance from the branch to the fire, then lifted one brow, implying the bra would have needed wings to reach that far.

Megan opened the Thermos and drank directly from it, then wiped her mouth with the sleeve of Jack's leather jacket. "Can you get your sled unstuck?"

"Not without a block and tackle and two hundred yards of rope," he said, still eyeing her suspiciously.

It was killing him that she wasn't reading him the riot act—she'd have to remember this strategy in the future.

"I went after your survival gear," he growled.

"Was the water very deep?"

He eyed her again. "Just over my head."

Megan took off his jacket. "Here, slip this on. It's already warmed up."

"No, you keep it."

"I'm actually starting to feel hot," she countered, tossing it to him. She turned and pulled his shirt off the branch and tossed that at him, too. "Wipe your hair dry. And if you hand me the dry sack, I'll see what goodies we have."

He pulled the liners out of her soggy boots and set them beside the fire to dry, then stood up, picked up her snowsuit, and draped it over another branch, then he finally set the dry sack beside her. He slipped into his jacket and obediently started wiping his hair with his shirt.

Megan took pity on him; he was cold and tired, and adding tension to that mix was cruel. "Look, I know we needed my gear if we have to spend the night out here. I . . . I just didn't want anything to happen to you," she whispered, feeling her face flush—and not due to the roaring fire.

He stopped wiping his hair.

She shrugged, hoping to appear more nonchalant than she felt. "I guess I've gotten used to having you around this past week."

"I'm not going away, Megan."

"I know."

He came over and sat beside her on the boughs, taking her hands and holding them in his. "I need to talk to you about what I said that day I sent you away."

She tried to pull back, but he held firm.

"I didn't mean it, Megan. I'd walk through the fires of hell before I'd ask you to do that."

"I know."

"What do you mean, you know?"

"I figured that out about five minutes after my plane took off. I was looking down at the nesting sites we'd been working together, and realized that anyone who handled those goslings and eggs the way you did wouldn't ask me to end my pregnancy."

He pulled her to his chest and wrapped his arms around her in a fierce hug. "I knew you wouldn't do it. But nothing I said was working, so I decided to make you hate me so much you'd pack up and leave on the supply plane that very day," he whispered into her hair.

"It worked."

His embrace tightened. "I am so damned sorry for what I put you through."

"And I'm sorry I realized what you were doing too late."

He leaned back to look her in the eyes. "I love you, Megan. When I first arrived on the tundra and you greeted me, I felt like I was being run over by a herd of caribou."

She opened her mouth, but he pulled her back against him again. "Shhh, just listen. I want you to think about us getting married. We can live here in Pine Creek, or wherever you want. I can work from anywhere." He cupped her head to his shoulder, stroking her hair. "Don't answer me right now. I just want you to think about it."

She tried to pull away to speak.

"Shhh," he said again, holding her in what was starting to feel like a desperate hug. "Just let what I said sink in for a while. Just . . . just give me a chance."

She mumbled into his shoulder, but he just squeezed her tighter. The poor guy was shaking like a leaf, and Megan suspected it had nothing to do with his dip in the lake—despite his feeling as icy as a wet polar bear. She gave up trying to explain that he was making her cold all over again, and wrapped her arms around his waist inside his jacket to share what little heat she had left.

The baby gave a sharp kick.

"Holy hell," Jack said, jerking back to stare down at her belly. "He just kicked me!"

"He does that sometimes," she said, smiling at his shocked expression. She reached out and took his hand and set it on her stomach. "Wait a minute and he'll do it again. Damn, now you've got *me* calling it a him!"

As if on cue, her belly started thumping like a snare drum. Jack laughed out loud and bent down and kissed the spot where the baby was kicking—then just as suddenly straightened, his face a dull red. He scrambled back to the fire and started stoking it again, even though it was roaring brightly enough to be seen from space.

Megan leaned back against the tree with a smile, running her fingers softly over her belly. Here was the man she'd fallen in love with on the tundra. Whenever he'd worked up the nerve to kiss her, he would turn red, get sort of clumsy, and all but apologize. One time after kissing her senseless, he'd turned and walked straight into the tent pole, bringing the entire canvas down on top of them. She was beginning to suspect his nerdiness wasn't an act after all, since Jack Stone didn't appear to have any more finesse than Wayne Ferris.

She was glad the nerd hadn't disappeared completely.

Apparently realizing he was about to start a forest fire, Jack turned his attention to the dry sack. He pulled out a mess kit, a neatly coiled rope, a hatchet, some power bars, and a small plastic container. Megan knew the container held fishing line, a mirror and compass, several lighters, and an ozone light stick to purify water for drinking.

"No radio?" he said, pulling out the sleeping bag and peering inside the empty sack.

Megan shrugged. "We always carry the satellite phone. Besides, that sack is rarely ever opened because we rarely get into this kind of trouble." She looked him directly in the eyes. "I'm sorry, Jack. I should have listened to you about not traveling back on the lake. I was being stubborn and stupid."

He unrolled the sleeping bag and shook it open, then motioned for her to move so he could lay it out over the boughs. "You're not in an exclusive club, sweetheart. We'd be here at least a week if I listed all my transgressions." He sat down beside her. "Don't ever apologize for following your passion, Megan. That's what I love the most about you."

"My passion?"

"Your passion for life, sweetheart. I swear you actually glow with energy when you get involved in something." He turned to face her, his expression almost eager. "So what first attracted you to me? Be honest, now."

Good Lord, he really *didn't* have a clue, did he? No guy in his right mind asked a woman that. "Honestly?" she clarified.

He nodded very seriously.

"Your size."

It apparently took a moment for that to assimilate before he suddenly turned away and started messing with the fire again.

"Hey—you asked for my honest answer, and I was first attracted to your size," she told his broad, muscular back. She rolled her eyes, since he couldn't see her. "It's not like you're puny or anything. You're just not supertall. Why are you so sensitive about your height, anyway?"

"I'm not. Or I wasn't until I met your family," he muttered. "With your gene pool, my son will be looking down his nose at me by the time he's twelve." Megan immediately wiped the grin off her face when he glanced over his shoulder at her. "You little brat," he said, his eyes narrowing. "You're laughing at me."

She immediately shook her head, then ended up nodding. "But in a sweet way. And only because I don't get why you're being so sensitive." She rolled her eyes right at him this time. "What sort of guy asks a question like that, anyway?"

"I thought women liked sensitive men. Aren't you always complaining that we don't talk about our feelings?"

Well, he didn't seem frozen to death any more. In fact, he looked rather hot. And sexy. And desirable. "I think we should go to bed," she blurted out without thinking.

He pretty near fell in the fire, scrambling to his feet. "I'm going to get some more firewood. Hit the bushes if you need to, then go to bed." He started to leave, then turned back. "Damn, I forgot you don't have any boots."

He walked over to the pile of gear he'd brought back from his own sled, and tossed her a pair of socks. Megan noticed that he'd also brought the two full bottles of beer as well as one of the empties. He picked up an empty bottle and shoved it in his jacket pocket—his hand re-emerging with her bra straps.

"Okay," she finally admitted. "If you must know, I destroyed my bra to tie my pants closed at the bottom so I could walk."

He tossed the straps at her with a laugh. "Good idea. At least your little swim didn't freeze your brain," he said. "After you put on the socks, go ahead and tie the pants closed. That should keep the socks dry while you to go to the bathroom. I might be gone a few minutes, but I'll stay within shouting distance. I need to find a spring for drinking water."

"That's about as easy as finding a needle in a haystack, especially in the dark."

"I have a hunch there's one close by," he said, walking out of camp.

Once again left staring at the spot where he disappeared, Megan decided that Jack's hunches were starting to annoy her. Ninety percent accurate, her ass. She was lucky if her hunches were right *half* the time.

She didn't bother putting on the socks or tying her pant bottoms closed, since she was going to have to take off the damn suit anyway. She walked a couple of yards past the tree while staying within sight of the fire, which only served to create more treacherous shadows than light her way. She stubbed her toe, cursed a bit, and hopped from foot to freezing foot with gritted teeth. She'd give her right arm for male plumbing for just five minutes!

She did her duty and ran stumbling back into camp without bothering to put the ski pants back on. She crawled up on the sleeping bag and stuck her feet in front of the fire, again gritting her teeth when they started to prickle as they thawed.

She finally put on Jack's socks, hung up his ski pants, and checked to see if her own pants were dry. They weren't, but she hadn't intended to put them on yet, anyway. She balled his slightly damp shirt up for a pillow, lay down, and pulled the edge of the sleeping bag over her bare legs.

She finally closed her eyes with a smile, listening to branches snapping and rotten logs quietly breaking as Jack gathered their night supply of fuel. So he liked her passion, did he? Well, she'd show him some passion. The man had to go to sleep sometime tonight.

He returned twenty minutes later, set down the wood, and surveyed camp. "You're not wearing the ski pants," he said, eyeing them on the branch.

"I thought it would be warmer if we don't wear much clothing, so our body heat can transfer to each other."

He sat down beside her and took off his boots, placing them within reach. He then pulled a compact revolver from the back waist of his pants and tucked it inside one of the boots.

Megan scooted over to make room for him to lie down. "You should take off your pants. They're damp."

He hesitated, eyeing her over his shoulder. "We're going to have to snuggle."

"If I remember correctly, you're a very good snuggler."

His cheeks flushed deep red. He quickly stood and dropped his pants but left his long johns on. "Scoot toward the fire. I'll sleep in the back."

"But then you'll get the edge of the sleeping bag to cover up with." It was only a single bag, and opened up, there wasn't enough material to both lie on and cover up with.

He picked her up when she didn't move fast enough and set her down closer to the fire. "You'll have me covering you," he said, crawling in behind her and on his side so they were spooned together.

He wrapped one arm around her waist and cupped her belly protectively, tucked his legs over hers, and settled down with a tired sigh. Megan stared into the roaring fire, listening as his breathing slowly evened out, and she knew he had fallen asleep. What was it with guys, that they could simply sleep on demand?

She wasn't so lucky, as her mind kept flitting from one thought to another. She thought about Kenzie and the creature they'd seen, and about Mark Collins and her samples he apparently wanted. And she thought about Jack's proposal, her heart telling her to go for it, and her practical left brain cautioning her to wait until she got the report from the investigator.

But then she thought about the two months she'd shared with Jack on the tundra, and how they had been the happiest two months of her life.

Megan finally turned in his embrace and whispered, "Make love to me, Jack."

Chapter Sixteen

Jack woke with a start, unsure if he had dreamed the words or if Megan really had said them. Either way was trouble. When he opened his eyes, Megan's face was mere inches from his, her expression expectant. Before he could say anything, she cupped his cheeks and touched her lips to his—not with her usual damn-the-torpedoes-full-speed-ahead urgency, but with endearingly gentle determination.

His arms automatically tightened around her. "This isn't wise, sweetheart," he whispered, even as his lips moved of their own volition across her jaw toward her ear. "You're just restless and edgy right now."

"No, I'm horny," she said, her hands gripping his hair to better direct his exploration of her throat. She tossed back her head to expose her neck, and arched into him with a shiver.

When in hell had she removed all her clothes?

"I want you, Jack. I want to feel you inside me."

It sure as hell didn't get any more direct than that, did it? And she hadn't called him Wayne, so she was fully aware of what she was asking. Having as little willpower as a bear in a honey hive when it came to Megan, Jack locked his mouth over hers before she could change her mind.

She rewarded him with a soft sound of approval and released his hair to slide her hands up under the hem of his shirt, not stopping until she reached her target. Jack knew she was particularly fond of his chest, since she'd told him often enough.

Being quite fond of hers, too, he covered one of her breasts with his free hand, surprised at how full it felt—until he remembered why. He handled her gently, letting his thumb brush softly across her distended nipple, which proved to be very sensitive. Megan's soft sound of pleasure turned into a full-blown moan as she arched into his touch, her legs moving restlessly against his as her fingers curled into the muscles of his chest.

Her response encouraged Jack to continue reacquainting himself with her beautiful body, all while drinking his fill of her equally delightful mouth. She obviously had the same thought, as one of her hands left his chest in search of a more interesting target.

Jack chased after her, actually surprised she'd waited as long as she had. "Slow down," he whispered into her mouth. "We've got all night, sweetheart."

She skillfully dodged his attempt to capture her hand and had her fingers wrapped around him before he could even rear back. Jack sucked in his breath and released a shuddering sigh.

Marauding Megan was back.

Lord, he loved her for knowing exactly what she

wanted and not being afraid to go after it. Obviously liking what she found inside his long johns, she made another interesting sound, which Jack answered with a shout when her fingers feathered over his scrotum.

"Take off your clothes," she murmured, wiggling around to tug at his shirt with her other hand.

He immediately sat up and pulled his shirt off over his head, then reached down and slid his long johns off without Megan's help, as she was still locked on her target, determined to drive him mad. Just as soon as he was free of his clothes, Jack grabbed both her hands and wrestled them over her head so he could kiss her again.

He should have remembered that this in no way disabled her. Now that they were both naked, her toes became her new weapons of choice. She ran one foot up the length of his leg and somehow managed to wiggle halfway beneath him so that he settled between her thighs.

Locking both of her hands in one of his without breaking their kiss, Jack slid his free hand down between them and had just found her sensitive little bud when he was poked—several times and rather sharply—in the belly.

"Holy hell!" he yelped, scrambling back so suddenly he fell off the bed of boughs. He stared at Megan's naked, moving stomach. She looked like she'd swallowed a basketball, it was so perfectly round—except when the tiny creature inside was doing calisthenics.

Dammit to hell, he couldn't make love to her with their baby in there!

Megan burst out laughing. "I wish you could see your face right now," she chortled. She stopped caressing her wiggling belly and reached out to him. "Come on, Jack. You're going to get frostbite."

He couldn't stop staring at her belly. "We can't . . . I'm not going to . . ." He finally looked at her. "Our kid will know what we're doing, Megan. He'll *feel* me when . . . when I'm . . ." He trailed off to a whisper, shaking his head because he couldn't even say it out loud in front of the baby.

She laughed at him again. "Of course he'll feel us. He's supposed to. Having his parents make love is reassuring to him. Come on," she said, wiggling her fingers as she reached out to him. "Show our baby how much you love us both."

Jack wiped a hand over his sweating face. He couldn't do it now if God Himself held a gun to his head. He climbed out of the snow and back into bed, pulling her down beside him so they were spooned together with her back to him.

She gave a frustrated huff, then started snickering. He threw a leg over hers to make her quit squirming. "Go to sleep. You need your rest. We don't know if we'll have to walk out of here tomorrow or not."

Her entire body expanded, then deflated with a heavy sigh. "You are such a nerd."

Megan didn't know whether to laugh or cry. Of all the parochial, nonsensical notions—imagine not being able to make love because the baby might feel it? Did he honestly think pregnant women didn't have sex? And now that she'd made up her mind to do it with him, she wasn't about to not do it for another few months, that was for sure.

Megan stared into the fire, listening to Jack's breathing

slowly even out again. How was she going to get him past this foolish notion? He said he loved her, so by God, he needed to prove it! Besides, she liked making love; she was a healthy woman who appreciated an athletic romp in bed with a sexy man, especially when that man was unequivocally into her.

And for the first time in five months, Megan was beginning to believe Jack truly did love her. Didn't he realize a sweet bout of lovemaking was just what she needed?

He was so clueless.

She smiled despite herself. Surely he was trainable. Her mistake tonight had been asking him to make love. He was a guy, wasn't he? And didn't guys have sex on the brain 24/7? She should have just quietly pulled down his long johns and climbed on top. He wouldn't have felt the baby in that position, and by the time he'd realized what was happening he would have been way too involved.

She grinned. He was sleeping now, wasn't he?

Megan decided she better give him another few minutes, just to make sure he was in deep dream sleep. She became almost giddy with anticipation. Was Jack about to have the best damn erotic dream of his life, or what?

Five minutes later she carefully removed his arm from around her, got up on her knees facing him, and was pleasantly surprised to discover that he hadn't bothered to put his long johns back on. Talk about a blatant invitation!

She crawled to the woodpile and tossed a few sticks on the fire, watching to see if Jack woke up. The fact that he didn't gave her hope. She crawled back over to him, peeled the edge of the sleeping bag off his hip, and softly sucked in her breath.

He was so beautiful, so perfectly, ruggedly male. He had a series of raised scars crossing the left side of his ribs, which he'd told her were from an encounter with a young bear when he was twelve. And the ugly mark on the right side of his stomach just above his hip bone he'd said was a souvenir from his military days. Megan suspected it was a bullet wound, since she knew there was an even more wicked scar on his back, implying the bullet had gone clean through. There were several other gouges and nicks on his beautiful body—some substantial, some not—that spoke of a hard and at times death-defying life.

She was finding it harder and harder to stay angry at him for breaking her heart. After all, what would she have done if their roles had been reversed in Canada? How brutal might she have gotten if she thought Jack's life was in danger?

Honestly? She would have done anything, said anything, to protect him because she had loved him that much.

"You look like you can't decide whether to castrate me or jump my bones."

Megan's gaze snapped to his, and she had to smile. "I don't want to castrate you."

"That's good." He lifted a brow in inquiry. "So does that mean you were going to take advantage of me in my sleep?"

She nodded.

"I'm sorry for panicking earlier. Now that I've thought about it, I seem to recall my parents making love while my mother was carrying me. It got a bit bumpy on occasion, but I remember having this warm, fuzzy sense of being totally immersed in their love."

Megan put her hands on her hips. "You can't possibly remember something like that. You weren't even born yet. Nobody can remember anything that happens before three or four years old."

He propped his head up on his hand. "I think we remember quite a lot, only it becomes so ingrained in us that we simply don't retain much of the details. I can still hear my mother singing to me. I remember how she smelled of cinnamon and vanilla, how she used to rock me for hours when I was sick, how she constantly flipped her hair behind her shoulder when it got in her way, since she wouldn't braid it when Dad was around because he liked it loose. I remember every minute of my life from conception to nine years old like it was yesterday."

Megan's heart broke all over again, this time for a little boy who'd had his mother ripped from his life far too soon. She instinctively hugged her belly.

Jack suddenly flopped onto his back, throwing his arms wide. "You might as well have your wicked way with me. I promise not to wake up until it's over," he said, closing his eyes and letting out a loud snore.

Now? He expected them to make love *now*, after practically bringing her to tears? Megan crawled back into bed and snuggled up against him with a sigh. She was going to have to sit this man down for a good talk one of these days, and explain that sad tales of his childhood were not exactly a turn-on.

He gently pushed her shoulder. "Hey, I thought we were going to make love."

"I've changed my mind."

He pushed her again, a little harder this time. "You can't just change your mind for no reason." His pushing hand started caressing her arm. "I thought you were horny."

"I was, until you started talking about your childhood."

He was silent for several seconds; then she yelped in surprise when he gently spun her around, picked her up, and sat her straddling his hips. "I've had a wonderful life, Megan. And now it's time we start making our baby's childhood just as memorable," he said, kissing her deeply.

Oh, what the heck. They were both naked, they were in a cozy little nest in front of a roaring fire, and Jack was obviously ready. So why not?

He started chuckling—while he was kissing her!—and Megan sat up with a growl. "Now what?" she snapped.

"I was just thinking this has got to be the longest foreplay in the history of our relationship."

"Foreplay? You call the last hour *foreplay*?" She wanted to smack him, but she pointed her finger at his face instead. "You are one second away from taking another swim in the lake, buster. Do you think you can possibly stay focused for ten minutes so we can actually do this?"

"Ten?" he repeated in surprise. "All this work for ten measly minutes?" He grabbed her pointing finger, gently bucking her off him and turning so he was looming over her. "I'll tell you what. You can have your ten minutes, but then I'm taking another . . ." He cocked his head in thought. "Another thirty minutes for myself." He lowered his mouth to within inches of hers. "You want to go first, or shall I?" he whispered, inching even closer but not quite touching her lips, apparently waiting for her answer.

Megan reached down and wrapped her fingers intimately around him, grinning when he jerked in surprise. "I'll go first." She used her other hand to push his shoulder, sending him onto his back, and rolled with him until she was once again straddling his thighs. "Pay attention and see if you can't learn a little something about foreplay, will you?"

"Yes ma'am!" he said in a half-shout when she started fondling him in earnest.

She lovingly tortured him for several minutes, until she could see beads of sweat breaking out on his forehead and the cords in his neck bulging. Deciding he was one second away from losing control when his hands balled into fists at his sides, Megan finally took pity. She wiggled forward until she was directly over him, braced her hands on his sweating chest, then gently lowered herself down over his shaft.

They both moaned, the sound mingling with the crackling fire to drift off into the stillness of the night. "Oh God, that feels good," she whispered, moving slowly as she adjusted to the fullness, then quickening the tempo. "It's been way, way too long," she ended with another moan.

His hands went to her hips, his fingers gently kneading her flesh as he slowed her motions, moving his own hips to alter his angle and depth. His actions increased her pleasure, and Megan tilted back her head and closed her eyes, savoring the feel of him moving inside her. He brought one hand to her feminine center and used his thumb to caress her sensitive bud while he continued to guide her gentle rocking.

"Go on, sweetheart," he softly petitioned. "That's my girl. Go visit our beautiful place."

Megan felt herself tightening, spiraling inward, deep into the depths of the magical place he always took her. She crested with a shout of release, her entire body convulsing in waves of blinding heat. Time stopped and the physical world receded as she floated in a wondrous landscape of colorful, energized light.

"Come back to me, Megan," she heard from a distance. "That's it, sweetheart, come back so we can go there together."

Megan suddenly found herself back in Jack's embrace; he was stroking her hair, gentling her with soothing whispers as wave after wave of energy continued pulsing through her.

"That's my girl," he whispered in her ear. Megan realized he was sitting up, she was still straddling him, and he was still embedded deeply inside her. "Was it as beautiful as ever?" he asked, calming her with caresses to her body and tender kisses to her face.

"You weren't there with me."

"I'll go with you next time, I promise."

He lifted her off him, then turned them both until she was lying on the sleeping bag. Kneeling between her legs, he pulled her backside up onto his thighs, and Megan realized that the baby wasn't in his way in this position.

He slowly entered her, his gaze locked on her face with such intensity, waves of heated awareness washed through her again. "Beautiful Megan," he whispered, slipping deeply inside her, then pulling nearly out, then sliding even deeper. "I see our magical place every time I look in your eyes."

She reached out, wanting to hold him, but he took her hands and set them over her head, wrapping her fingers around a fir bough. "Lie still," he tenderly commanded, grasping her hips, "and let me watch you blossom. I'll go with you this time, I promise."

He set a gentle and thoroughly mesmerizing rhythm, and Megan felt herself focusing inward again, sensing she wasn't alone this time. Jack definitely was present; she could feel the power of his energy threatening to take her into a storm of such intensity that she cried out.

"Shhh," he soothed, even as he quickened his pace. "You can let go, sweetheart. You're always safe when you're with me," he said, touching her intimately as he continued his gentle assault. "Come with me," he commanded, thrusting deeper.

The storm he had conjured sucked her into its swirling vortex, and Megan was suddenly floating through a wondrous landscape of shimmering light. And this time Jack was right beside her as they explored the beautiful world together. The colors were intensified tenfold, the warmth more penetrating, the sense of wonder intoxicating.

"We can't stay," Jack whispered, cupping her head in his hands and kissing her deeply. "We'll come back again soon, I promise. But you need to sleep now."

She reluctantly let him lead her back, not wanting to leave such euphoric beauty where she felt so warm and safe—and so loved. She yawned, cuddling into his embrace.

"That's it, little one, let me hold you in my arms. Dream with me, Megan, and let me introduce you to our son."

She snuggled against him with a sigh of profound contentment. She didn't know how he did it, but every time they made love, he carried her off to this beautiful place that existed only when she was with him, and then she would wake up in his arms, feeling utterly and completely loved. It had happened the very first time they'd made love, and had only intensified over the next month. If she didn't know better, she might wonder if Jack really did possess some sort of magical power that . . .

A beautiful woman suddenly stepped out of the shimmering ether, carrying a baby in her arms.

Chapter Seventeen

It was just breaking dawn when Megan opened her eyes to find herself wrapped up like a mummy in the sleeping bag. The fire was roaring, her clothes were in a pile beside her, and Jack was nowhere to be found. He'd left a beer bottle full of water next to her clothes, along with a power bar—which meant he'd had at least one more stashed someplace yesterday.

Megan squirmed free of the sleeping bag and sat up, only to scramble back under the covers when she realized how cold it was. She reached out one hand to her clothes, sighing in relief to find that Jack had set them by the fire to warm up. She pulled everything under the sleeping bag with her, then contorted in every position imaginable while getting dressed.

She was panting by the time she slipped into her boots and stood up. Not bothering to put on her ski suit yet, she headed behind her favorite tree to take care of business, then hustled back to the fire and slipped into her suit. She grabbed the bottle of water and power bar and headed toward the lake in search of Jack.

She spotted him standing beside his snowmobile, his feet planted wide and his hands on his hips. And though he was a fair distance away, she'd swear she could see a look of disgust on his face. She took her time walking out on a snowpack hard enough that she barely sank in, eating the power bar and drinking water that tasted faintly of beer.

The closer Megan got to him, the more her heart raced with the memory of last night. He looked . . . he looked . . . oh damn, she had fallen in love with him all over again!

"Good morning," she said when she finally reached him.

Jack started to say something, but when his gaze met hers he snapped his mouth shut without saying a word. Two flags of color appeared on his cheekbones. Megan took another bite of her breakfast to cover her smile. The man was actually blushing!

Over their lovemaking last night?

He was such an easy mark. "Do you think you'll be able to get it up soon—I mean unstuck soon, or are we going to have to walk? Or," she purred, "we could just cozy back up to the fire and wait for the cavalry to arrive."

His cheekbones turned nearly purple. He walked around her and headed to shore, still without saying so much as good morning. Megan polished off the last of the power bar and gulped down the rest of her water as she grinned at his back. She was such a bad person, but really, a saint couldn't have passed up an opportunity like that. Teasing Jack was easier than shooting fish in a barrel.

She stuffed the wrapper and bottle in her pocket and walked around his sled, eyeing it in sympathy. It was stuck up to its running boards in slush that had frozen solid overnight. They'd need a chisel, if not a blowtorch, to free the damn thing.

She turned in a circle studying the landscape, trying to figure out where they were, and realized she had absolutely no idea. She hadn't been this far north on the lake in ten or twelve years. Megan started walking to the ledge sticking up through the ice, curious about where her sled had gone in.

She could see the tracks Jack had made dragging her out, the rope he'd used, and her helmet lying on the ice several yards away. There were more tracks indicating where he'd walked up onto the north side of the ledge, where the ice wasn't weak. From there his footprints moved down into the water. She couldn't see any sign of her sled, since the hole had skimmed over with a thin layer of ice, and she gave an involuntary shiver. Jack must have stripped off his clothes on the ledge, gone into that dark, freezing lake to get the dry sack, then scrambled back out and quickly dressed.

She really shouldn't have teased him this morning.

There were other tracks going in and out of the hole, as well. Megan walked toward them, giving the ledge a wide berth, and stopped beside the carcass of a half-eaten fish. So, she'd been right, some . . . thing had been fishing. Something heavy. The impressions in the snow were deep, seven or eight feet long and about three feet wide, and if she wasn't mistaken, some of them looked to be from a tail. She hunched down and touched the snowpack where what appeared to be a wing had brushed against it, then stood up and started following the tracks away from the hole.

"Get back here!" Jack shouted.

She turned to see that he was stopped halfway out to his sled, his arms full of the fir boughs from their bed. Had he just shouted an order at her?

"Excuse me?" she shouted back.

"I don't need you wandering off and getting lost. Get back here and help me."

She propped her hands on her hips. Oh, she was sooo glad she'd teased him this morning. "I never get lost!" she hollered. "And I don't respond well to orders being shouted at me, either."

He dropped the boughs. "O-kay then," he said, his voice turning dangerously low—just like her father's did when he was nearing the end of his patience. Somehow, no matter how softly her papa spoke, his voice carried an unreasonable distance, just as Jack's did now. "Would you please come back here and help me get this sled out?"

Megan eyed the tracks leading out onto the lake, heaved a heavy sigh, and started trudging back to his snowmobile. He was mad at the sled, not her, and now was not the time to push him over the edge. Besides, the sooner they got home, the sooner she could ask Kenzie about the creature she'd seen.

But someday soon, she would have to find out what happened when a self-professed pacifist exploded. He could deny it until the cows came home, but Jack Stone was a warrior, and when warriors exploded . . . they rarely took prisoners. That's why a smart woman learned the consequences of going too far *before* she found herself married to one.

Megan stopped to pick up some of the boughs he'd

dropped, and tossed them down with the others when she reached his sled. "Do we have something we can use to chisel the ice?" she asked, deciding to defuse the tension with a show of cooperation.

Good Lord, she was turning into her mother!

He took off his jacket and rolled up his sleeves—even though it was likely only ten degrees out—then pulled a small hatchet from his belt. He got down on his knees and started chopping the ice along the running boards.

"Great. Do we have another hatchet I can use? Wasn't there one in your saddlebag and one in the dry sack?

"I'll chop, you watch for planes."

Wow, a whole sentence. She was making progress. She plopped down on the fir boughs with a sigh. Since he seemed to be more in the mood for listening than talking, Megan decided to broach the subject of how they'd gotten into this mess in the first place.

"Um . . . about what we saw last night," she said.

He stopped chopping.

"I think we should keep it to ourselves."

He straightened to his knees, studying her. "Why?"

"Well . . . in the first place, nobody would believe us."

"And in the second?"

"If they did believe us, then everyone in town would likely get all scared. And when people get scared, they sometimes do foolish things."

"Like?"

Megan sighed. This wasn't going at all well. "Like they might decide to hunt it down and kill it."

"It," he repeated. "Exactly what is *it*, Megan?"

She lifted her shoulders. "How would I know? I saw exactly what you did, and I swear, I've never seen anything like it before."

"Exactly what did we see?"

Okay, if he wanted her to spell it out, she would. "We saw what must be a long-lost descendant of a dinosaur. You know, like they think the Loch Ness monster is? Only our creature seems to be a cross between a ptero-dactyl and a . . . a large lizard of some sort. It can fly, so maybe it's a winged reptile . . . or something or other."

Oh, that had sounded intelligent. But she'd be damned if she would say what it really looked like.

Jack apparently had no such reservations. "You don't think it looked like a dragon?"

"Dragons are mythological. And what we saw was definitely real, so it's likely reptilian."

"And the slime I found at the break-ins? Was that from a reptile?"

"It couldn't be. Reptiles have scales and they're dry. Amphibians are slimy."

He sat back on his heels. "So we're talking about two different creatures, then? Is that what you're suggesting?"

"I have no idea who or what broke into those shops. Maybe the kids concocted some sort of slimy goo to throw you off their trail."

"Forensics can't break it down to any known sub-stance in their data banks."

They were getting off track here. "You're assuming one thing has to do with the other, Jack. Just because we saw something last night that we can't identify doesn't mean it's responsible for your break-ins."

He studied her in silence for several seconds, then started chopping again.

"I'm just saying we should keep this our little secret," she said through gritted teeth. "What would be the point of telling anyone?"

He stopped chopping and looked at her. "So you don't think I should ask Kenzie Gregor what the creature is?"

Megan couldn't stifle her gasp of surprise, and she wanted to kick herself when Jack's eyes narrowed at her response. She quickly tried backpedaling. "What makes you think Kenzie would know anything about this? Have you even met him?"

He started chopping again.

"Jack," she growled, just as a fast-moving plane crested the mountain to their east, diving toward the lake and swooping over their heads with a high-pitched roar.

Megan scrambled to her feet and started waving and shouting. The plane nosed up into a steep turn, circled around, and roared past them again, this time not a hundred feet above the lake a few hundred yards away.

"It's Matt!" she yelped, watching it circle a nearby island before finally setting down on its skis and taxiing toward them.

"You're not riding back with him. He flies like a maniac," Jack said, coming to stand beside her.

"He won't fly like that with a pregnant woman on board," she called back, running toward the four-seater Cessna that had come to a stop a hundred yards out on the lake. But she skidded to a halt, her excitement turning to dread when she saw Kenzie climb out the passenger door.

Instead of rushing to her, Kenzie stood hunched over beside the plane, his hands braced on his knees as he sucked in large gulps of air. He looked so sick, Megan realized this was probably his first plane ride. She turned her attention to Matt, who was speaking into his radio mike. He finally climbed out his side, focused not on her but somewhere over her shoulder.

"Did you radio Dad to tell him you found us?" she asked Matt, drawing him to a stop in front of her. She finally got his attention, his expression fierce as he gave her an assessing, visual inspection.

"I just spoke with your mother, and she's calling him now. Grey and Robbie headed out on snowmobiles around midnight last night to look for you. Why in hell haven't you been answering your satellite phone?"

"Because it's at the bottom of the lake," Jack said, walking up beside her. "Along with her sled."

Matt snapped his gaze to Jack. "What happened?"

Megan stepped between them. "I got ahead of my headlights and ran into open water," she said. "Jack fished me out."

She heard a heavy sigh behind her, just before Jack took hold of her shoulders and moved her off to the side. "My sled's frozen in the slush," he told Matt, who was suddenly looking amused. "We were chopping it out while waiting for someone to show up. Why don't you take Megan back with you, and I'll finish getting it free."

"And if you can't get it free?" Matt asked.

"Then I'll walk back."

Matt eyed him in silence, then nodded.

"I'll stay and help," Kenzie said, finally joining them, though he looked as if a soft breeze might knock him over. He extended his hand. "Kenzie Gregor."

Jack shook it. "Jack Stone. And I'd appreciate the help, if you don't mind riding back on a sled designed for only one rider."

"I'd just as soon walk back, thank ye."

"I think we should *all* fly home," Megan said, not

wanting Jack and Kenzie to spend any time together. She looked at Jack. "Dad or Robbie will come back with you tomorrow to get your sled and see about pulling mine out. We can't leave it in the water for more than a week without getting fined by Inland Fisheries."

Jack shook his head. "I'll get mine out now, then come back with your father tomorrow or the next day." He turned and started walking away.

Megan ran to catch up with him, grabbing his sleeve to make him stop. "Jack, I want you to come back with us now."

"No, you just don't want me alone with Kenzie," he told her quietly, turning so the others wouldn't hear. "Which makes me wonder, are you worried about his welfare or mine?"

"Fine, then. I hope you both get frostbite," she snapped, turning to flounce off to the plane.

He pulled her around to face him before she had taken two steps, completely ruining her dramatic exit. "Forget those DNA samples and everything else for today," he told her, seemingly unaware of—or more likely ignoring—her outrage. "The moment you get home, I want you to go to your doctor and get checked out. You might have gotten some lake water in your lungs and you could develop pneumonia. Have your mom go with you."

"Any other orders before I leave, Chief Stone?"

"As a matter of fact, yeah," he said, pulling her against him and kissing the scowl right off her lips. He leaned back just enough to look her in the eyes. "Fasten your seat belt, and see if the name Walker works for you, for our son."

"We're having a girl!" She shoved him away, and this time she *ran* to the plane.

She climbed in the passenger side and fastened her seat belt. "I don't care what I dreamed last night; you're a girl," she told her belly, giving it a pat. "And don't you worry, I'll teach you to hold your own in this world. Especially against men."

Matt climbed in beside her with a chuckle. "Sorry, sis, but you're having a boy."

She gave her brother-in-law a smack in the arm. "I wanted to be surprised!"

"Hey, don't kill the messenger. I didn't decide the kid's sex, his father did. Speaking of which, I see he's back in your life." He put on his headphones before she could form a comeback. He started the engine, ran through his preflight check of gauges and controls, then gave the plane enough throttle to turn them facing up the lake into the slight breeze. Megan stared out her window, watching Jack and Kenzie on their knees, chopping the sled free.

As the plane's skis skimmed over the snow and rose into the sky, her gaze moved to the shoreline, where she could see the fire trailing up a thin plume of smoke. When Matt banked left toward Pine Creek, Megan lost sight of their cozy little camp, effectively putting the most wonderful night of her life behind her.

Chapter Eighteen

"*I* would ask what yer intentions are toward Megan."

Jack stopped chopping and looked across his snow-mobile's seat at Kenzie. "Funny, I was just about to ask you the same thing."

If his expression was any indication, the huge Scot obviously didn't like having his question answered with another question.

Jack was beginning to see why Grand-père admired these historically fierce Highlanders. Kenzie Gregor could be a throwback himself; despite his modern clothes and short hair, Jack could easily picture the man on a medieval battlefield, wearing a kilt and wielding a sword with lethal accuracy. The guy was well over six feet tall, and when he'd taken off his jacket and rolled up his sleeves, Jack had seen enough muscle to make a bear turn tail and run.

Or make a woman's heart melt?

"Megan's like a sister to me," Kenzie said as he began chopping again.

"It's just as well you feel that way about her. She doesn't particularly like tall men, anyway."

Kenzie looked over the sled at him, his eyes narrowed. "For the last five months she hasn't liked men in general. I'm still waiting to hear your intentions, Stone."

"I intend to marry her, preferably before our son is born."

"Are ye, now?" Kenzie said, suddenly amused. "Then I hope you're prepared to drag her kicking and screaming to the altar. I didn't exactly see her returning yer kiss a moment ago."

Jack shrugged and started chopping again. "She'll come around."

"Matt said you did what ye did because Megan was in danger in Canada. He also said ye think the problem may have followed her here."

Jack straightened and wiped the sweat from his forehead with his sleeve. "News runs through your families like fire through sagebrush. Yes, I think she has something Mark Collins wants."

"And ye don't want her to give it to him?"

"A man was murdered because of the information Megan has. So she's going to give it to me, and I'm going to turn it over to the Canadian authorities." He began chopping the ice away from the rubber track, being careful not to damage it.

"Ye intend to let the authorities deal with Collins?"

"Yes. Once I turn over the information, Mark Collins will leave Megan alone, and that's all I really care about. What was the favor you asked Megan for the other night, when you came to her house?"

Kenzie bent down and started chopping again, this time up toward the ski. "That's none of your business."

"Anything that involves Megan is my business."

"It's a simple favor a brother would ask of a sister, so ye needn't worry about it."

Jack flinched at the sound of metal striking metal. "I'd appreciate it if you didn't chop off the ski," he said, tossing down his hatchet and standing up. "Let's see if we can rock it loose."

Kenzie also stood up, tossed down his hatchet, then grabbed the running board of the sled. Jack did the same on his side, and they alternated lifting until Jack skipped a time and lifted when Kenzie did. The track suddenly broke free.

Jack walked to the front, grabbed the handle on the ski, and lifted it free. Kenzie did the same, and together they dragged the heavy snowmobile forward twenty feet onto the packed snow. Jack stepped back to the handlebars and turned the key. The starter engaged, but the sled didn't start. He flipped the choke, turned the key, and the starter whined and the engine sputtered, but it still didn't start.

He plopped down on the seat with a muttered curse and gave Kenzie a speculative look. "You know anything about snowmobiles?"

Kenzie shook his head. "About as much as I know about airplanes, which is that I don't care for either." He eyed the sled. "I'd be more help if it were a horse."

"Tell me something, Gregor. Before MacBain interrupted you that night of the break-in, were you trying to kill me to protect your little pet, or just disable me?"

"What in God's name are ye talking about?"

"You ambushed me when I started after whatever the hell it was that ran out of that store." Jack shrugged. "I was wondering just how far you'd go to keep your dragon a secret."

"A dragon? Ye think I have a pet *dragon*?" Kenzie actually took a step back. "Are ye touched in the head, mon?"

"No, I believe that of the two of us, I'm probably the more grounded. Where you, my friend, seem to be straddling two worlds."

The towering Scot crossed his arms over his chest. "Am I now? And just which two worlds would those be?"

Jack reached over and gave the key another turn on the off chance the sled would start. The engine only whined and coughed, so he gave his attention back to Kenzie. "I'd say you're standing on the wrong side of society's door right now, Gregor. Or maybe you're simply wrestling with life in general." He stood up, squaring off against the giant. "I don't want Megan caught in the middle of this, so drop whatever favor you need from her."

"Caught in the middle of what, exactly?" Kenzie asked, his expression implying he had no intention of dropping anything.

"Megan and I both got a good look at your pet last night when it crossed in front of our headlights, then flew toward that mountain," he said, pointing east. "Megan startled it when she came through that opening in the peninsula, and she broke through the ice when she tried to avoid hitting it. She knows that you know where it lives."

"She's guessing."

"She's a scientist, Gregor, and what she saw last night is akin to waving a bone under a dog's nose. So either you get rid of the beast, or I will—before it goes from stealing doughnuts to hurting someone."

Kenzie stared at him in silence, apparently trying to decide how much of a threat Jack really was. Then he suddenly headed back to where the sled had been stuck, grabbed his jacket, and started walking toward shore.

"One week, Gregor. Then I start hunting your pet," Jack called.

Kenzie lifted a hand to indicate that he'd heard, and kept walking. Jack glared down at his snowmobile, wondering if confronting the Scot directly had been wise, or if he'd just plastered a bull's-eye on his own chest. Because if Grand-père was correct, he had just backed the brother of a very powerful drùidh into a corner.

Jack was just popping the cap off his second Canadian lager when he spotted the two snowmobiles three miles down the lake, headed toward him. He crossed his feet at his ankles, settled back against the cowling of his sled with a sigh, and used the bottle cap to draw in the snowpack.

He outlined an upright body with a long tail, took a sip of his beer, then added a set of large wings coming out its back. He glanced up to find that the snowmobiles were about two miles away, took another sip, then added a head to his sketch, complete with beady little eyes, a long snout, and flared nostrils.

Yup, it sure as hell looked like Puff the Magic Dragon to him.

The muted whine of the two sleds told Jack they were about a mile away. He checked the position of the sun, figured it was about an hour before noon, and took a long guzzle of the ice-cold beer, swishing it in his mouth before swallowing. He sure would love to have a power bar right now, or even better, another roast beef sandwich slathered with mustard. He tilted the bottle all the way up and drained the last drop of beer just as the sleds stopped ten yards from his feet and suddenly went silent.

"Morning, gentlemen," he said when the two men pulled off their helmets. "Nice sleds. I see they're both two-seaters."

They sat on their snowmobiles, eyeing him. Well, Robbie MacBain was eyeing him. Greylen looked more like he was deciding exactly how he intended to kill Jack.

"You promised to bring my daughter home safe and sound."

"She is safe and sound," Jack told him. "And I had Matt Gregor take her home, so she'd get there quicker. You don't happen to have any food, do you? Megan ate my last power bar this morning."

Grey's scowl intensified.

Robbie unzipped his saddlebag and tossed Jack a package of beef jerky.

"Thanks," Jack said, setting down his empty bottle and ripping open the small bag. He pulled out a strip of jerky and shoved the whole piece in his mouth.

"What happened?" Greylen asked.

Jack chewed. He knew he was pissing off Laird MacKeage, but he wasn't exactly in a happy mood himself. He'd lost a three hundred dollar helmet, his brand-new sled was likely ruined to the tune of another thousand bucks, he was hungry and tired, and his knee was hurting again. And then there was the fact that as soon as Kenzie told his brother about Jack's planned hunt, he was going to have a damn drùidh dogging his heels.

He finally swallowed and stood up—smudging his drawing with his boot as he did so—and walked over to where his sled had been stuck. He drove his empty beer bottle into a small patch of slush that hadn't frozen, filled it up, then faced the men as he held the bottle between his hands to warm it.

"Something ran across in front of us as we were heading down the lake, and Megan had to leave the trail to avoid hitting it." He used the bottle to point toward the ledge. "She broke through over there. I fished her out, then built a fire to warm her up and dry her clothes. It was my decision to stay put until daylight, when either I could get my sled out, or you came and got us."

"What was the something?" Robbie asked.

"What were ye doing running the lake at night?" Greylen asked at the same time.

Jack answered Greylen, as he still hadn't decided how much to tell them about the creature. "The trail we were following came out on the lake ten miles north of where we wanted to be, so we decided to connect up with the ITS trail another six or seven miles south of here. We weren't speeding, and we were following the club trail."

"Until something ran out in front of you," Greylen said, climbing off his sled. He walked over to Jack. "So what was it that caused my daughter to leave the trail, Stone?"

Jack took a guzzle of the melted slush and wiped his mouth with the back of his hand. If Megan wanted to keep secrets, then *she* could lie to her father. "I'm not sure, exactly." He pointed toward shore. "It was headed that way, last I saw it. I was more worried about Megan than it."

Robbie got off his sled and walked toward the ledge. Greylen followed. Jacked dug another piece of beef jerky out of the package and stuffed it in his mouth, wondering how Megan expected to keep the creature a secret, considering it had left tracks a blind man could follow. He trudged after the two men, washing down the jerky with another gulp of lake water.

"Megan said we have a week to get your sled out before you get fined," Jack said. "It's only in about ten feet of water."

Robbie stopped beside the tracks Jack had made dragging her out. He looked at the frozen rope still lying on the ice, then toward shore, and then at the tracks on the ledge leading into the water. "You pulled her out, but then you went in yourself. Why?"

Yup, the guy definitely knew how to read signs. "For her survival equipment. I knew everything was in a dry sack, and I had hoped to find a radio."

Megan's father wasn't paying attention to their conversation; he was staring at the black ice covering the hole where his daughter's sled was. He suddenly bent down and picked up her ice-caked helmet, the broken shield falling onto the snowpack with a muted thud. Greylen stared at it in silence for several seconds, then lifted his gaze to Jack. "I would thank ye, Chief, for saving my daughter's life."

Jack nodded. "You're welcome," he softly returned,

his shoulders relaxing for the first time in ten minutes. He started walking to shore. "I was just about to break camp when you arrived. Any chance of my hitching a ride back with you?"

"Your sled isn't running?" Robbie asked.

Jack shook his head. "I think something burned up in it when I hit the slush. I'll have to hire Paul Dempsey at Pine Creek PowerSports to tow it home for me."

"Then how come you didn't get in the plane with Matt?" Greylen asked.

"I don't fly unless I'm at the controls. Did you meet Kenzie Gregor on your way up the lake?"

"I thought he was with Matt," Robbie said.

"He stayed and helped me get my sled out, then decided to walk home. I have the impression he doesn't much care for anything with an engine, especially if it goes faster than a horse," he said, heading for shore again.

While packing up camp, Jack watched through the trees as the two men made their way over to the tracks the creature had made, studying them in silence. MacBain looked toward the mountain, then in Jack's direction, before finally turning to speak to Greylen.

Oh, yeah. MacBain definitely knew about the creature, though it seemed Greylen was only now learning about it. Jack wished someone would tell *him* what in hell a mythological creature was doing roaming around Pine Creek, Maine, in the twenty-first century. *And* why none of the men in the three families seemed surprised by that fact?

He snorted as he bent down to pick up the sleeping bag. Because they had two drùidhs on board, that's why—one of which was Greylen's youngest daughter.

Jack wondered when Megan intended to let him in on that particular little secret.

And she was worried about *him* being a shaman? Her own sister could probably turn the world inside out at the crook of her finger!

Jack went utterly still. Holy hell. Was the dragon some old boyfriend who had broken a MacKeage girl's heart?

Chapter Nineteen

$\mathcal{J}$ack threw down his pen and rubbed his face with a frustrated sigh. He glanced at his watch, saw it was nearly midnight, and decided to give himself twenty more minutes before he set out on his rounds.

The snowmobile trip from hell—and a bit of heaven, too—had ended thirty-six hours ago, when Robbie and Greylen had finally dropped Jack off at his house. Megan had been nowhere in sight, but he hadn't expected her to be. Most likely her parents would be keeping her within arm's reach for a while, once Greylen told Grace how close they'd come to losing their daughter.

Megan and Camry had to stay at Gù Brath for a couple of days anyway, until Megan's busted pipes were repaired. It seems both Pine Creek and Frog Cove had experienced a bit of a crime wave while Jack had been away. It would probably take Simon a week of Sundays to recover, and another week to finish writing all the reports. That's why Jack had given him today and tomorrow off and was pulling double duty tonight. He wondered if he could get the selectmen to ante up for another patrolman.

He eyed the four yellow pads laid out on his desk, on which he'd been adding copious notes. The first pad, LITTLE BASTARDS, had certainly grown; the irony being that he'd been the target of their latest prank. He shook his head with a chuckle. He had to give them credit; they were getting damn creative.

They'd had the nerve, and apparently the tools, time, and stamina, to trick out his police cruiser with enough accessories to make a hot-rodder jealous. His brand-new SUV now sported a brush guard, air horns mounted on the roof, oversize mud flaps with chrome reclining lady emblems, a bug shield that had CHIEF written in bold letters across it, and a sun visor and rear roof spoiler. None of the additions were store-bought new, which meant either a local salvage yard or several personal vehicles had also been victimized. Jack was leaning toward the salvage yard, as no private citizens had reported anything missing yet.

And that was just the visible stuff. When he'd started his cruiser to come to work this morning, he'd nearly been deafened by the tuned exhaust pipes they'd installed. Heads had turned when he'd idled through town, and his ears were still ringing.

The hoodlums must have frozen their little brass balls, as they'd done the work right in Jack's driveway on a night the temperature had dropped to minus two degrees. They sure seemed determined to thumb their noses at him, didn't they?

He had six days left before he—or Kenzie Gregor—closed the book on the break-ins, so Jack figured he should able to finally burn his LITTLE BASTARDS pad by then, too. He'd made a few phone calls and quietly done some checking around this afternoon, and was pretty sure who the culprits were.

The solution he'd come up with involved his beautiful new sled, but he simply didn't have the heart to see those kids taken from their single mother and placed in a foster home or detention hall. They were intelligent—at least the older boy was—and Jack wanted to redirect their creativity before the juvenile courts bled it out of them.

Now all he had to do was to talk Paul Dempsey into coming on board when he went to see him tomorrow morning.

So LITTLE BASTARDS was being dealt with, and hopefully THE BREAK-INS pad could also be burned at the end of the week—unless he had to hunt down the beast himself.

Which left MEGAN's pad and the one titled MARK COLLINS.

And that's where things started getting complicated. The reason Megan was having to get her pipes repaired was that someone had broken into her house the night they'd been stranded up the lake. Camry had been at Gù Brath with her worried mother, thank God, while Greylen had been out searching. With no one else living out on Frog Point in the winter, the burglar had had the entire place to himself.

Or he did until the little bastards had shown up to decorate their police chief's cruiser. That's what Jack speculated had happened; whoever had been searching Megan's house had been forced to beat a hasty retreat out her bedroom door that led onto the deck facing the lake. Unfortunately, he hadn't closed the door behind himself, and the bedroom heating pipes had frozen, burst, and spewed water everywhere.

This break-in had definitely been a professional job; the guy hadn't made a blatant mess, and he'd been methodical in his search before he'd been interrupted. Jack's gut tightened at the memory of walking through her house with Greylen and Robbie MacBain yesterday afternoon. The three of them had agreed Mark Collins had likely hired someone to look for what Jack had explained were DNA samples Megan had taken in Canada. Which meant the man had been lurking in town all this time, waiting for an opening.

The three of them had also agreed that he would probably try again, since he hadn't completed the job. They had not agreed, however, on how to deal with the threat he posed. Greylen wanted to use the samples for bait and Robbie wanted to send them to the Canadian lab but not announce that fact so the man would try again. Jack wanted to send the samples in, then call Mark Collins directly and tell him what was going on so the bastard would redirect his energy to saving his sorry ass.

The samples had been overnighted to Canada this morning, and tonight MacBain was sleeping in Megan's cold house. Jack had finally agreed to wait until he got word back from the lab as to what had killed those animals before he decided how to handle Collins.

These Scots were hands-on people who were in the habit of dealing with trouble their way, rather than waiting for someone—even law enforcement—to deal with it for them. Wanting to show he could fit into their little clans, Jack had decided to let them play cops and robbers if it made them feel better. All he cared about was that Megan was safe—which she certainly was, now that everyone was up to speed and she was sleeping in a fortress. If her family wanted to deal with Collins, that freed Jack up to deal with the hoodlums and Puff the Magic Dragon.

Jack gathered up his yellow pads and locked them in the bottom drawer of his desk, then stood up. He stretched out the kinks in his muscles and shut off his desk lamp, plunging his office into darkness. He had no compunction about killing a creature that shouldn't exist, because he sure as hell knew it couldn't be the results of good magic or anything else that served mankind.

His only reservation had to do with his future clansmen, and why they were protecting it.

"Nice ride," Paul Dempsey drawled, looking out his showroom window at Jack's cruiser.

"It's sort of growing on me," Jack said. "In fact, it's the reason I'm here."

Paul shook his head. "I don't work on trucks. You need to take it to the dealer in Greenville. They have the equipment to fix that noisy exhaust."

"But you have the equipment to fix my snowmobile. Since you're swamped with work, I just want to borrow your shop and your tools in the evening, when you're not open."

Paul look surprised. "You're going to fix it yourself? I had to explain the difference between a four- and two-stroke to you, the first time you came in here."

"I have my own mechanic."

"Who?" Paul asked with eager interest. "Is he for hire?

If he knows four-strokes, I'll put him to work immediately *and* put your sled first in line."

This was turning out even better than he'd hoped. "I'd have to speak with him first, but I can almost guarantee he'd go to work for you. The problem is, he can only work afternoons. But he could stay after you close and help get you caught up."

Paul shook his head. "I'm not hiring a high school kid." He pointed at Jack. "And if you're smart, you won't let one of them anywhere near your sled, especially with a wrench in his hand. We're talking about cutting-edge technology here."

"Which they're teaching at the tech school in Greenville," Jack countered. "Those kids are more knowledgeable about today's engines than you probably are. It's no longer simple high school shop, it's vocational-technical schooling."

Paul's eyes narrowed. "Who are we talking about? What's the kid's name?"

"Tommy Cleary."

"No way! I'm not letting that brat anywhere near my shop!" His face reddened and he pointed at Jack again. "And you expect . . . you're asking me to leave Tommy Cleary in my shop after-hours?" he sputtered. "*Alone*?" He shook his head. "I'd be robbed blind!"

"Or you'd find yourself with the best damn mechanic you've had in years," Jack calmly returned. "From all accounts, Tommy's a genius when it comes to anything mechanical."

"Says who?"

"Say his tech teachers," Jack told him, stepping closer and lowering his voice when a man and woman walked into the showroom. "He did a damn good job on my cruiser. And his teachers tell me Tommy can trouble-shoot problems better than a mechanic with twenty years of experience. The boy's got a gift, Dempsey, and it's being wasted."

"No," Paul growled, his attention going to the young couple eyeing the sporty racing sled in the front window. The man was sitting on it while the woman was studying the price tag. Paul looked back at Jack. "No. No. No!"

"Do you have any idea what it would do to Joan Cleary to have her boys taken away from her?" Jack asked, moving to block Paul's view of his customers.

"Goddammit, Stone, that's not fair. Tommy's been in trouble before, you know. All of the Cleary kids have. I know Joan Cleary's had a rough go of it, but I will *not* hire that juvenile delinquent son of hers."

"Why not?" Jack asked calmly, again moving to block Paul's view.

Paul glared at him. "Why not? Dammit, because . . . because he's just a kid!"

"He turned eighteen last week. He graduates in three months, and you'll be able to have him full time after that. Can you imagine how much his paycheck would help out his mother?"

"No. No. No!"

"And when word gets out that you've got a gifted mechanic, you'll be booked a month of Sundays ahead."

"What I'll be is bankrupt. Because the minute word gets out that Tommy Cleary is working here, every-one will start taking their repairs to my competition in Greenville."

"That would depend," Jack drawled, moving directly in front of Paul again, "on what sort of spin you put on it. If you make a huge deal over the fact that you stole Cleary right out from under your competition's nose, your customers will think you're a genius and that Tommy's the only one they want working on their engines."

Paul eyed Jack speculatively. "You've already spoken to my competition? Before talking to me?"

Jack shook his head. "I'm giving you first shot at Tommy. If you don't snatch him up, I'm headed to Greenville from here." He lowered his voice to a conspirator's whisper. "I tell you what: I'll give you until noon today to decide. Sell that guy over there a sled, then give the tech school a call and ask them what kind of mechanic Tommy is. But come noon, I'm offering him to your competition."

Paul caught Jack's sleeve when he turned to leave. "Joan Cleary used to be one hell of a fine-looking woman before Eric Cleary wore her down, may the bastard's soul rot in hell. She really could use Tommy's paycheck, couldn't she?"

"About as much as you could use a good mechanic. And Tommy could use some direction and purpose in life, and his little brothers could use a better role model. It's a win-win opportunity for everyone, Paul."

Paul thought furiously for several seconds, then suddenly puffed up with importance. "Have him stop in after school today, and I'll see if we can't work out a deal about hours and wages until he graduates."

"How about tomorrow afternoon instead?"

"Why not today?"

"I couldn't very well offer Tommy anything without speaking with you first, could I?" he said, turning and walking away.

"Dammit, Stone. Did you just set me up?" Paul called out as Jack reached the door.

He turned to the suspicious store owner. "No, Dempsey, I believe I just shored up your bottom line." He looked over at the young couple now in a heated discussion over the snowmobile the guy obviously thought he needed. "If I might make a suggestion?" Jack said, drawing their attention. He nodded toward the workhorse Paul had talked him out of three weeks ago. "It might not look as sporty as this one, but it would make a great family sled. Take my word for it, there's nothing like riding the trails together."

That said, Jack walked out to his cruiser, whistling a happy tune. He climbed in, then checked his watch. He should leave for Greenville by two-thirty to be at the tech school when it let out at three. His mood heightened even more when he thought of Tom Cleary riding home in the police chief's beautifully tricked-out cruiser.

Jack had no idea what the Cleary boy looked like, other than Ethel's description of a gangly teenager with over-long blond hair and likely tattered clothes. Which meant he could be any one of the thirty or so young males pouring out of the tech school, as *tattered* appeared to be the newest thing. Since he'd arrived too late to go inside and have Tommy paged, Jack stopped his cruiser directly in front of the main entrance, hoping one of the boys would give himself away when he saw his latest prank in broad daylight.

One boy did suddenly stop dead in his tracks and gape, though most everyone—male and female—stopped and stared. But this particular boy seemed more disconcerted than awestruck. He looked around nervously, then suddenly bolted.

Jack muttered a curse. Of course he'd run. Didn't they always? He climbed out of his cruiser and chased after him. "Tommy, wait!" he called to the kid. "I need your help."

Apparently Tommy wasn't the helpful sort, since he continued sprinting around the corner of the building, then zigzagged through a parking lot filled with every imaginable make and year of vehicle. The boy scaled the thirty-foot-high snowbank at the end of the lot in three easy strides, then disappeared down the other side. Jack followed at a flat-out run, acutely aware of the shouts of encouragement cheering Tommy on, as well as the small assembly of students joining the chase.

Jack also scaled the snowbank, crested the top, and saw his quarry disappear into the woods. "Big mistake, Tommy boy. You're on my turf now." He turned to look at the parade of students preparing to scramble up the snowbank behind him. "Sorry, people, this is as far as you go," he told them.

He was answered by a barrage of questions, several muttered curses, and sounds of general disappointment.

"What'd Tommy do?"

"Are you going to arrest him?"

"Leave him alone, he didn't do anything!"

"He's getting away, cop. What's the matter, you out of shape from eating too many doughnuts?"

"Do I *look* out of shape?" Jack asked with a laugh. "Come on people, go home. Tommy's not in trouble, I just want to ask a favor of him. So please be upstanding citizens and go home and do your homework."

He then turned and scrambled down the back side of

the snowbank, stepped into the woods where Tommy had, and studied his tracks a few seconds before heading off at a forty-five degree angle to the left.

Within ten minutes Jack was standing behind a tree watching a huffing and puffing Tommy heading straight toward him. The boy kept looking over his shoulder and had started stumbling a bit in his panic, and when he looked forward Jack could see the hunted look in his eyes.

Jack stepped out directly in front of him. "Whoa, there," he said, steadying the kid when he yelped in surprise and nearly fell. "Easy, Tommy. I just want to talk to you."

"I didn't do nothing," the boy said, panting heavily.

"Oh, I wouldn't say the improvements to my cruiser are nothing. They turned my poor little wannabe into a real truck."

Tommy's eyes widened in surprise, and he suddenly plopped down in the snow to catch his breath. "How come you ain't winded?" he asked.

"I don't even work up a sweat running through the woods." Jack hunched down in front of him. "I have a proposition for you, Tom, and you only have tonight to think about it, because I want your answer tomorrow morning before you head off to school."

"What sort of proposition?"

"I burned up the engine in my new snowmobile, and I want you to fix it."

"You do? Me? Why?"

"Because you can. And if you get it purring like a kitten again, I can get you a mechanic's job at Pine Creek PowerSports."

Tommy snorted. "Dempsey won't hire me. I already

tried to get a job from him last summer. I offered to sweep floors and wash windows, but he wouldn't even talk to me. He sure as hell won't let me near any of his sleds or ATVs."

"He will now, if you can get my snowmobile running smoothly. And if you do right by him all spring, you'll have a full-time position once you graduate."

A spark of interest blossomed in Tommy's eyes. "Why would he hire me now, when he wouldn't before?"

"Because I have more pull than you do. Being chief of police has its perks, and I'm not above using my badge to my advantage."

"Then why are *you* doing this for me?"

"Because I can."

He shook his head. "Why should I trust you?"

"Because you have only two choices. One way gets you a weekly paycheck and respectability; the other gets you room and board at the county jail. You're not a juvenile anymore, Tom. If you get caught for your crimes, not matter how harmless they are, you'll pay adult consequences. Then who's going to help your mom deal with your brothers?"

"You've talked to my mom?" he squeaked.

"No. And I don't intend to unless you force my hand." Jack stood up. "This will stay just between us, providing the pranks stop. Be in my office at seven tomorrow morning with your answer."

"Wait!" Tommy said, also standing up. "I need to know why you're doing this!" He ran to catch up with Jack. "You don't even know me."

"Yes, I do," Jack told him. "I *was* you, except my stunts weren't nearly as creative."

"What stunts?" Tommy asked, back to being suspicious.

"The *Fart* Gallery?" Jack said with a chuckle. "Let me ask you something, Tom," he said, turning serious. "When you and your brothers were working on my cruiser, did you see anyone nosing around, three camps down from my house? Or did you see or hear anything unusual? A snowmobile on the lake, maybe a car driving away?"

Tommy stepped over a fallen log, then gave Jack a sidelong glance. "I don't know what you're talking about," he muttered.

"This is important," Jack told him, veering onto a game trail so the walking was easier. "Somebody broke into Megan MacKeage's house, and there was a lot of damage."

"It wasn't us!" Tommy yelped.

"I know it wasn't. But I sure could use your help finding out who it was."

Tommy walked beside him in silence for several hundred yards. "We did see a car parked at the end of the camp road. It had New York plates on it, and the windows had iced up, so we knew it had only been sitting there a short while, because they wouldn't have fogged up if it had been there all day. But we didn't see anyone around or hear anything."

"What make and model was it?" Jack asked, heading down the lane toward the school.

"Lincoln Town Car, 2006. White. It had a rental sticker on the bumper," he told Jack, just as the school bus passed them. "Damn, I missed my bus."

"Not a problem," Jack said, giving him a friendly slap on the back. "I'll give you a ride home in my cruiser."

Chapter Twenty

After dropping Tom off, Jack drove to TarStone Mountain Ski Resort. He slowly rumbled up and down the parking lot looking for a white Lincoln, then drove up to the entrance of the three-story hotel. He asked the horrified doorman to leave his cruiser where it was parked, stepped inside the bustling lobby, and walked past the line of patrons at the registry desk.

"Is Greylen MacKeage available?" he asked the clerk who spotted his badge and came over.

"No, sir, he's not. But Callum MacKeage is available. Or I could page his brother, Morgan, if you prefer."

Jack didn't want to go to Gù Brath and chance running into Megan. "I'll speak with Callum, thank you. Would you please call Greylen and ask him to come over here? And also give me a printout of your guest list that would include what they're driving?"

"I don't know if I'm supposed to do that, sir."

"I'll handle this, Derek. Thank you," a gentleman

said as he appeared in a doorway behind the counter. "Chief Stone, if you would come this way," he offered. "And bring me that printout he requested, would you, Derek?"

Jack strode around the counter and walked past what could only be another giant MacKeage, though this one appeared to be several years Greylen's senior. He looked as if he should have retired fifteen or twenty years ago, but here he was in a suit and tie, his physique that of a much younger man, his eyes sharp with intelligence.

What in hell was in the water around here?

"Chief," the man said, extending his hand. "I'm Greylen's cousin, Callum MacKeage."

Jack shook his hand. "Call me Jack, please. It's good to meet yet another member of Megan's family. I asked your clerk to call Greylen to come here."

"I already called him when Derek told me you were here. Grey's on his way, and so is Morgan, his brother. Do ye have some news for us about Megan's burglar?"

"I have a description of the car he was driving, and I'd like to see if he's registered here."

The door to the office opened and another giant walked in, this one a few years younger than Greylen. Jack decided he was bottling up the water from his well and selling it as a growth elixir.

"Chief," the man said, extending his hand. "Morgan MacKeage, Megan's uncle. Have you caught my niece's burglar?"

Jack shook his hand. "Please call me Jack. As I was just explaining to Callum, I found out what the guy is driving, and I'm assuming he's staying here."

"Why?" Callum asked. "There are other hotels in town."

"Because this is where I would stay if my target's family conveniently owned a hotel."

Both men narrowed their eyes at him. Jack sat down without waiting for an invitation, and looked around. He realized Callum had brought him to Grey's office when he saw the pictures of all the girls when they were young. He stood up and walked over to look at one in particular.

"This is Megan. How old is she here?"

"Nine," Morgan said, coming to stand beside him. "She's sitting on Lancelot." He waved at the wall of seven individual pictures of Grey's seven daughters on horseback. "Each girl was given a draft horse for her fifth birthday. Their uncle Ian had a passion for the big, docile beasts."

"I don't believe I've met Ian," he said, studying the other photos, immediately picking out Camry. Even as a kid, Jack could see she was a hellion.

"No, you haven't. Ian left us nearly three years ago."

"Sorry," he murmured.

The door opened and Greylen walked in, carrying a computer printout. "What's up, Stone?" he asked, walking around his desk and sitting down. "Ye have some good news for us?"

"No, I'm hoping you do," Jack said, sitting across from him. "I'm looking for a guest of yours who would be driving a late-model, white Lincoln Town Car with New York plates."

Greylen pulled a set of glasses out of his shirt pocket and studied the printout. A minute later he set the pages down on his desk and pointed to a spot on one of them. "Peter Trump, room 316." He hit the intercom button. "Derek, could you please print out Peter Trump's history for me, and also tell me when he'd scheduled to check out," he asked, releasing the button.

"Trump has a history here? How do you know?"

Grey tapped his finger on the page. "We have a code for repeat guests, so we can reward their patronage."

Jack leaned back in his chair. "Peter Trump is likely an alias. What did you take for an ID? Does it say?"

"Credit card," Greylen read. "Which would be viable, or we'd have known it was fake when he checked in. We always run them through first thing, to hold the funds."

Jack shrugged. "It's easy to get a card under a false name. The good thing is, Trump doesn't realize we know who he is or where he's staying. It's just a matter of my knocking on door 316 and asking him to come down to the station for questioning."

To a man, the three MacKeages gave Jack scowls that would have made a bear tremble.

He immediately shook his head. "We're doing this my way this time, gentlemen, and we're doing it by the book. I have to show the selectmen I'm doing something to earn my paycheck. So far, it looks as if I've been running around chasing my tail. What's Megan up to today?" he asked, standing up and heading to the door. "Has her mother let her out of her sight yet?"

"Megan was locked in the lab with Kenzie when I left Gù Brath," Grey said, following him.

Jack pulled open the door, then turned and held up his hand to the three men following him. "I'm going up alone," he said, checking his gun tucked in the back of his belt, under his jacket. "Just give me a master key card and point me to the stairs."

He turned and nearly ran over Derek.

"Um . . . here are the printouts," Derek said, handing them to Greylen. "And Mr. Trump left his departure date open-ended."

"Thank you. Would you also get Chief Stone a master key?" Grey said, looking down at the printouts he'd just received. "Peter Trump has been here five times in the last six months. First time was August 23." He looked at Jack. "Not a week after Megan got home." He looked back at the printout in his hand. "He stayed two weeks. Then he was here again in early October, when he stayed one week. Then November and December. He arrived this last time on January 10." He looked at Jack again. "That would be shortly after Megan went to work for Mark Collins."

Jack took the key card from Derek, walked into the lobby, then turned back to the men. "The stairs?"

Morgan pointed to the left. Jack pushed through the heavy fire door, walked up two of the steps, then turned and bent down to peek through the tiny window in the door. Yup, the three Scots were scrambling in three different directions, apparently intending to cover his ass.

Jack turned and headed upstairs with a smile. Nothing like having a few giant Highlanders watching his back.

He made it partway down the hall of the third floor, then stopped with a muttered curse. His jacket was police issue. When Trump checked the peephole and saw Jack's badge, he would likely start shooting through the door. He slipped off his jacket and tossed it on the floor next to the wall, pulling his gun from the back of his belt and holding it down by this thigh.

Greylen stepped off the elevator and walked toward

him. "Let me knock on his door," Grey said. "He should recognize me and not get suspicious."

Jack nodded. It was a good plan. They walked to room 316 together; then Jack hung back and waited. Grey knocked, then knocked again, but nobody answered.

"Mr. Trump, are you in there?" Grey asked. "We're having a water problem with the room below ye, and we need to check your bathroom, sir."

Still nobody answered.

Grey reached in his pocket and pulled out his own master key card. But just as soon as he stuck it in the slot, Jack nudged him aside and opened the door while staying out of the direct line of fire. The door swung open into what appeared to be an empty room.

With his gun leading the way, Jack slowly entered the two-room suite, checking the closets and bathroom and both rooms thoroughly. He lowered his gun with a sigh and Grey finally entered the room.

"He's gone," Grey said, stating the obvious. "He packed up and left without checking out."

"Which probably means he's not coming back," Jack said, tucking his gun in his belt as he continued exploring the room. He picked up the trash can, dumped the papers in it onto the desk, and rummaged through them. "Don't let housekeeping clean in here until I have Simon Pratt check for fingerprints," Jack said, shoving all the papers back in the trash can. "With luck, our guy might be in someone's database. There's a chance he's never coming back, but there's also a good chance that he suspects his car was seen and has changed vehicles and checked into another hotel either here in Pine Creek or in Greenville."

"I would guess the last, since he can't know we've

sent off the samples," Grey said. "Mark Collins emailed Megan yesterday and asked how her survey was coming along."

"Did she answer him?"

"Aye, she sent him an email saying she thought there was a mountain lion in the area to be developed."

"Perfect," Jack said. "Mentioning the cat makes it appear that she doesn't suspect a thing."

"Megan just realized this morning that her laptop is missing. She had me go over to her house with her to get it, but she couldn't find it."

Jack dismissed the news with a shrug. "The samples are what Collins want."

Grey moved directly in front of Jack. "I'm worried that Megan herself might be a target now. She told me this morning that she had taken extensive notes on what she'd observed around the dead animals. That's why she went after the laptop this morning, when she remembered her notes and wanted to read them."

"Shit," Jack hissed. "If Collins gets hold of her computer, he might decide Megan is just as much of a threat as those samples are." He glared at Grey. "She has to stay at Gù Brath until . . . dammit, it could take weeks to get Collins off our backs."

"Or an instant, for the right man," Grey said very softly.

Jack shook his head. "I don't know where in hell you people get your sense of justice, but taking the law into your own hands is not acceptable."

"Collins is now threatening my daughter's life, Stone. In my day, we made sure such threats couldn't come back to haunt us." Grey walked to the hall door. "I will give you the same amount of time to deal with Collins that you gave Kenzie to deal with his problem. One week, Stone—and then I will take matters into my own hands." His eyes hardened even more. "And if you fail, you will leave Pine Creek forever—alone."

Jack stared at the empty doorway. O-kay. It didn't get any more direct than that, did it?

Jack pulled out his cell phone, called Simon, and told him to come to the resort to take fingerprints. He then slipped the phone back in his pocket with a sigh. It was time to start thinking like his ancestors.

Taking advantage of his foul mood, Jack went to the MacKeage stables to wait for Kenzie. He knew the Sasquatch was using a horse to travel to and from the cabin where he lived with the priest, because Jack's badge had gotten the doorman to talk about a lot of things, including Kenzie's frequent visits to Gù Brath since Megan had moved back home.

Jack had also learned from the affable doorman that Miss Camry MacKeage was a huge flirt, but that she was all talk and no action. Presumably he told Jack this so Jack wouldn't get his hopes up, seeing how he was new in town and all. Not that it mattered, anyway, as the doorman had heard that Camry was flying to France in a few days because of what some scientist there had discovered about ion propulsion—which, the doorman had explained, was Camry's area of expertise.

So Jack sat on a bale of hay and let some horse named Snowball nuzzle his shoulder. He was surprised to realize he was going to miss Camry. She had grown on him over the last couple of weeks, and he was sorry she was leaving.

The large stable door suddenly slid open and Kenzie

Gregor walked in, stopping short when he spotted Jack.

"How's your favor going with Megan?" Jack asked.

Kenzie walked to a stall and led one of the huge draft horses into the aisle. "It's going quite well, thank ye."

"And your pet? How's that little problem coming along?"

Kenzie gave Jack a warning glance and went back to bridling his horse. "I told ye I'd take care of it, and I will."

"No, actually, you never did tell me you would."

Kenzie turned to face him. "The beast won't be breaking into any more shops. He's sick, and I fear he may be dying."

"Well, that takes care of that problem," Jack said, standing up to leave.

"Ye don't understand, Stone. I intend to do everything in my power to save him."

"Or your brother's power?"

Kenzie looked momentarily startled, then narrowed his eyes. "What has my brother got to do with this?"

Jack shrugged and stepped outside, Kenzie following. "You save that creature's life, Gregor, you better find a way to send it back where it came from."

"I will deal with it," he said, leading his horse toward the path heading up the mountain. He stopped, swung up onto its bare back in one easy motion, and gave Jack a speculative look. "Camry and Megan were talking at lunch today, and Camry mentioned a word I haven't heard before. Would ye happen to know what *shaman* means?"

"What it means, Gregor, is that you Celts aren't the only magic act in town," Jack said, walking away.

* * *

Jack's foul mood continued through the rest of the day and into the evening. It also was likely responsible for the heart-pounding nightmare he had that night, in which he repeatedly found himself battling one monster after another as he frantically tried to get to Megan, who was struggling in the icy water of a tundra lake.

Each time he was just about to reach her, another adversary got in his way. Kenzie Gregor tried to cut him in half with a large bloody sword, Jack barely deflecting each blow with his tiny hatchet. Then a faceless Mark Collins stood with his small army of students, forcing Jack to hack his way through them, their cries of betrayal caught up in Megan's scream for help. The dragon flew at him next, shooting fire from its nostrils as its tail lashed at Jack, trying to knock the hatchet from his hand.

And just when he thought he'd defeated any and all foes and could finally save Megan, Jack found Greylen MacKeage blocking his path. Looking a good forty years younger, wearing a gray and red, dark green, and lavender plaid and holding an ancient and bloodied sword in his hand, the fierce Highlander was the final gauntlet he had to run in order to reach the woman he loved.

The hatchet dangling in his hand at his side and blood seeping from his wounds, Jack's entire body trembled with exhaustion and apparent defeat. He could only watch helplessly as men from three different clans pulled Megan from the icy water and then flew off, carrying her to an impenetrable fortress on a distant mountain.

"Ye failed, Stone," Greylen said, moving to block his way when Jack tried to follow. "You've disgraced your ancestors by failing to protect what's yours. Ye don't deserve a family of your own, especially my daughter and grand-son. We'll raise the boy to be a powerful warrior."

"I don't want him to be a warrior!" Jack cried out. "And neither does his mother."

"Turn around, Stone. See what your way has gained you."

Jack slowly turned and saw Kenzie, the dragon, and Collins and his students regrouping, preparing them-selves to come at him again.

"*You* possess the skills of a warrior, Stone," Greylen said, drawing his attention again. "But ye refuse to use them."

"I prefer peaceful solutions to problems."

"And so you will continue to fight the same fights, refusing to see that sometimes a man must act decisively, even when it goes against his nature."

"I fought *them*," Jack said, nodding behind him with-out taking his eyes off Megan's father.

"Aye, but your blows were ineffectual, and instead of solving anything, ye only postponed the inevitable. Did ye not hope to avoid taking action yourself by giv-ing Kenzie a week to deal with the dragon? And so your problems come at you again, and my daughter and her child pay the price of your hesitation."

Jack dropped his chin to his chest. "There has to be a way I can save her," he said, more to himself than to Grey.

"There is, Coyote."

"What is it, then?" Jack asked, looking up, only to find his grand-père standing beside Greylen, the two men ap-pearing to be different sides of the same coin.

"You must embrace your dark side," his grand-père said. "And acknowledge the shadow your heart creates when you stand in the light. One does not exist without the other, Coyote—which means *you* cannot exist unless you accept both."

"If I acknowledge the shadows, will I get Megan and my son back?" he asked, looking up to find himself in his pitch-black bedroom, his sheets soaked with sweat and his heart pounding in dread.

Jack untangled himself from the bedding, showered, dressed, and went to work, his mood from yesterday compounded tenfold by the nightmare he couldn't seem to shake—which vividly echoed the fact that he hadn't seen Megan since Matt Gregor had whisked her off to Gù Brath in his plane.

Jack's day continued its downward spiral when he walked into the police station and found John Bracket in their makeshift holding cell. The man had a cut on his forehead and blood on his shirt, and was hollering at Ethel to get him a lawyer.

And Jack realized he was looking at yet another monster he hadn't fully dealt with: just like a battered wife, he had hoped this particular problem would solve itself. But here it was, haunting him again.

"Did Mrs. Bracket finally press charges?" Jack asked Ethel.

"No, we did. John Bracket got in an accident on the way home from some bar in Greenville, and sent our sand truck off the road. It plunged into Pine Creek."

"How's the driver of the sand truck?"

"He's at the hospital with Simon. They both needed stitches."

"Both? What happened to Simon?"

"Bracket split open Simon's cheekbone when the boy tried to handcuff him to bring him in."

Jack bit back a curse. "If I'd pressed charges last week when Bracket punched me, this wouldn't have happened."

"It would have eventually," Ethel said. "He'd have gotten out on bail, gotten drunk again, and something just as ugly would have happened." She shrugged. "It's always the same vicious cycle."

"This particular cycle stops today. We're drawing up a list of charges that will keep him locked up for a couple of years, and pray that's long enough for him to find some religion."

"I've already done the paperwork, and a sheriff's deputy is on the way to transport John to the county jail," Ethel said, just as the phone rang. "I put your messages on your desk," she finished, picking up the phone.

Jack walked into his office, sat down at his desk, and stared at the opposite wall. It wasn't just time to *think* like his ancestors; it was time he had a heart-to-heart talk with them.

Jack's mood did an immediate one-eighty when he walked into Pine Creek PowerSports that afternoon and found Tom Cleary hunched over the partly dismantled engine of his sled. Tom actually looked like a mechanic: he was wearing clean coveralls, his hair was shorter—though it looked like his mother had cut it—and he had on safety glasses and steel-toed boots.

Paul Dempsey was hovering over the boy as if he expected Tom to pick up a sledgehammer and start thumping away.

"Will it be ready by tomorrow morning?" Jack asked, bending down to peer into the massive mess of metal.

"If I work on it all evening," Tom said without bothering to look up. He did nod toward Paul. "And if Mr. Dempsey quits telling me what to do next."

Paul harrumphed and walked to the door leading into his showroom.

Jack gave Tom a pat on the back. "There's a fifty dollar tip for you if you get it done tonight. I need my sled tomorrow morning for a run up the lake."

"It'll be ready for you," Tom said, just as he pulled a large piece of metal off the top, exposing the guts of the engine. "You just burned up a piston, is all," Tom said, shining a light down one of the four large holes. "But you didn't score the cylinder, so it'll be an easy fix."

"Thanks, Tom."

"Mr. Stone? Thank you for . . . for everything."

"You want to thank me, give half your paycheck to your mother and encourage your brothers to behave, okay? And call me Jack. You're a workingman now; you've earned the right."

"I already told Mom she could have most of my paycheck," Tom said. "And I promise the pranks will stop."

Jack gave him a nod and walked into the showroom just as Paul was flipping the Open sign in the door to Closed.

"You're a good man, Dempsey," Jack told him, climbing on one of the large red ATVs. "And smart, too, for hiring Tom. He's going to make you lots of money."

Paul puffed up a bit. "I gotta admit, I was judging the book by the cover. Everyone in town has watched those Cleary boys grow up rough-and-tumble, and I guess we're all guilty of visiting the sins of their father on them."

Jack nodded. "Giving him this chance to prove himself . . . well, you're a good man."

Paul's face reddened, and he fiddled with the price tag on the ATV Jack was sitting on, then suddenly got a sparkle in his eyes. "Say, did you know a lot of the snowmobile trails around here double as ATV trails in the summer? What are you planning to do for fun when the snow melts?"

"I'm planning to buy myself a boat and a large cooler for food and beer, and I'm going to fish this lake dry."

"Oh, man," Paul said, rushing over to a rack of brochures, pulling one out, then rushing back. "Have I got the perfect boat for you!"

Chapter Twenty-one

"You know you're certifiably crazy, don't you?" Camry said as she drove their "borrowed" trail groomer up the ski lift path of TarStone Mountain in the pitch dark. "Which means I must be crazy, too," she muttered, giving Megan a sidelong glance before turning left into a narrow cutting in the woods. "I mean, it's one thing for a panther to actually be a man, or for Robbie's dead mother to turn into a snowy owl, because that makes convoluted sense for the magic we grew up with. But a *dragon*, Meg? Hold on!" she yelped when the right track of the snowcat rolled up onto a fallen log.

Megan braced herself so she wouldn't slide into Camry. "Why not a dragon?" she asked as soon as they leveled out. "If they don't exist, where did the idea for them come from? Somebody had to have seen something that looked like a giant lizard with wings. Who could make up a creature like that?"

"The same person who made up all the mythological beasts," Camry countered. "Someone with a really warped imagination. Either that, or they smoked a lot of pot back then." She looked over at Megan. "Dragons don't exist, sis. You must have seen something else."

"Jack saw it, too. And I just know Kenzie is hiding it in one of the caves on Bear Mountain."

"You figured that out just because Kenzie smells funny?"

"That, and because when I alluded to seeing the creature, he got all guarded and suddenly had to leave."

"Exactly what are you two doing downstairs in the lab for several hours each day?" Camry asked, bobbing her eyebrows. "And how come you lock the door?"

"We're . . . doing a project together." Megan was reluctant to lie to her sister, but she was even more loath to break her promise to Kenzie. "He's working on a belated wedding gift for Matt and Winter, and I'm helping him," she explained, which wasn't all that far from the truth. "And he wants it to be a surprise."

Camry snorted. "I think he's just using that as an excuse to spend time with you."

"He says I'm like a sister to him," she countered. "And besides, he knows Jack is back in my life."

"Is Jack back in your life?" Camry asked softly. "What went on between you two the night you fell in the lake?"

"Jack saved my life."

"And you were so beholden that you slept with him, didn't you?"

In an attempt to cover up what she knew was a blistering blush, Megan grabbed the handle on the dash. "Look out!" she yelped, bracing herself for a bump that didn't come. "Sorry," she muttered, sitting back and smoothing down her hair. "I thought I saw another log in the headlights. Turn here."

"That road won't take us to Bear Mountain. The one we want is farther up."

"No, this is it. Turn left."

"But this one goes to Robbie's house."

"Then stop," Megan said, having to grab the dash handle again when Camry brought the snowcat to a sudden halt. Megan looked over at her sister, just able to make out her expression in the soft glow of the dash lights. "When was the last time you were up here?" she asked.

"Three or four years ago," Camry admitted.

"I swear this is the trail we took with the horses when Winter and I took Matt to see Bear Mountain this past fall. But the snow makes everything look different. Still, I say we turn here."

"And if it does come out at Robbie's, and he catches us?"

"He's staying at my house tonight, remember?"

Camry gave the snowcat the gas and turned left. She suddenly laughed. "This is fun, Meg, even if it is a wild goose chase. I told you sneaking out from under Mom's and Dad's noses would be just like old times."

"We shouldn't have lied to them."

Camry snorted. "Like they'd have let you go traipsing off in the woods at night after what happened up the lake. Don't worry, Chelsea will cover for us. And it makes perfect sense that we'd spend the night with her in Bangor. You do need a new laptop."

"I still feel guilty for sneaking out and then stealing the snowcat."

Camry stopped the snowcat again and looked at Megan. "So do you want me to turn back or not?"

"No! I am finding that dragon. I just wish everyone would quit trying to keep the damn thing a secret. Dad, Robbie, and Kenzie know that I understand the magic, so what are they protecting me from?"

"Maybe from Jack?" Cam speculated. "They still consider him an outsider, Meg. Maybe Dad and Robbie are afraid you'll slip up and inadvertently tell him. They haven't explained our family secret to Jack yet. Surely you remember what it was like for Heather, Elizabeth, and the other girls when they wanted to get married. Hell, Walter left Elizabeth standing at the altar. It took Robbie three days to find him, and another two days to convince him we aren't all insane."

Megan looked down at her lap. "How am I going to explain the magic to Jack?"

"You're not. Daddy and Robbie are. That's the rule."

She looked up at her sister. "But what if he thinks we're all crazy and he runs like Walter did? Jack can hide where even Robbie won't be able to find him. He's hidden practically his whole life and is obviously very good at it."

"Robbie has Matt and Winter to help him now. Jack can't hide from them." Camry leaned forward to look Megan in the eyes. "You've fallen back in love with him, haven't you?"

Megan simply nodded.

Camry pulled her into a hug. "I'm so happy for both of you." She chuckled and patted Megan's belly. "I mean for the three of you." She straightened with a groan and gave the snowcat the gas again. "So this definitely means I can't date. Your marrying Jack makes the curse six for six."

"Poor Cam," Megan said with teasing sympathy. "Don't

worry. You'll run into the right guy one of these days, and the curse will be the last thing on your mind. It happened to me, and I promise it will happen to you, too."

"But I don't want it to happen to me. I like being single. If I feel like going to bed at six in the evening, I can. And if I want to stay at work until three in the morning, I can do that too, because I don't have someone calling me every hour asking me when I'm coming home."

"No, you only have Dad giving you a hard time when you visit," Megan said with a laugh. "Here. Turn here. Dammit, we're in town!"

Camry stopped the snowcat just as they crested the snowbank of a plowed road. She looked up and down the street, then over at Megan. "It's only a quarter mile to the main road, and then a short distance to the lake. And we know Frog Cove is frozen solid; they've been driving trucks on it for the last month. I say we go for it. It'll shorten our run by at least ten miles if we just head up the cove and cut into the woods where Bear Brook comes out."

Megan involuntarily shivered. "We don't know how thick the ice is around Bear Brook."

"Then we'll go all the way up to Talking Tom's cottage on the point and then backtrack. There's a trail leading from there up to the top of Bear Mountain, isn't there?"

"Yes. But what if someone sees us going through town?"

"There are more snowmobiles than cars around here this time of year, and they'll think our snowcat is one of the club trail groomers." She started to give the machine gas, then hesitated. "Where's Jack tonight? Does he make patrols around town?"

"I have no idea what Jack is doing. Apparently he's been so busy with police work, he can't even find the time to come see me."

"There has been a bit of a crime wave lately, sis. Have you seen his police cruiser?" Camry asked with a laugh, easing the snowcat over the snowbank and onto the street. She drove down the residential lane, made a quick stop to check for traffic, then darted across Main Street and into the town park. "It doesn't matter if anyone does see us," she said as they cruised onto the lake. "They can't tell who's inside here, and if they call the resort, Thomas will cover for us."

"You're going to get that poor man fired," Megan said, looking around to see if anyone had noticed them. But it was eleven o'clock on a Tuesday night, and the town seemed deserted.

"So what's the plan if we do find ourselves nose to nose with a dragon?" Camry asked. "Did you bring some doughnuts?"

Jack stood in the middle of the Frog Point camp road and aimed his flashlight down at the lifeless body of Peter Trump, specifically at the half-inch metal spike sticking out of his back. "So he simply tripped and fell on that survey stake," Jack said, repeating what Robbie MacBain had just told him.

"He made the mistake of glancing over his shoulder to look for me," Robbie said, "and he tripped, tried to catch himself, and landed exactly like you see him."

Jack lifted his gaze. "He just . . . fell."

Robbie sighed, seemingly in an attempt to hold onto his patience. "I wanted him alive as much as you did, Stone. He's our best chance to nail Collins."

"He was. So why didn't you simply take him down at the house?"

"Because of Megan. I didn't want her coming home to a mess, if there was a struggle. Nor does she need that kind of negative energy in her new home, especially with the baby on the way. So I let him see me, knowing he'd run, and I intended to bring him down out here in the road."

"I would say your plan worked." Jack moved the flashlight beam on the ground around the body, stopping when he spotted the gun. "How come he didn't shoot you?" he asked, walking closer to stare down at it.

"I never gave him a target. He did fire his weapon as he ran out of the house. You should find a bullet lodged in the siding by the lakeside door."

"Where's *your* gun? I'll need to take it for evidence."

"I don't have one."

Jack lifted his gaze to Robbie. "I see. You expected Trump to come search Megan's house again, and you were waiting for him unarmed?"

Robbie lifted an eyebrow. "I didn't say I was unarmed, I said I don't have a gun."

Jack pulled out his cell phone with a sigh. O-kay, then. "I'm calling the state police, as they like to be in on this dead body stuff. Why don't you go to my house and make yourself comfortable, as I imagine we're both going to be here awhile. The key's under the mat."

"We need to find out if he sent Megan's laptop to Collins."

"I'll check his pockets for a hotel key or receipt. If he hasn't sent it yet, it'll be in his room or his car. If he has, we'll deal with that problem after we clean up this one."

Robbie still hesitated. "I wanted him alive, Stone."

"So did I," Jack said, speed-dialing the state police.

With a sum total of three hours of sleep in the last twenty-four, Jack finished tying his backpack down on the rear rack of his idling sled, climbed on, and headed up the lake just as the sun was breaking over Bear Mountain. He didn't have a clue where he was going; he simply trusted that he would recognize his destination when he got there. He wasn't wearing a helmet because he hadn't bothered to buy a new one, and the crisp February air would go a long way toward keeping him awake.

He still hadn't seen Megan, and he was beginning to think the gods were waiting for him to get his act together before they let him see her again. But then, she hadn't exactly been beating down his door, had she?

Oh, yeah, that's right. She was otherwise occupied, doing a mysterious favor for Kenzie Gregor—like helping him give his slimy pet a bath or something.

Jack reined in his anger, redirecting his thoughts to more pleasant things, like the sweet sound of his purring engine. He checked his speedometer and smiled when he saw he was cruising at an effortless sixty miles per hour. Young Tom Cleary was fifty bucks richer this morning, and Jack was eight hundred bucks poorer but immensely pleased.

Back on the lake on a snowmobile, Jack found his thoughts once again drifted to Megan, so he mentally went over the list of equipment he'd brought. It had been difficult packing for an unknown destination, but he felt prepared for just about anything. He'd taken climbing gear, his gut telling him he was headed for high ground, along with several wool blankets and a collapsible bucket. His equipment also included snow-shoes, his high-powered rifle, plenty of power bars, the knife his father had given him for his eighth birthday, and his hatchet.

Twenty minutes later, Jack let off the gas and hit the brake, bringing his sled to an abrupt stop when he noticed the solitary mountain rising up from the lake five or six miles ahead. It was almost a perfect dome, and he estimated it to be more than a thousand feet tall. He could see several sheer cliffs peeking through the dense evergreens covering it, and he let out a pained groan. Even though he was prepared, he'd been hoping he wouldn't have to actually climb to his destination—not on three hours of sleep.

He checked the position of the sun, guessed he'd been traveling for a little over half an hour, and realized the mountain was sitting directly at the north end of the forty-mile-long lake.

O-kay, he decided, giving his sled the gas and quickly bringing it up to speed; if his ancestors wanted him to climb, he would climb.

Which is exactly what Jack found himself doing half an hour later, though he didn't have to use a rope and harness. He'd found a faint but definitely man-made path leading up the mountain, and realized he was not the first Native American to come here searching for answers.

There was a slight hum in the air that filled Jack with a sense of peace. The higher he climbed, the stronger the hum grew, until even his bones began to vibrate in perfect harmony with an energy as ancient as time itself.

His ancestors were singing, beckoning him closer to

their circle of power. By the time he reached the top, Jack couldn't tell if he was still in his world or theirs. He stood in a small opening in the forest and looked around.

He had definitely arrived at his destination.

He slid his backpack off his shoulders with a tired groan, leaned it against a crooked old pine tree, and dug out his hatchet. He found several alder saplings growing on the edge of the clearing, apparently just waiting for someone to need them. He cut down a dozen, and carried them to the center of the opening, where he drove them in the snow in a circle about ten feet wide. He returned to his pack, got out the coil of rawhide he'd brought, and started lashing the alder tips together, forming a dome.

He pulled out the colorful, slightly tattered wool blankets next, rubbing them fondly as he breathed in their familiar scent. Vivid memories cascaded through his mind: Grand-père wrapped in his favorite blanket, huddled in front of a roaring fire, seemingly oblivious to the snow falling on and around him; three more blankets exactly like these, covering his mother and father and brother as they traveled to the afterlife; Jack's trembling body huddled inside one of them as he fought the fever the bear attack had brought on when he was twelve.

"Stop dawdling, Coyote," Grand-père whispered through the trees. "We've been waiting what seems like forever for this day. Get on with your task."

"I'm coming," Jack muttered, tossing the blankets beside the alder dome. He picked one up and shook it out, then carefully placed it over the structure, repeating the process until his shelter was completely covered.

Picking up his pace, he built a fire just a few feet from the tiny entrance he'd left in the dome. Then, while the roaring fire did its job of making glowing embers, he went in search of water. He found a bubbling spring just beyond the clearing and knew he was standing on sacred ground. The wise ones had thoughtfully provided every necessity for anyone seeking their counsel.

Jack knelt down and drank before plunging the bucket in the spring and lugging it back to the clearing. He set it beside the dome, crawled inside, and began tramping down the snow. He cut fir boughs and covered half the floor with them, then covered the boughs with one of the two remaining blankets. He went out and shoveled as many embers as he could into the dome, just inside and to the right of the door, well away from the fir boughs. He built the fire back up, poured the bucket of water over the wool blankets covering the poles to thoroughly soak them, then went back to the spring and refilled it.

He came back and crawled inside his cozy little lodge. Knowing he'd soon be awash in sweat, Jack quickly undressed, neatly folding his clothes and setting them in a pile. Then he stretched out on the blanket with his hands clasped behind his head for a pillow, closed his eyes with a sigh, and decided to have a little nap while he waited.

He woke up to a current of superheated air moving over his sweat-soaked body as several men entered the dome, led by Grand-père. His grandfather, Shadow Dreamwalker, followed, along with several other men Jack didn't recognize. He thought one was a Viking, judging from his clothes. Another one wore the suit of a Crusader, and one looked to be wearing a Civil War uniform from the northern army, if Jack wasn't mistaken.

No women, only men, and all warriors.

"Aren't there any scholars among you?" Jack muttered, sitting up when Grand-père nudged him aside to make room to sit down. The lodge continued to fill up, and Jack realized he was the only one who was naked. Apparently apparitions didn't sweat. He reached for his clothes, but the Viking was sitting on them.

"You are already in touch with your gentler ancestors," Grand-père said with a harrumph. "It's your shadow side you need to get in touch with today, Coyote."

A spot of daylight appeared near the bottom of the dome, and Jack saw his brother, Walker, wiggle under the steaming wool wall and sit quietly behind the Crusader. Walker caught Jack's eye, smiled, and gave him a wink.

"I hope you are comfortable, Coyote," Grand-père said, "because I fear this may take us awhile."

Chapter Twenty-two

It was noon the next day before Jack found himself cruising back down the lake. He felt surprisingly well rested, though his head still hurt from the rousing arguments he'd had with his ancestors, which had inevitably ended with long-winded lectures from each of them. Walker had dropped off to sleep after only two hours, and every so often Jack had glanced at his brother with envy.

When the Old Ones had finally left just before dawn, Jack nudged Walker awake, and had just finished dressing when their mother entered the lodge looking for her older son. She and Walker had sat with Jack while he'd eaten a breakfast of power bars, and they'd chatted about any number of mundane things. Jack was sad his mother hadn't brought his son for him to play with, but Jack's father was babysitting. Walker was immensely pleased to learn the baby might be named after him. Then, when Jack's eyelids had grown heavy, his mother had cradled his head in her lap and sung him to sleep.

When he'd awakened just before noon, he'd been alone and a bit chilled because the fire had long gone out. He'd quickly dismantled his makeshift shelter, hiked down the mountain to his sled, and raced toward Pine Creek with a firm resolve and a heart filled with hope.

Maybe the Old Ones did know what they were talking about when they'd explained there was no escaping his shadow; that he'd always find it right behind him, attached to his heels. And it was at that precise place of attachment, the Ancients had said, that Jack needed to focus his energy if he wished to be effectual. He couldn't walk in only one or the other; shadow and light were complementary, not adversarial.

Yeah, yeah, he got it now.

While he'd had their collective wisdom at his disposal, Jack had asked for suggestions on how he could deal with each of the current problems he was juggling. That little request had started a whole new round of arguments—between him and his ancestors, and then between the Old Ones themselves. Hopefully the results would be worth the headache.

Which was why when Jack entered Frog Cove he veered east toward the Bear Mountain shoreline instead of toward his home on Frog Point. He stopped on the lake in front of Matt and Winter Gregor's cabin, shut off his sled, and was just climbing the porch stairs when he heard a pickup pull up out back. He walked to the end of the porch just as Matt Gregor got out of the truck and spotted him.

"Chief Stone," Gregor said, coming toward him. "What can I do for you?"

It appeared Matt was a to-the-point kind of guy. Jack usually got along well with men with that quality.

"As a matter of fact, I've come to ask you for a favor," he told Matt, getting directly to the point himself. He stepped back when Gregor climbed the stairs and faced him. "I'm in need of some sort of natural disaster," Jack explained, ignoring Matt's raised eyebrow. "Nothing too big or destructive, just a simple . . . oh, earthquake, maybe?"

Matt just stared at Jack.

"It would be up on the Canadian tundra, so you don't have to worry about people getting hurt. And if you could limit its scope, even the animals should fare okay."

Matt folded his arms over his chest. "Are you drunk, Stone?"

Jack sighed. "Look, I know you don't really know me, other than what Megan may have told you. But I promise, I'm perfectly sober and admittedly desperate. Believe me, it's a hell of a lot harder for me to ask you for a favor than it will be for you to grant it."

"And this favor is a limited, nondestructive earthquake somewhere up on the Canadian tundra," Matt repeated. "May I inquire why you've come to me? I build jet engines, which have nothing to do with geological science."

"Engines don't have much to do with magic, either," Jack said. "But drùidhs are supposed to serve the good of mankind, and this earthquake will definitely be a good thing for a lot of people—especially Megan."

Matt eyed Jack with guarded interest. "*Drùidh* is a rather unusual word for you to use," he said softly.

"But one you're quite familiar with."

"Says who?"

"Say my ancestors." Jack shrugged. "And for all I

know, there may have been a few of *your* ancestors kicking around in my dream, too. Look, the bottom line is, I know you're a powerful drùidh. So I'm asking you to create a natural disaster for me, just big enough to expose the oil sitting under that tundra. Once it's common knowledge that it exists, the company Mark Collins is working for will lose its competitive edge. The Canadian government will hold on to the mineral rights, and it will be their decision what to do with that oil. Collins will no longer have any reason to come after Megan, and your father-in-law won't go after Collins. Everyone wins—except for Mark Collins and the oil company he's working for."

Matt was silent for several seconds, then quietly asked, "If you're so knowledgeable in the ways of our ancestors, why don't you simply create your own natural disaster?"

"Just because I know what needs to be done doesn't necessarily mean I can do it."

Matt continued studying Jack, this time the silence stretching interminably. "So the reason that man was murdered in Canada, and you sent Megan home, and the threat followed her here, is all because there's oil under the tundra?"

"Yup. And best as I can figure, someone hired Collins to make sure the oil wasn't discovered until they could secure the rights to that area. That's why he planted one of his students in the survey Megan was working on: to report if something was discovered. But once the government knows the oil is there, Collins will be out of a job and Megan will be safe."

"And so you need an earthquake just big enough to make the oil . . . what? Bubble up to the surface?"

Jack nodded. "The moment the seismic alarms go off, that section of tundra will be crawling with geologists. They'll find the oil, and it will be on every news station around the world by noon that day."

"You want an earthquake," Matt repeated yet again. "So that Greylen won't have to deal with Collins himself."

"Simply getting rid of Collins will only solve Megan's problem temporarily. The oil company would just hire another Mark Collins, and the new man would discover Megan was part of the original mess."

Matt nodded. "That makes sense." He looked directly at Jack. "In fact, everything you've told me so far makes sense—except that I can't quite reconcile how you're handling Megan's problem with how you're handling my brother's."

"I gave Kenzie a week, and I'll honor my promise," Jack told Matt. "So instead of brewing a storm cloud over my head, why don't you wave your magic wand and send that slimy beast back where it came from?"

"Because Kenzie has asked me not to."

Great. Just damn great. "So anything the brother of a powerful drùidh wants, he gets? Even if it means a dragon is running around Pine Creek, breaking into shops? What happens when someone is working late in one of those shops? Are you willing to tempt fate just to indulge your brother?"

Matt laughed, though he sounded anything but amused. "Hell, Stone, I all but sold my soul for Kenzie. Tell me, what lengths would you go to for Megan and your son? Or for any member of your family? Would you be willing to walk through the fires of hell for them?"

"I already have." Jack turned and walked off the porch toward his snowmobile. He stopped on the edge of the shoreline and looked back. "The sooner that earthquake happens, Cùram, the better for all of us. And I'd appreciate it if we could keep this little matter between ourselves."

"Megan hasn't told you about the magic yet," Matt stated. He suddenly lifted one brow. "Or is it you who haven't told her yet, Coyote?"

Jack smiled. "We'll both get there eventually."

Matt nodded. "Then I will keep this between us. And I will stay out of your matter with Kenzie, as well. My brother must walk his own path, just as you must walk yours." Then he grinned at Jack. "Keep your television tuned to the news tomorrow morning, Stone, and see what happens when shadow and light work in harmony."

Jack gave Matt a wave and walked down the steep shoreline to his sled. O-kay. Either he'd just put Canada on the map as the newest nation to give OPEC a run for its money, or he'd turned it into the next world disaster-relief recipient.

He zoomed across the cove and up onto his lawn, grabbed his pack, and headed around the house to his porch, taking the steps two at a time. He opened the screen door and spotted an envelope taped to the window.

He dropped his pack, tore open the envelope, and read the invitation written in Megan's bold scrawl.

YOU ARE INVITED TO GÙ BRATH AT SIX TONIGHT.

Jack shoved the note between his teeth, unlocked the door, picked up his backpack, and walked into his house with an eager smile. Nothing like ignoring a girl for a few days to get her to take matters into her own hands. Maybe after dinner with the parents, he'd take his little warrior for a moonlight stroll and see if she wanted to rip off his clothes again.

Chapter Twenty-three

𝒟inner turned out to be a birthday party for Elizabeth's youngest boy, with nearly every kid in town in attendance. Grace told Jack he was welcome to join the adults in the living room; no, he wasn't expected to bring a present; yes, Megan was around someplace. "Feel free to hunt her down," Grace had offered just as the birthday boy—Joel, Jack thought his name was—demanded his gram's attention in the kitchen. Apparently there was a major crisis over the cake's looking like Big Bird instead of Curious George.

Feeling a bit overdressed in the tie and blazer he wore under his police jacket, Jack lingered in the huge foyer of the MacKeage fortress for several minutes, working up the courage to venture into the chaos. In that time he witnessed no fewer than a dozen kids, ranging in age from five to thirteen, sliding down the curving banister at breakneck speeds—with no adult to supervise them. The kids did appear to have a method to their madness, though. The older ones slid down first; then one stayed at the bottom to catch the younger kids while the others guarded the youngsters sliding past them on their way back up the stairs to do it all again.

Several other girls and boys came charging down the hallway with wooden swords, engaged in a fierce battle over a confused but definitely excited puppy. Jack scooped up one of the female combatants just as she was about to be flattened by an older kid catapulting off the end of the banister. He swung the toddler up against his chest and found himself face-to-face with beauty personified—wielding a sword as long as she was tall.

"Poweeceman," the girl said, patting the badge on his jacket. She used her sword, smacking him in his head, to point at the ongoing battle. "Save Puddles."

"You'll probably need several pair of handcuffs in order to do that," Camry said with a laugh, taking the girl from him. "Which one are you?" she asked the toddler.

"I'm Peyton, Aunt Campy," the girl said, putting her hands on her hips in disgust—her sword missing Jack only because he managed to duck.

Camry laughed and set her down, then patted her bottom to send her on her way. "Go save Puddles yourself," she instructed. "We MacKeage women fight our own battles, young lady."

The girl took off after the disappearing mob of young clansmen, her sword held over her head as she let out a battle cry that shook the rafters.

Before Jack could say hello or ask where Megan was, Camry slipped her arm through his and dragged him into the chaos. "Come on, Jack. Let's get you a drink."

* * *

Completely oblivious to the party going on outside her
father's office, Megan sat perfectly rigid, hugging herself in an attempt to still the tremors forming deep in
her stomach. If she didn't move, didn't breathe, didn't
feel, maybe she wouldn't turn into a bottomless pit of
anguish.

"Who told you this?" she asked Carl Franks of Franks
Investigations.

"You said you wanted a thorough report," Carl told
her, shifting uncomfortably in his chair across the desk.
"So I found the driver of the logging truck who hit
them. I got his name off the accident report and found
him living down in Edmonton, Alberta. He's around
seventy-five now, but he certainly remembered the accident. He never got behind the wheel of a rig after that
day. I was surprised he was even willing to talk to me
about it. It was obviously still painful for him."

Megan hugged herself tighter to stave off the tears
welling up inside her. "And he told you Jack watched
his family burn up? His mom and dad and brother?"

Carl nodded. "Seems Mr. Stone had pulled his car
onto the side of the road because his two boys were
fighting in the backseat. The younger boy had punched
the older one and given him a bloody nose, so the
father gave the kid a time-out under a tree. The truck
driver's load of logs shifted when he came around the
curve a bit too fast, and when he tried to get his rig
under control, he ended up slamming into the back of
the Stones's car. He told me both vehicles burst into
flames. That's when he spotted this kid running out of
the woods, and had to pull him away when the boy
went to open the door of the mangled car." Carl shook
his head. "The driver figured they were dead, because

there wasn't much left of their vehicle and he couldn't see any movement inside. But the boy fought him, kicking and screaming, and continued trying to get to his family. The kid burned his hands, and the driver eventually dragged him half a mile down the road, back around the curve so they couldn't see the accident. He had to practically tie him down while they waited for another vehicle to come along."

Megan used her shirt sleeve to wipe the tears running down her cheeks. "And the accident report said the boy's name was Coyote Stone?" she asked, her throat raw with emotion.

Carl Franks stood up and grabbed the booklet he'd laid in front of her, then paced to the hearth, sticking a finger inside his collar to loosen his tie. He opened the neatly typed report, and leafed through the pages.

"Coyote Stone was brought to Edmonton, and a social worker there changed his name to Jack in hopes it would help him get adopted. But the boy," Carl said, looking up then quickly back at his report, "who was nine at the time, just up and disappeared from his foster home. They found him ten days later walking along a road that headed north." He looked up again, shaking his head in wonder. "The kid had made it halfway to Medicine Lake. They put him in several more foster homes after that, but he ran away from all of them. There's speculation that his great-grandfather helped him the last time. They never saw Jack Stone again until he was fifteen," Carl said, no longer reading his report. "But when they placed him in a foster home that time, he disappeared again and didn't turn up until I found a record of him having joined the Canadian military at age twenty."

Carl walked over and set the report back on the desk in front of her. "Everything's in there, Miss MacKeage. I did exactly as you asked and was very thorough. The only thing I couldn't discover is what Jack Stone did in the military. Those five years are classified information." He started edging toward the door. "I'll just send you a bill, okay? I'll let myself out," he said, going out the door.

Megan stared at the report, no longer bothering to wipe the tears flowing down her face. Jack had never lied to her about his childhood; he'd merely left out the heart-wrenching details. She hugged her belly, suddenly deciding she *would* name their son Walker, after Coyote Stone's older brother.

What must go through a nine-year-old's mind after witnessing something like that? Did he blame himself for their deaths, because his father had stopped to give him a time-out for fighting? Was that why he was a self-proclaimed pacifist?

And those ten days he'd spent trying to get to his great-grandfather . . . how had he eaten? Where had he slept? He had to have hitched rides with people; who would pick up a nine-year-old kid and not call the police?

There was a knock on the door just before it opened. "Some guy told me I'd find you in here," Jack said, walking up to the desk. "Is there a reason you didn't warn me about—Megan! What's the matter?" he asked, rushing around the desk and hunching down in front of her. "You're crying. Why? What did that man say to you?"

The dam holding back her emotions exploded, and Megan threw herself into Jack's arms with a wailed sob and clung to him fiercely.

"Megan! What's wrong, sweetheart?" he asked, holding her tightly. "Tell me what's wrong!"

"M-my answer's yes, Jack," she said between sobs. "Yes, I'll marry you. Tomorrow, if you want. Or right now. W-we'll find Father Daar and get married tonight."

"And this is making you cry?" he asked with a chuckle, trying to lean away to look in her eyes. But when she wouldn't stop clinging, he sighed softly and just held her, her head tucked under his chin as he gently swayed them in a rocking motion. "Okay, then," he whispered into her hair. "We'll get married first thing tomorrow morning." He tried once more to see her face, this time succeeding. "What brought this on all of a sudden? And why is your decision to marry me making you cry?"

Megan tried to regain her composure; she really, truly tried. But when she pictured the man in front of her as a little boy watching . . . "You watched your family die!" she wailed, burying her face in his shirt again.

He went perfectly still. "What are you talking about?" he whispered tightly. "What's going on?"

"I kn-know the whole story," she sobbed. "About the accident, and how you tried to save them. The truck driver even told Frank how he dragged you down the road to get you away from—Oh God, it must have been horrible!"

Jack took hold of her shoulders and forcibly set her away from him. Megan shuddered, blinking through her tears, and saw him pick up the report sitting on the desk. He silently thumbed through it, his face completely void of expression. "You sent someone to Medicine Lake to investigate me?" he asked ever so softly, stopping at one particular page for several seconds, then moving on. He finally brought his gaze back to her. "You couldn't have just asked me?"

His eyes were distant, and Megan felt a cold, bottomless fissure open between them.

"No, wait, I forgot. You don't believe anything I tell you." He tossed the report down on the desk, the soft sound making Megan flinch. "I just remembered I have stuff to do tomorrow," he told her. "So I guess the wedding's off. Not that I'm in a hurry to hitch myself to a woman who doesn't trust me—much less one who's marrying me out of pity."

He turned and headed for the door.

"Jack, wait!" Megan cried, grabbing the report and running over to the hearth, where she tossed it onto the glowing embers. "I haven't even read it. I don't need to anymore!"

"It doesn't matter," he said, quietly closing the door behind him.

Megan chased after him but he was already down the hall, and she had to wrestle her way through a mob of children before she finally reached the front door just as it was closing. She wrenched it open and ran onto the bridge spanning the rippling brook below. "Jack! Wait! Please wait!" she pleaded.

He stopped at the end of the bridge and turned to face her.

"I'm sorry. I didn't trust you when you first came here, so I hired someone to check out your story. But I trust you now, Jack. I burned the report because I trust you."

"Really? Enough to tell me what the favor is you're doing for Kenzie?" he asked, his emotionless voice carrying across the expanse between them.

"Please don't ask me that," she pleaded, stepping toward him, her hand outstretched. "I-I gave him my word."

"And your little ride to Bear Mountain last night with your sister?" he asked. "Did you promise not to tell me about that, either?"

She took a step back, bumping into the door.

"I'm chief of police, sweetheart. You don't think I'd hear about a TarStone Resort snowcat roaming through town in the wee hours of the morning? So where'd you and Camry go until six this morning?"

Silence spanned the distance between them.

"I see," he said finally. "Funny how trust can be selective." He touched his fingers to his forehead in a brief salute. "I'll see you around town."

At that, he turned and walked off into the night.

Megan watched until he disappeared into the shadows, then went back inside, running past the people heading to the dining room as her mother carried in the cake. She ran up the stairs to her childhood bedroom, threw herself down on her bed, and stared up at the ceiling, unable even to cry.

She'd hurt Jack badly. She'd seen it in his eyes and heard it in his voice, and feared he was so wounded, he might never be able to forgive her.

The door opened and her mother walked in, quietly lay down on the bed beside her, and also stared up at the ceiling in silence.

"I've really done it this time, Mama," Megan whispered into the moon-softened darkness. "I think I broke his heart tonight." She turned her head toward her mother. "Will I be able to mend it, the way he did mine?"

"I don't know, baby. Women are more resilient than men are in matters of the heart, because hope is the very fabric of our being. If it wasn't, the human race would have died out several hundred generations ago, since we wouldn't have brought children into a world wrought with war, hunger, pain, and heartache." Grace looked over and smiled sadly. "But men . . . men aren't as lucky. For them, everything seems to be cut and dried. Black and white. All or nothing."

"I told Jack I trusted him, but when he asked me about Kenzie and the dragon, I couldn't tell him."

"Why not?"

"Because I promised I wouldn't."

"And your promise to Kenzie is more important than your love for Jack?"

Megan rolled onto her side and propped herself up on one elbow to face her mother. "Are you saying I should have broken my promise?"

"I'm saying that you shouldn't have given your promise to Kenzie to begin with. He asked you for a favor, and that you keep it between yourselves, but you were under no obligation to go along with his terms. You could have told Kenzie that Jack came first in your life."

"But he wasn't really in my life at the time."

"And when he was? Did you tell Kenzie you could no longer keep his secret? That you'd either have to stop whatever your favor is, or tell Jack about it?"

Megan threw herself onto her back again, blinking up at the ceiling. "I hadn't thought about that. Kenzie dictated the terms of the favor, and I just blindly went along with it." She frowned over at her mother. "I am such an easy mark. I want everyone to like me, and I can't live with myself if they don't. Look at how much I covered for Winter this past fall when she was fooling around with Matt." She sighed and stared back up at the ceiling. "I can see now that my heart wasn't anywhere near as broken as I let on when I came home. I knew deep down inside that Jack had sent me away for a good reason, but I still carried on like an idiot." She looked at her mother again. "I was afraid everyone would think I was a failure for running home to my parents, pregnant and without a husband."

Grace laughed softly. "You did cry a lot." She propped her head up on her hand and squeezed Megan's arm. "But the only person who has to like you is the man you love, baby. If your heart belongs to Jack Stone, then he is your priority. He should have your unconditional trust, respect, and total devotion. And Jack strikes me as the sort of man who would return those qualities in spades, given the chance."

"He would," Megan whispered. "So how do I fix it?"

"You start by telling Kenzie you can no longer abide by the conditions of his favor, and that if he wants to continue whatever it is the two of you are doing down in the lab every day, then he has to let you tell Jack. If not, then you can't continue to help him."

"And the dragon?"

"You stop pussyfooting around that damn thing and tell Jack everything you know about it."

"But that would be telling him about the magic. And the rule is, Daddy and Robbie have to tell him."

Grace gave Megan a motherly smile and patted her arm. "The day you gave away your heart, your responsibility to your father transferred to Jack. The men in this family might *want* to control every situation, but that doesn't mean we have to let them." She sighed. "I still say Walter wouldn't have panicked if Elizabeth had been the one to tell him our family history. It's much less intimidating for a man to hear something like that from the woman he loves instead of from his future father-in-law—especially when that happens to be Grey."

"But how do I tell Jack?"

"With love, baby," she said, patting her arm again. "And timing. You pick the proper time and place, preferably right after he's eaten. Men are much more agreeable when their bellies are full."

Megan sighed. "Thanks, Mama. I think I get it now."

"Do you? Because it's not as simple as walking up to Jack and reciting a laundry list of all your secrets. You not only have to trust him completely, you're going to have to make him feel that he can trust you with his secrets."

Megan scrunched up her face at her mother. "And if he won't tell me his secrets?"

"Then it's not really love, is it? That's how your heart knows it's the real thing," Grace said, slipping a strand of Megan's hair behind her ear. "Along with trust, devotion, and respect, you also need intimacy between you. Those are the four cornerstones your love should stand on."

"Like you and Daddy. Do you think Jack and I will have what the two of you have thirty-four years from now?"

"Yes," Grace said, rolling off the bed and standing up. "Why don't you stay here tonight, rather than going back to your house? You and Camry must be tired from your ride up Bear Mountain last night."

Megan sat up with a snort. "How does everyone know about that?" Her eyes widened in alarm. "Does Daddy know?"

"Does it matter?" Grace asked, walking to the door.

"It's not your father you must answer to now, but Jack." She arched one eyebrow when Megan opened her mouth to protest. "Are you about to tell me you wouldn't mind if Jack snuck off in the middle of the night without telling you?"

"Of course I'd mind."

Grace nodded. "You're not seeking permission like a child, Megan—you're discussing something you feel strongly about. There's a huge difference between the two, and it goes a long way to creating an equal and honest relationship."

"I get it. Truly. Go back to the party before the cake's all gone."

"You'll be okay?"

"I'll be just peachy," she said, lying back down and folding her hands over her belly with a smile. "Walker and I are going to lie here and figure out how we're going to explain the magic to Jack."

"Walker?"

"I'm having a boy, and we're naming him after Jack's brother, Walker."

Grace rushed back to the bed and gave her a huge hug. "Congratulations! Your father is going to be so excited to have another grandson."

"Let's not tell him just yet, okay? Or else he'll spend the next three months trying to talk Jack into changing his last name to MacKeage." She shook her head. "Just like he's tried with every son-in-law who gave him a grandson."

Grace walked back to the door. "He almost got Walter to change his name," she said with a laugh. "Until Elizabeth and I sat Walter down and explained that he wouldn't be turned into a toad if he didn't." She

opened the door. "Walker. I like that. Walker Stone."
She smiled. "Maybe Walker MacKeage Stone?"

"Maybe. Though I'm leaning more toward Walker
Coyote Stone," Megan said, laughing at her mother's
puzzled look. "I'll tell you why once I clear it with my
future husband."

After all, her first obligation was to Jack.

Chapter Twenty-four

$\mathscr{J}$ack turned up the volume on the television, then returned to packing his gear as he listened to the news. The Great Discovery, which had happened three days ago, was still making the headlines. Canada certainly was on everyone's map now.

And Cùram de Gairn was a lot more powerful than Jack had realized, not to mention a genius. There had been a small natural disaster, all right, but it hadn't been crude oil that had bubbled to the surface. Instead the earthquake had spawned several frothing geysers of the purest, sweetest water ever discovered, from what was being referred to as the largest subterranean aquifer in the world. And the upside was the First Nation People living in that area were scrambling to bottle the clear liquid gold for international export.

Jack buckled his pack shut, then walked over and picked up his rifle. He opened and closed the breech to double-check that the weapon wasn't loaded, then replaced the regular scope with a night-vision scope. He slipped the rifle into the sheath attached to his pack, then clicked the remote to turn off the television before heading into his bedroom to change.

He wasn't proud that he'd been avoiding Megan for the last three days, as well as ignoring the three notes she'd left taped to his door asking him to dinner three nights in a row—including tonight. But until this dragon business was settled one way or another, he was in no frame of mind to deal with their relationship.

Assuming there was a relationship to salvage when he got back. Killing the dragon would likely drive the last nail into the coffin of his and Megan's future, which meant he was about to condemn himself to weekend visits with his son.

Kenzie's time was up and Jack hadn't heard anything, though the man had kept his promise that there wouldn't be any more break-ins. In fact, the police business had been downright slow lately. It might have something to do with the two-foot snowstorm two days ago, or maybe the small army of state police cruisers in town all week investigating Peter Trump's death had put a damper on crime. Ethel certainly wasn't complaining. And Simon was back on the job, sporting four stitches on his left cheekbone. He was all but strutting around, having discovered that a facial scar received in the line of duty was a total chick magnet.

Dressed in thin long johns and clothes that afforded him easy movement, Jack grabbed his gear and headed out to his snowmobile. He secured his pack to the rear of his sled, started it up, and raced across the cove toward Bear Mountain, veering north to land well away from Matt and Winter's cabin.

It was maybe an hour shy of sunset, and Jack wanted to start his trek up the mountain while he still had some daylight left. He reached shore at a point of land where a crooked old cabin was tucked in the pines, and parked between it and an even more rickety shed. Settling his pack on his back, he slipped into his snowshoes, pulled out his rifle and loaded it, then found a trail heading up the mountain on the other side of the shed. The trail looked plenty wide enough for a snowcat to maneuver up. But no one had been here since the snowstorm; the only tracks he saw were from four-legged creatures.

So where, he wondered as he trudged up the mountain, would he choose to live if he were a dragon?

Megan heard the snowmobile start up and immediately ran to the lakeside window, where to her dismay she saw Jack heading onto the lake. She gasped when she noticed what looked like a rifle sticking out of his backpack; she ran out on her deck and uselessly shouted at him as he zoomed away.

"Dammit to hell, Jack," she cried, watching helplessly as he shot across the cove toward where Talking Tom's cabin stood empty. "How do you always know exactly where to go?" She rushed back inside and dialed Camry's cell phone.

"You need to meet me at the resort's garage right now," she said when Camry picked up, not even giving her a chance to say hello. "We have to borrow the snowcat again and get up to the cave! Jack just left on his snowmobile in the direction of Bear Mountain, and he's got a rifle with him. I'll meet you there in ten minutes."

"You think he's hunting the dragon?"

"Kenzie's week is up. Where else would Jack be going with a rifle?"

"But we'll never get there in time, Meg. And it's not five o'clock yet, so the garage will be full of workers. I can't just waltz in and take one of the groomers. Besides, you said Jack took his snowmobile. He'll be there before we can even get the snowcat started."

"His sled does okay on the wind-packed lake, but it isn't designed for the powdered snow he'll find in the woods. He's going to have to snowshoe up the mountain, and then he still has to find the cave. Just steal the damn thing when no one is looking. We have to get up to the cave *now*!"

"Okay, okay. But meet me where Matt's road hits the main road instead of at the garage. I'll grab the snowcat, head straight through town, and we'll approach the cave from the opposite direction. If we're lucky, we'll get there before him." There was a sudden pause. "Um . . . then what?"

"Then I guess I introduce Jack to William."

The trail Jack was following broke into a high meadow just as the sun set over the mountains on the west side of Pine Lake. The first thing he noticed was the construction going on at the top of the meadow, where a cliff jutted more than a hundred feet above the trees. He also heard gushing water on the other side and knew it was Bear Brook making its way down to the lake.

Jack also felt a bracing energy humming through the air, and realized he was looking at the future home of Megan's sister and brother-in-law. He remembered now that Megan had said Winter and Matt were living in the cabin by the lake only until their house was finished.

Which looked to be a couple of years away at least, judging by the size of the foundation tucked against the cliff, as if they were going to make the sheer granite wall part of their home.

If he were a dragon, he wouldn't live anywhere near a construction site that was bustling with workers all day. So where, Jack wondered as he scanned the mountaintop, would he want his lair to be? It should be high enough to see anything approaching, preferably a cave, or at least an outcropping of ledge for shelter, probably with a southern exposure.

Jack scanned the meadow again in the waning twilight, aware of the absence of tracks large enough to belong to the creature he and Megan had seen on the lake. But then, Kenzie had said the dragon was sick, so maybe the beast was already dead.

Hoping he was that lucky, Jack started up the northern tree line of the meadow. A half hour and a couple of miles later, he came to a groomed snowmobile trail. He stopped and took out his water bottle for a long drink while deciding in which direction to go.

Not wanting to risk meeting any snowmobilers who might wonder what he was doing up here at night carrying a rifle, Jack continued straight across the trail and plunged back into the woods before turning south, aiming toward another sheer cliff he could see in the distance.

He was closing in on it about an hour later when he stopped and went perfectly still. There was just the slightest of breezes, but it was enough to carry the faint scent of the slime he'd found at the break-ins. Since he was heading into the breeze, Jack knew he was going in the right direction.

Despite it being totally dark out but for the moonlight filtering through the trees, he quickened his pace, bringing his rifle to his chest and working the bolt to slide a shell into the chamber. He kept his finger on the safety and his eyes semifocused to watch for movement.

The smell grew slightly stronger as he got closer to the cliff. But it was another twenty minutes before he found a well-trodden path, which he followed directly up to an opening in the cliff. Jack stopped just outside the entrance to the cave, quietly slipped out of his snowshoes, and listened for any sounds within.

Not hearing anything, he quietly stepped into the mouth of the mountain. There was a good chance Kenzie Gregor was inside, and an even better chance the man would do everything in his power to stop Jack from killing the dragon.

Using his rifle to lead the way, with one finger on the safety and another on the trigger, he silently inched deeper into the winding cave. He was just reaching in his pocket for a small penlight when he realized that instead of getting darker the farther he got from the entrance, it was actually getting lighter. The smell of kerosene and wood smoke mixed with the foul odor of slime.

Damn, the dragon wasn't alone.

The winding corridor he'd been following suddenly opened into a cavernous room so tall he couldn't see the ceiling, and large enough that he could just barely see the far end. Light from a small fire reflected off the dark walls, and several lamps were strategically placed on ledges. But it wasn't the dragon curled up on a large nest of straw that nearly brought Jack to his knees.

No, it was seeing Megan sitting next to the beast.

Kenzie was nowhere in sight; Megan was completely alone with the creature, and utterly defenseless. Jack raised the butt of his rifle to his shoulder. "Slowly move away from it, Megan," he said softly, walking to the center of the cavern. "Please, sweetheart, just stand up and back away."

She turned at the sound of his voice but didn't seem overly surprised to see him. She did stand up, but instead of backing away, she stepped directly between Jack and his target.

"His name is William Killkenny," she said. "And he's a nobleman from ninth-century Ireland."

Jack lowered the barrel of his rifle but kept the butt at his shoulder.

"He's here because he heard that Kenzie might be able to help him become a man again." She glanced over her shoulder when the dragon groaned in his sleep. "A witch turned him into a dragon to teach him a lesson," she said, lowering her voice and stepping closer, though she stayed between Jack and the beast. "It seems William burned her cottage in the forest because he thought she was disrupting his hunting. In retaliation she put a curse on him, claiming that until he learned how to treat defenseless old women, William Killkenny would roam the earth as a monster."

"Know why a dragon?" Camry asked, walking around Jack, her arms full of straw. She set it down next to the sleeping beast, then stood beside her sister. "Because back in the ninth century, dragons were everyone's worst nightmare. Even though they're mythological, they were the big, bad boogeyman parents used to keep their children from straying into the woods. So instead of turning William into a frog or something, she turned him into a nightmare."

"Which doesn't make sense, when you think about it," Kenzie Gregor said, walking past Jack. He was carrying two buckets of water, which he set down by the fire before going to stand beside Megan and Camry. "It's impossible for a man to make amends when he's a frightening creature, since no one will let him get close enough to give him the chance."

Jack could only stare at the three of them in silence. Did they honestly expect him to believe the dragon was a ninth-century nobleman, much less that he'd *traveled through time* to get here?

"I know what we're telling you is unbelievable," Megan said, stepping closer, her large green eyes shining with . . . aww hell, she looked close to tears. "Which is why I've been so reluctant to say anything to you." She stopped directly in front of him. "You see, my whole family is . . . well, we're sort of . . . different. The magic is *real*, Jack. My father and Callum and Morgan, and Robbie's father, Michael, are from twelfth-century Scotland. And Matt and Kenzie are from the tenth century."

For the life of him, Jack still couldn't say anything.

Megan rubbed her arms as if chilled, though it had to be near eighty degrees in the cave. "You have my word that our baby will be normal, just like you and me. I don't possess the magic, I'm only a child of it. As are Camry and all my sisters, except Winter. Winter is . . . she's a . . ."

"She's a drùidh," Camry said. "And so is Matt. And the old priest who lives up on TarStone used to be a drùidh until he turned his power over to Winter. Father Daar's real name is Pendaär, and he's eighteen hundred years old. He's also the reason we're all here, if you ask me."

"You told us your great-grandfather was a shaman, Jack," Megan said, looking utterly vulnerable. "You must have seen the magic at work. Things had to have happened that you didn't understand and couldn't explain." She gestured toward the dragon. "William is just one of those things. He shouldn't exist, but he does. And for him to die as a dragon would be tragic.

"Please don't kill him, Jack," she whispered. "Help us save him, instead. If you possess even an ounce of your great-grandfather's gift, or if you can just remember what herbs he used, please help us save William so he can live long enough to learn his lesson." She reached out and touched Jack's chest, tears running down her cheeks. "He deserves to die as a man, not as the nightmare he is."

Jack blew out a deep sigh, wondering what had made him think he could have killed the dragon even if no one had been here when he found it.

"I won't kill him," he said, holding his rifle out from his side.

Megan threw herself against his chest with a sob of relief. "I'm sorry," she whispered, hugging him tightly. "I've been an idiot for not telling you before now. I-I was scared."

"Of what?"

She looked up into his eyes. "I was afraid you'd think I was . . . that I was too weird to love," she said with a sob, burying her face back in his chest.

He tucked her head under his chin and held her, watching as Camry and Kenzie—who looked decidedly uncomfortable—got busy all of a sudden. Kenzie poured one of the buckets of water into a pot and set it in the fire, and Camry, making a disgusted face, picked up the dragon's tail and stuffed straw under it.

O-kay. He wasn't going to kill the beast, but was he going to help them save it?

"Megan's been teaching me how to read," Kenzie said, somewhat defensively.

"To *read*?" Camry echoed, spinning around in surprise. "*That's* the big secret? But that's not something to be ashamed of. You live in this century now, Kenzie, and if you can't read, you'll be at a huge disadvantage."

Jack asked, "Gregor, what happens if I do manage to save your smelly friend? What's to stop him from breaking into the shops again? I imagine a healthy dragon won't be easy to control."

"I've already decided to leave Pine Creek," Kenzie said, his expression hopeful. "My calling is not here in the mountains. I'm afraid William Killkenny is only the first of many displaced souls who will be seeking me out in hopes I can help them transition back into human form."

"Why would displaced souls think you can help them?" Jack asked in surprise.

"Because up until this past winter solstice, I was just like William. I've led countless lives as various animals, though never as a mythological creature." He eyed Jack directly. "If I can get William well again, I intend to take him and the old priest with me, to find a new home of our own. Somewhere by the sea, I'm thinking."

Megan broke free, catching Jack by surprise. "You're leaving?" she cried. "But why?

"Because I must, lass. Destiny is calling me." He smiled at her. "But Maine has a wonderfully rugged coast, I've heard, much like Scotland's. I'll still be close enough for you to visit."

Jack slid back the bolt of his rifle, emptied the chamber and magazine, and put the bullets in his pocket. He slid off his backpack, took off his jacket, and rolled up his sleeves as he walked over to where the dragon was sleeping.

He visually inspected the horse-size creature from nose to tail, noticing the slime oozing out from under its scales like sweat. It was a decidedly strange-looking animal, now that he was seeing it close up. It looked . . . well, it looked exactly like a nightmare *should* look.

The beast had pointed ears about the size of a man's hand, with two short appendages between them similar to giraffes'. Its head was shaped like a horse's, only its snout flared to huge nostrils. It had scales for skin, like a fish or snake, which directly contradicted the slime. Unless the foul-smelling stuff was a form of sweat, and the beast was already sick at the time of the break-ins.

Jack took hold of its nose and peeled back its lip to see inside its mouth. The gravely ill dragon never even opened its eyes. Jack sat down beside it, placing his hand on its side where he thought the heart should be. Feeling a strong, powerful thump, he slid his hand along its torso, stopping at its distended belly, and felt a violent, gurgling rumble under the scales. He wiped his hands on the straw before turning to the silent threesome watching him expectantly.

"Okay, Gregor," he said, "I need you to find me a few things in the forest."

When Gregor nodded, Jack looked at Camry. "How did you and Megan get here tonight?"

"By snowcat. It's parked a couple hundred yards away."

"Good. I need you to go to my house and get a few things. Under my bed is an old leather satchel. Could you get it and some of the old wool blankets in the closet in my bedroom?"

Camry nodded.

"And while you're there, grab the six-pack of beer out of the fridge." He eyed the dragon, then sighed. "I think we may be in for a long night."

Camry ran out of the cave. Jack rattled off a list of plants that Kenzie should be able to find in the woods in the middle of winter. "You might have to dig in the snow for some of them. Will you recognize the plants I just named when you see them?"

Kenzie also nodded, grabbed the empty bucket, and strode out the cave entrance. Jack wiped his hands on his pants again as he walked over to Megan, and took hold of her shoulders.

"I intend to go to my grave claiming I'm not a shaman," he told her. "But I do seem to . . . know stuff." He pulled her into his embrace. "Thank you for trusting me with your family secret."

"My father and Robbie would have told you before we got married," she said into his shirt. She leaned back and looked at him. "We *are* still getting married, aren't we?"

"Well, I don't know," he said, giving her a lopsided grin. "I'm still waiting for you to propose to me."

"For *me* to propose? But I'm a traditional girl. You have to do the asking, and I'm supposed to decide whether or not you deserve me."

Jack choked on a laugh. "Traditional?" he sputtered. "There isn't one traditional bone in—"

She grabbed his cheeks and squished them together to shut him up, and pulled his head down to give him a kiss that was anything but traditional. In fact, it was downright hot. And needy. And really quite demanding.

Deserve her? Hell no, he didn't deserve her, but he sure as hell wasn't about to tell *her* that.

A loud, rumbling groan came from the bed of straw, and Megan finally broke the kiss and buried her blushing face in his chest. Jack held her tightly against him and chuckled. "You want to know what's really wrong with William?" he asked, gently rocking her back and forth as he eyed the restless dragon.

"What?" she asked into his shirt.

"William Killkenny is paying the price for his crimes. He's got a bellyache."

She popped her head up and blinked at him. "A bellyache? You mean he's not dying?"

"I'm not saying he couldn't," Jack said. "If he truly is from the ninth century, then he's not used to modern food, especially doughnuts and candy bars. Not only has he stuffed himself full of refined sugar, he's taken in a fair amount of modern chemicals and preservatives, which his ancient system doesn't know how to digest."

"Then how are we going to cure him?" Megan asked, looking as if she already knew the answer and didn't like it.

"We clean out his innards."

She backed away, shaking her head. "Oh, no. We are not giving him an . . ."

Jack burst out laughing. He walked to the fire, grabbed a stick, and lifted the pot of boiling water out of the flames. "No, I think we can avoid that particular procedure. We'll just steep some herbal tea, get it down his throat, and wait for nature to run its course." He laughed at her horrified expression. "Hey, that sort of thing doesn't make you queasy, does it? Because in about three months, you're going to be experiencing it firsthand—although on a decidedly smaller scale."

She lifted her chin. "I've been babysitting little Angus for Robbie and Catherine all fall, and I've changed dozens of diapers." She got a sudden gleam in her eyes and stepped toward him, lowering her voice. "But let's not tell Camry exactly what we're doing, okay? Let's just surprise her."

Jack grinned broadly. "Oh, don't worry, we won't tell Camry. Or Kenzie."

Chapter Twenty-five

It was late the next afternoon before a very silent Camry stopped the snowcat in front of Megan's home, and an equally silent Jack and Megan climbed out. But just as soon as Camry drove off—speeding straight down the camp road toward Main Street—they both burst out laughing.

"When I'm ninety years old," Megan chortled, "I'll still remember the look on Cam's face when she finally realized what was happening."

"She sure can move fast when she needs to," Jack said, his arm coming around Megan's shoulders as he guided her up the porch stairs.

"We are sooo going to pay for this," she said, turning the doorknob, only just now realizing that she hadn't locked up when she'd left in such a hurry yesterday. Was it really less than twenty-four hours ago? It seemed like a lifetime, she was so tired. "Do you think they'll be able to get the smell out of the snowcat?" she asked with a giggle.

Jack pulled her to a halt just as she started to open the door. "Whoa. You won't get the smell out of your house if you go in there with your clothes on."

"You want to undress out here?" she squeaked, looking around.

Jack started peeling off her jacket. "The only other person living out on this point is the chief of police," he drawled, tossing her jacket in the porch corner, then grabbing the hem of her sweater. "And I'm pretty sure it's his sworn duty to protect your modesty," he continued as he pulled her stinky sweater over her head.

Megan shuddered when the foul smell brushed over her nose. Since he was doing such a fine job of undressing her, she decided to do the same for him. But he captured her hands when she tried to unzip his jacket, and held them to his chest.

"If I go in with you, I'm not leaving until tomorrow morning," he told her, his steel blue eyes locked on hers.

She wiggled free and unzipped his jacket. "I imagine your house is quite cold by now," she said, slipping the jacket off his shoulders. She let it fall to the porch and immediately started undoing the buttons on his shirt. "And I have this really big hot water heater, so we can scrub each other silly without worrying about running out of hot water." She sent his shirt after his jacket. "And I've always wondered what it would be like to sleep in a real bed with you."

He swiftly pulled her undershirt off over her head. "Okay, get ready. We'll strip down to our underwear, then get in the house before our skin figures out it's suppose to goose-bump."

She had to giggle at that. "How come you're not yawning every five minutes? You've been up as long as I have, and did most of the work."

He tapped the tip of her nose, then unbuckled his belt and unzipped his fly. "Because I'm not growing a baby." He stopped to pat her stomach. "How is he, anyway?"

Megan slipped out of her boots. "Shhh. He's having a nap."

"Oh," he said, bending down to unlace his own boots. "We'll probably have to burn our clothes and use a whole bottle of shampoo to get the smell out of our hair. Slip off your pants and run inside."

"Okay, on the count of three, we run," Megan said without bothering with her pants. "Okay . . . three!" she shouted, giving Jack a nudge and bolting into the house.

He was one step behind her, when Megan suddenly skidded to a stop. "Mom! Dad! What are you doing here!"

Could it *possibly* get any worse?

Jack gathered his clothes, boots, pack, and rifle in his arms, and walked home barefoot. *Yes, Laird, I was trying to strip your daughter down to her birthday suit on the front porch so I could have my wicked way with her—first in the shower and then in an honest-to-God real bed for a change.*

Jack took his own porch stairs in two strides, dropped his boots, and discovered his main door was locked when he ran into it trying to rush inside. He tossed the rest of his clothes in the snowbank, *including* his pants this time, then blatantly mooned God and Frog

Point when he bent down to retrieve his key from under the mat.

Dammit to hell. He couldn't lose the image of Grace MacKeage staring at him and Megan in shocked surprise, and the stove poker falling out of Greylen's hand with a clang.

Instead of turning toward his bathroom, Jack went to the cupboard, pulled down the scotch, and drank straight from the bottle.

There hadn't been any vehicles parked in the driveway, so how had they gotten here? Jack took another swig of the scotch, relishing the burn sliding down his throat as he walked to an east window. He looked outside and spotted a snowmobile parked on the lake in front of Megan's house. Well, that explained that. He wrenched open the woodstove door and set a match to the waiting kindling.

Taking another swig, he walked back out onto his porch, grabbed his rifle and pack, and set them inside. No need leaving a weapon available, in case the laird decided to come over for a little fatherly chat. Jack went back to the woodstove and added some logs, then stood naked in front of its stingy heat. How was he going to marry Megan without ever having to face Grace Mac-Keage again?

The whiskey finally reached his tired muscles, and Jack knew he'd better get in the shower while he still had the strength. Dammit to hell, Megan was supposed to scrub his back—and he had intended to thoroughly scrub her front.

He turned on the shower, waited until the water ran hot, and stepped under the spray. Maybe he could sneak over later tonight, after her parents went home.

He snorted, dumping half the bottle of shampoo down over his head. The way his luck was running, he'd probably crawl into bed with Camry.

Despite his total exhaustion, Jack came fully awake when his blankets moved and a slightly chilled but sweet-smelling body slid into bed beside him. He smiled into the darkness. "Have you no shame, woman, sneaking over here after what just happened at your house?"

She snuggled against him with a shiver. "You seem to have more than enough shame for both of us," she said with a giggle. "I didn't know a person could turn that red. Or that *every* inch of skin blushes," she finished, her cold hand sliding down his torso and finding a particularly sensitive area.

Jack sucked in a gasp and quickly chased after her wayward hand. "How come you're so cold?" he asked, pulling her hand up and holding it against his chest.

Her toes started a slow, sensuous journey up his leg. "I just threw on my boots and bathrobe to run over here."

Jack rolled to face her, tossing his leg over hers while still holding on to her hand. "What time is it?" he asked, gasping again when her lips brushed his collarbone.

"It's three hours past our shower date," she said between kisses, her lips traveling up his clean-shaven jaw to his mouth. "You have a very comfortable bed, Jack," she whispered, continuing her journey to his cheekbone and then his ear. "Let's see if our magical place is just as beautiful on a real mattress. Will you take me there?" she whispered directly in his ear.

"S-sure," he half-growled, half-yelped when she softly bit his earlobe. "Okay, that does it," he said, rolling onto

his back and pulling her with him until she was straddling his waist. He released his grip and immediately
captured both her breasts in his hands, making her
moan, first in surprise and then pleasure as she leaned
into him.

She wiggled provocatively, lifted up on her knees, and
with Marauding Megan determination, settled down over
his shaft with another sweet sound of pleasure.

"You seem to have started without me," he barely got
out when she began moving on him.

She groaned, increasing her tempo. "You're catching
up quickly, though." She dropped her head back to arch
her breasts into his hands, her own hands bracing herself on his chest as her fingers flexed into his muscles.

He felt her muscles tightening, her body pulling in
on itself, and he let go of her breasts to take hold of
her hips. "Slow down, sweetheart," he desperately petitioned. "Make it last."

"Next time," she said even more desperately, grabbing
one of his hands and pushing it down between them.
"Come with me, Jack. Now!"

With a growl of resignation and no small amount of
anticipation, he gently began to intimately caress her.
She always promised to go slow next time, and when
next time came, she was even more demanding.

Maybe he'd get her calmed down in thirty or forty
years.

Every coherent thought in his head suddenly vanished when Jack felt her heading into their magical
place, dragging him with her on a cresting wave of
blinding heat. His shout of release blended with hers,
and together they traveled through the cosmos, flying
hand in hand, their three hearts beating as one.

Megan collapsed on top of him with a groan, snuggling her head under his chin with a sigh. "Okay," she muttered against his neck. "You deserve to marry me."

He pulled the blankets up over them. "That's it?" he said, holding her in place to catch every last lingering contraction. "That's your proposal?"

"I am not asking you to marry me, Jack. I'm telling you we're getting married in March, on the spring equinox. My family's got a thing for the solstices and equinoxes. You got a problem with that, Coyote?"

"No, ma'am."

She dropped her head down to his neck with another yawn. "Good. Because William and Kenzie and Father Daar will want to attend, so we need to have it before they leave." Jack felt her smile against him. "I'm going to be the first one in my family to have a dragon as a groomsman."

Jack snuggled her against him with a resigned sigh. He'd bet his boots he was going to be the first one in his family, too.

Epilogue

At precisely 7:08 p.m. on March 20, the exact time of the vernal equinox and during one of the worst spring blizzards in recent history, Jack finally kissed his very pregnant bride in front of an eighteen-hundred-year-old priest, two drùidhs, six time-traveling highland warriors, and a whole slew of MacKeages and MacBains—none of whom thought it at all strange to have a dragon in the wedding party.

Well, a few of the spouses did—especially Walter Sprague, Elizabeth's husband. The poor high school principal had nearly fainted when William had walked into Gù Brath's huge living room with Elizabeth on his arm, then taken his place beside Kenzie and Matt, the other two groomsmen. Jack had considered asking Simon to be his best man, but seeing how there was to be a mythological creature in attendance, he had asked Robbie MacBain instead.

"Come on," Megan said, dragging Jack down the

makeshift aisle behind the procession of wedding attendants as they headed toward the dining room. "We've got to keep William away from the buffet table. He's going to make himself sick again."

"If he can't learn that sweets will kill him, how does Kenzie expect William to survive long enough to learn how to treat defenseless women?" Jack asked, grinning like the happy man he was.

"Oh God. He's headed for the cake. Quick," Megan said, shoving Jack toward the huge wedding cake in the far corner of the room. "You go distract him while I fix him a plate of vegetables."

William will love that, Jack thought with a snicker. The dragon certainly looked a lot better than he had a month ago, though. He'd lost a good deal of weight and he smelled pleasantly earthy instead of rank. His large, batlike wings were folded neatly against his body, and his scales were dry and appeared almost polished, glittering iridescent when the light hit them just right. Someone— Camry, Jack suspected—had even gotten William to wear a red silk bow tie.

Camry hadn't flown to France after all, but had locked herself in her mother's lab, where she had proceeded to wear out a fax machine and email server as she hotly debated with the scientist in France who claimed to have solved the ion propulsion thing. Whenever she surfaced, she was usually muttering something about some arrogant French idiot who couldn't have calculated his way out of a wet paper bag if the equation had been written on his hand in indelible ink.

When she wasn't faxing and emailing and cursing her French counterpart, Camry was teaching Kenzie and William to read, as well as the rules of their modern new world. William was actually more man than beast, and he could even talk, though he usually refused to, except to Kenzie and Camry.

Camry now stepped in front of William and the poor beast stopped dead in his tracks, nearly tripping on his tail when he came nose to snout with his tutor—whom Jack suspected was more tyrant than teacher.

Then Megan's mother walked into the dining room on her husband's arm. Jack had managed to avoid Grace for two weeks after the skivies incident, before she had finally cornered him in his office, obviously having conspired with Ethel, who had transformed from a proficient clerk to a meddling mother hen to both Jack and Simon. Jack had been forced to spend a rather uncomfortable hour with Grace; he suspected she knew exactly how uncomfortable he was as she'd chatted with him about the weather, and babies, and Native American folklore.

Speaking of babies, Megan was waddling worse than William now. Little Walker was growing large, and Megan complained to anyone who would listen that the boy always did calisthenics when she was ready for bed. Jack's hand cupping her belly was the only thing that settled Walker down, so he continued to let her believe he had the magic touch.

"Could I please have everyone's attention!" Megan suddenly called from beside the cake table. "Thank you all for coming out in this blizzard for our wedding." She held out her hand to Jack, her simple gold wedding band glittering in the chandelier light. "I have a few announcements I wish to make."

Having absolutely no idea what his bride was about to announce, Jack stepped up beside her nervously.

"First, because I can't wait another two months for

you to find out, Jack and I are having a baby boy," she said, patting her belly. "And his name will be Walker MacKeage Stone."

Jack breathed a sigh of relief. As announcements went, that hadn't been so bad. They'd had a few arguments over Walker's full name, and Jack had been adamant Coyote wouldn't be one of them. He had promised he'd consider it for their next son, but what he *hadn't* told her was they'd be having only girls from here on out.

"And second, some of you may not know it yet, but this is Father Daar's last night with us. He, Kenzie, and William," she said, nodding toward the dragon in the corner of the room, "are leaving tomorrow for the coast. They don't know where they're going to end up exactly, but likely someplace Down East."

There were a few murmurs, and Father Daar harrumphed and got all red in the face when several people walked over and hugged him.

"Stop acting like this is my damn funeral," he protested, waving his cane in the air to shoo them away. "I am *not* too old to begin a new adventure. And somebody has to go with those pagan fools, to keep them out of trouble," he added, pointing his cane at Kenzie and William.

"And lastly," Megan continued, drawing everyone's attention again, "I want to give my wedding present to my husband." She reached behind the cake and picked up a large brown envelope, which she handed to Jack.

Jack's heart sank. They were supposed to exchange wedding presents? They were giving themselves to each other until death did them part; they didn't need to exchange *stuff*. He took the envelope with a smile, though he felt like a moron. He hadn't gotten her anything!

"Go ahead, open it," she encouraged, nudging his arm.

Jack slid his finger under the flap, opened the envelope, and peered inside. Apparently unable to wait for him to pull out the piece of paper, Megan pulled it out for him, then all but shoved it under his nose.

Jack had no idea what he was looking at.

"It's a deed," Megan said, shaking the paper, as if that would help him read it. "I bought Springy Mountain. But the deed's in both of our names, and we can build a little cabin up there."

Jack knit his brows, still not getting it.

Megan shoved the deed back in the envelope. "It's the mountain where we spent the night," she explained in soft exasperation. "Including the land where you saw the cougar markings. So now we never have to worry about that area being developed."

That said, she folded her hands over her belly under her lovely full breasts, and looked up at him expectantly.

Jack glanced at their equally expectant audience. "Um . . . my wedding gift for Megan . . ." He shot her a warm smile. "I couldn't exactly bring it here tonight, because it's . . . You see . . ."

The lightbulb finally came on, and his smile widened. "I bought you a really fast boat, so we can shoot up the lake to the cabin we're going to build. Isn't that great, sweetheart!"

Letter from LakeWatch

Dear Reader,

Every day I am privileged to witness an abundance of animals going about their daily business in my little corner of this mysteriously interconnected world. And whether their creatural antics move me to laughter or tears, I am forever in awe of their powerful sense of survival, innate curiosity, and playfulness.

At any given moment, I can look out a window here at LakeWatch and see something happening. My short list of visitors consists of common birds, squirrels, loons, osprey, eagles, fox, raccoon, deer, moose, and the occasional coyote. My husband, Robbie, and I have watched rutting bucks battle it out in our woods, ospreys plunge into the lake for their dinner, and chickadees land on unsuspecting visitors in search of a treat. We have stifled giggles as we watched baby raccoons swat at the wind chimes outside our bedroom window at one in the morning, and we've sucked in horrified breaths as a really brave or really dumb squirrel challenged a skunk under our bird feeder.

All of which makes me wonder if some animals might possess a sense of humor, or if I'm merely projecting an endearingly human trait upon them. For that matter, do creatures mourn? Can they feel pride? Regret? Hate? Compassion? Love?

I do know it never fails to surprise me how they interact not only with people but with each other. Crows are the town criers of the animal kingdom; toss out some food, and the black-feathered busybodies broadcast the news to every scavenger within earshot. In minutes, our front lawn can look like the local landfill as seagulls come swooping in from every direction. (This doesn't exactly endear me to the neighbors, but since my sons have returned and are now my nearest neighbors, there's not much they can do about their mother's penchant for feeding the crows, is there?)

We used to have chickens here at LakeWatch, and one afternoon I remember looking out my front window to see a crow and one of my hens engaged in a tug-of-war. Each had an end of some poor worm in its beak, and each refused to give up its prize. It was a comical sight, as my fluffy blond hen went eyeball-to-eyeball with that equally determined crow. Needless to say, the worm was the ultimate loser when it finally snapped in half. Both birds quickly swallowed their treats, then immediately began hunting for their next victims—acting as if the wild-domestic interaction was a common occurrence.

Another time, I was sitting on my back porch when

it suddenly dawned on me that my crows were being unusually raucous. I scanned the field to discover a fox standing on its hind legs, stretched full length up against our small shed near the woods. I then noticed a cat (not one of mine) lying on the roof of the shed, calmly staring down at the outfoxed vixen. The crows were perched in the surrounding trees, cawing their little heads off as if shouting, "Fight! Fight!"

So what does any of this have to do with my writing? Well . . . if you've learned anything about me these past few years, it's that I have a powerful appreciation for animals. I can't help but draw parallels between my feathered and four-legged friends and people— especially the characters in my stories. From observing Mother Nature, I have come to *expect* the unexpected. It no longer confounds me to be writing happily along, blithely headed down my intended literary path, and have one of my characters suddenly do or say something I hadn't anticipated. Sometimes I don't even realize what's happened until *after* it's happened!

Jack Stone caught me completely off guard when he first stepped onto the page. The guy was pointing a high-powered rifle at Megan and Kenzie, for crying out loud. I don't care that it wasn't loaded; that was not a nice thing for my hero to be doing.

At this point—which was quite early in the story—I wondered if I was even going to like Jack. Would he be one of those characters who caused me all sorts of trouble, or would I fall head over heels in love with him myself? Honestly, I am very open-minded when it comes to my stories; I'm just as curious to see what's going to happen next, when I'm writing, as you are when you're reading. After all, if I already *know* how things are going to turn out, why spend months locked in my studio merely toying with the details?

I don't meticulously plot out my books, or use a storyboard or scene cards. Heck, I don't even know my full cast of characters when I type "Chapter One" on that first page. (Please don't mention this to my editor, as she'll likely have a heart attack!) For me, telling a story is as unpredictable as life itself; I have no way of knowing what's going to happen tomorrow or next week or next year, much less in the next chapter.

We can certainly try to plan our future, but how often does it unfold exactly as we envisioned? And if we *could* know the future, would we really *want* to? If a caterpillar knew it was going to be some bird's dinner within hours of becoming a butterfly, would it even bother to emerge from its cocoon? Could you fall madly in love with someone if you knew you were going to fall out of love with him in a few years?

When we open our eyes each morning, we understand that the decisions we make today will shape our tomorrows. And so it is with my characters. They are just as hopeful as we are that the choices they make will be the right ones. Should they go next door and ask that cute guy if they can borrow a cup of sugar? Should they finally hand in their resignation at work? Should they sign up for that business class they've always wanted to take?

My characters might think they've got their lives all planned out when we first meet them, and they might even think they know exactly how they'll react in any given situation. But guess what? They are often as surprised as I am by how they *do* react. Just as when my hen grabbed that worm and looked up to find a crow on the other end, my characters must ultimately decide for themselves if the prize they're after is worth fighting for.

I *so* fell in love with Jack Stone.

Did you?

Until later, from LakeWatch,

Janet

Catch up with love...
Catch up with passion...
Catch up with danger....
Catch a bestseller from Pocket Books!

POCKET STAR BOOKS
A Division of Simon & Schuster
A CBS COMPANY

POCKET BOOKS
A Division of Simon & Schuster
A CBS COMPANY

Available wherever books are sold
or at www.simonsayslove.com.

17660

Do you have a passion for the past?

Don't miss any of the bestselling historical romances from Pocket Books!

Never say never in this dazzling new series from **New York Times** bestselling author Liz Carlyle!

Never Lie to a Lady ❧ She'll play along with his wicked game…for her own pleasure.

Never Deceive a Duke ❧ Desire can never be deceived—or denied.

❧

To Scotland, with Love ❧ Karen Hawkins
A handsome Lord has her *shaken*—and stirred!

Beware a Scot's Revenge ❧ Sabrina Jeffries
Revenge is a dish best served *hot*.

Madame's Deception ❧ Renee Bernard
When a innocent young beauty takes control of a bordello, can her seduction be far behind?

If You Deceive ❧ Kresley Cole
Can this ruthless Highlander ever learn to love?